PRAISE FOR
THE FLOATING AMSTERDAM FLOWER SHOP

'A gorgeous escapist read — a beautiful story
about healing and the power of flowers.'
Heidi Swain

'This beautifully written story set on the enchanting waters
of the canals of Amsterdam was a delight to read.
A much needed and joyful respite from the world.'
Rachel Burton

"As beautifully crafted and uplifting as any
florist's bouquet. I loved this story!'
Samantha Tonge

'It was a joy to be transported to The Floating Amsterdam
Flower Shop. We've never needed hopeful books more, and I
recommend this to anyone who wants to feel their heart lifted.'
Kate Storey

'What a blooming lovely story! The Amsterdam setting is joyous
and makes for an enviable romantic escape. Take me there!'
Kate Frost

PRAISE FOR ANNABEL FRENCH

'A charming and evocative read that
will have you wishing you were there.'
Rebecca Raisin

'A sun drenched read that conjures up the scent of summer.'
Julie Caplin

'Swoony and romantic!'
Leonie Mack

'Oh la la! This is the perfect escape.'
Bella Osborne

'The kind of romance that ticks all my boxes.
The perfect, escapist holiday read.'
Sarah Bennett

'Beautifully written – a real gem of a read!'
Lucy Coleman

The Floating Amsterdam Flower Shop

Annabel French is a bestselling author of several contemporary romantic fiction stories for HarperCollins, including her chateau series. Based in southeast England with her family, when she's not busy locked in her study writing, or daydreaming, she can be seen in the great outdoors, running after her dog, Skips. This is the first novel in her floating shop series.

Also by Annabel French:

Summer at the Chateau
Christmas at the Chateau
Wedding at the Chateau

The Floating Amsterdam Flower Shop

ANNABEL FRENCH

avon.

Published by AVON
A division of HarperCollins*Publishers* Ltd
1 London Bridge Street
London SE1 9GF

www.harpercollins.co.uk

HarperCollins*Publishers*
Macken House, 39/40 Mayor Street Upper
Dublin 1, D01 C9W8, Ireland

A Paperback Original 2025
1
Copyright © Katie Ginger 2025

Katie Ginger asserts the moral right to
be identified as the author of this work.

A catalogue record for this book is available from the British Library.

ISBN: 978-0-00-873644-6

This novel is entirely a work of fiction.
The names, characters and incidents portrayed in it are
the work of the author's imagination. Any resemblance to
actual persons, living or dead, events or localities is
entirely coincidental.

Set in Sabon LT Pro by HarperCollins*Publishers* India

Printed and bound in the UK using 100% Renewable
Electricity at CPI Group (UK) Ltd

All rights reserved. No part of this publication may be reproduced,
stored in a retrieval system, or transmitted, in any form or by
any means, electronic, mechanical, photocopying, recording or
otherwise, without the prior permission of the publishers.

Without limiting the author's and publisher's exclusive rights, any
unauthorised use of this publication to train generative artificial intelligence
(AI) technologies is expressly prohibited. HarperCollins also exercise their
rights under Article 4(3) of the Digital Single Market Directive 2019/790 and
expressly reserve this publication from the text and data mining exception.

This book contains FSC™ certified paper and other controlled
sources to ensure responsible forest management.

For more information visit: www.harpercollins.co.uk/green

*Thank you to everyone
who has supported me along the way*

Prologue

The smell of the London underground in summer was not one Rosie liked to inhale. However cheerful she tried to be – and she always aimed to look on the bright side – cheesy feet, body odour and whatever food someone had brought with them lingered in the hot, stuffy air, and she did her best not to breathe in too deeply. Head down, Rosie swayed as the train surged around a bend in the line, hot air brushing her neck. She was always grateful for her pixie cut in this sort of weather. Not so much in the winter though. The man next to her rocked backwards, his armpit hitting her in the face.

'Sorry,' he mumbled as the shock sent her phone tumbling from her hand, and she tried her best to reach down and get it without showing anyone her knickers or taking up too much room.

'No worries,' she replied cheerfully. 'It's not damaged.'

But he'd already gone back to ignoring her. Rosie swiped again at the screen and returned to scrolling through Instagram.

Images of brightly coloured, dreamy destinations flashed past her eyes, and she longed to be anywhere but on this packed-out tube train inhaling someone's unwashed hair. An image of the *Bloemenmarkt*, the world's only floating flower market, located in Amsterdam, filled the screen and her heart hummed. Her evening flower course had come to an end now and ideas had already begun circulating as to what she could do with the skills she'd learned. She could open her own business, or at least run a sideline alongside her dull design job. Flowers had always been her passion and she couldn't believe she hadn't thought of taking a course before. Now she knew how to pick blooms that complemented each other and arrange them in ways that filled the recipient with joy, she was determined to find a way to make that her living. Not before time either. She was nearly thirty and hadn't yet found a career she could stick to. She had no idea why. It was just that most jobs seemed so . . . boring, and no matter how much she tried, the thought of a new job, a new start, a new opportunity, always excited her, pulling her in another direction. But if she could find a career that involved flowers, she just knew she could make it work permanently. That must be why she hadn't managed to stick to anything for very long: her heart had simply lain elsewhere.

Out of the tube station, Rosie sucked in great lungfuls of fresh air (or at least the nearest you got to it in London) and walked through the local park admiring the flowers in bloom. She knew the names of them now, thanks to the course and her mum. Ignoring the stab of pain that always plunged into her heart when she thought of her, Rosie plonked herself on one of the benches, brushing her short hair back behind her ears.

Children were playing badminton, their parents sitting on a picnic blanket watching them closely, talking and laughing as they sipped from paper cups. Rosie remembered days like this with her parents, when she and her sister were small, and she tried her best not to think about what day it was. She returned to scrolling on her phone and watched a reel of an influencer spending a day in Amsterdam. Something about the city had always appealed to her. Not least because her mum had always wanted to visit the floating flower market but had never had the chance. As a botanist, she'd loved everything to do with flowers and plants, taking Rosie and her sister to Kew Gardens more weekends than she could count. She'd always shared pictures of the floating flower market, describing the tulips. Flowers that meant perfect or deep love. It had made her feel warm and snuggly, sat on her mum's lap, hearing her talk about it.

Nature had been her mum's passion, and it had always been Rosie's too, though after her mum had died, she hadn't allowed herself to indulge in it until recently. She'd been too scared of the feelings of loss it would bring up, and though it had stirred her grief, the floristry course had also made her happy in a way she hadn't been before.

Rosie watched as the video played on a continuous loop: people riding bikes, the famous canals. The city looked spectacular, green and vibrant, the colourful houses lining the streets, the houseboats moored and rocking gently on the tide. The food looked amazing too. Perhaps she should book a trip there? The bad thing about changing jobs so often was that she hadn't made many friends. London could be a lonely place at times, but with her family nearby and an ever-positive attitude, Rosie had never let it affect her too much. The good thing about not going out much was that she had a little money put by. She could afford it.

'Hey, you.' The bench shifted as Rosie's sister sat down.

Rosie looked over and smiled. 'Hey, Melody.'

Her sister's singsong voice perfectly suited her name. While her mum had been a botanist and insisted one of their daughters be called Rosie, after her favourite flower, their dad was a devout music fan, and Melody had been the compromise for their second child. They'd both hated their names growing up, only beginning to love them after their mum had died.

'You okay?' her sister asked.

The sentence was left unfinished, neither saying the words that still, even after all these years, hurt. The anniversary of their mum's death stabbed at both their hearts. Rosie had ignored it through the day, packaging it off into the little box of worry she tried not to pry into too often. It had been almost twenty years and though the pain wasn't as strong as it had been at the start, it still felt like there was a hole somewhere inside her. A dark, empty space that would never again be filled. She'd never quite identified where exactly it was, or how to fix it, and she lived in hope that it would simply shrink as the years passed. It never did.

'Getting there. You?' Rosie felt the hitch in her voice.

Melody looked over, her light blonde hair, the same shade as their mum's had been, escaped from the band it had been pulled back into. Her hands looked red and raw, made sore from where, as a nurse, she'd had to wash them repeatedly through her long, tiring shift. 'I've been on all day so I haven't thought about it. Well, I've tried not to think about it. Haven't been one hundred per cent successful. Have you called Dad?'

'I spoke to him this morning, and we'll see him this evening for dinner. Sometimes I think he copes better with it than we do.'

He always tried to be cheerful but had spoken openly about how much he missed his wife. He'd always been like that. His honesty about his feelings, letting them know it was okay to be sad, had helped them adjust to the silent space her mum used to fill. Rosie didn't know how he did it. She'd always struggled to speak of her mum, even now, especially to people who'd known her.

They sat in silence until her sister spoke.

'She loved life so much, didn't she? Making the most of every single day.' She shifted her body, turning to face her. 'Do you remember that day it was raining and everyone else was staying in, so Mum got us dressed in raincoats and boots and we went stomping through the streets, splashing in the puddles? How old were we then? Eight? Nine?'

Rosie smiled at the memory, the bittersweetness of having loved and lost mixing like oil and water in her veins. 'Something like that.'

Melody pressed her water bottle to her lips as Rosie looked at her phone. Her algorithm had paused on an image of the flower market and, suddenly, an idea struck her as though she'd been hit by lightning. She was done living life on a treadmill, every day the same, boring chores, the same dire job she didn't like, let alone love. She was done with it all. What she needed was something new. Something to get her teeth into. Something that spoke to the thing she was passionate about. And now, she knew what that should be.

'I'm going to move to Amsterdam,' she declared loudly as though voicing her thoughts meant she was affirming them to the world, and she couldn't back out.

Melody's water sprayed out of her mouth onto the path in front of them, narrowly missing a suited and booted man on his way home from work.

'Watch out!' He sidestepped and Rosie repressed a giggle as her sister spluttered and coughed.

'Sorry!' she replied. 'My bad. She wasn't expecting me to say what I just said.'

The man glanced back over his shoulder like she was mad. Maybe she was.

Melody wiped furiously at the dribbles coating her chin. 'No, I blimmin' well wasn't expecting you to say that!'

'It makes sense, Mels. Trust me. I'm going to move to Amsterdam and open a flower shop on the *Bloemenmarkt*.'

'The *what* what?' Mostly recovered, Melody coughed again and tried once more to have a drink.

'It's the Dutch name for the floating flower market in Amsterdam. It's the only one in the world. It'll be amazing. I can just see it now, exactly how it will be.' She closed her eyes, picturing the brightly coloured flowers like they were an Instagram photo. She'd live on a houseboat, or in a flat in one of the houses overlooking a canal. She'd have friends and a social life and every day she'd work with flowers and plants. Opening her eyes again, she sighed. 'I'm so sick of letting life pass me by and I hate my job. Like . . . really hate it.'

'More than waitressing at that Halloween-themed restaurant?'

'Definitely. That fake blood got everywhere. Bits of me were stained pink for days. I'm not sure proper fake blood is supposed to do that.'

'It's not.'

'I'm going to do it, Mels. I'm going to move and make something of myself. I'm nearly thirty – it's about time I started thriving rather than just surviving.'

Melody's perfectly arched eyebrows pulled together. 'Have you been watching life coaches on Insta again?'

'No,' Rosie replied defensively, then paused and added: 'Okay, maybe. But that doesn't mean they're wrong.'

'Listen, I love you – you know I do – but this isn't the first time you've come up with some kind of crazy scheme to change your life. You can be a little . . .'

'Optimistic? Hopeful? Go-get-'em?' She gave a jaunty pantomime air punch.

'Impulsive. You don't look before you leap and this is a big move, Rosie. It's not switching jobs or changing flats; it's moving to a new country, giving up the security you have here on a whim. And you don't have a job to go to.'

'Sometimes it's good to follow your heart.'

Melody sighed. 'You can't make this sort of decision in five minutes, Rosie. You need to sort out a job first.'

'I will. I'll find one, and Amsterdam's only a few hours away on the Eurostar. That's less than travelling to . . . I don't know . . . Scotland.'

'What's Scotland got to do with anything?' Melody shook her head at the unexpected tangent. 'Speaking of which, do you remember when you wanted to move to the Highlands and start a reindeer farm?'

'Okay, that wasn't one of my best ideas – I'll admit it.'

'You'd never even seen a reindeer in real life! And when

I made you go and actually face one, you screamed as soon as it opened its mouth and you ran away! You have to think these things through, Rosie. You can't just up and move countries.'

'Why not? We can do anything if we put our minds to it.'

'No, we can't!' She was getting cross now. Her voice was taking on that bossy nurse tone she used at work. 'We – you – need money, somewhere to live, a job—'

'Mum wanted us to be happy,' Rosie countered cheerily. She wasn't going to be daunted because, unlike some of her other dubious life decisions, this felt right somehow. 'And I'm not happy – not here. Not in the dead-end jobs I've been doing. The only thing that's made me happy was my floristry course and that's finished now—'

'But will Amsterdam make you happy?' Melody pointed to the phone screen. 'Moving away from everyone who knows and loves you.'

'I'll make new friends,' she replied. 'Everyone I know is married with kids and we hardly see each other. I don't blame them; life moves on, but the few friends I have – or rather had – aren't a reason to stay. And like I said, I not that far away from you and Dad. I'm not emigrating to Australia.' Rosie turned to her sister, almost pleading. 'I can't explain it, Mels, but every time I look at that picture, I get this feeling in my bones – in my gut – that this is where I'm meant to be. I need to make a change, and this is as good as any. Better, in fact, because I love flowers. I want to open a flower shop and where better than the only place in the world with a floating flower market? A floating. Flower. Market.'

'What did you have for lunch? That feeling in your gut could just be indigestion.'

Rosie smiled indulgently. 'Falafel, but it isn't repeating on me. What I'm feeling is happy, excited, hopeful!' She grabbed her sister's arm with both hands. 'Honestly, I can see it all now. Biking through the city, wandering the canals, eating *stroopwafels* and *bitterballen*.'

'Bitter what?'

'*Bitterballen*. Deep-fried, crispy snack balls.'

'Snack balls . . . ?' She pinched the bridge of her nose. Clearly it was all too much, today of all days. 'Just think about it, Rosie-Roo, please?'

The use of her childhood nickname grounded her a little, but the idea had taken root. Somehow, she just knew she had to take this chance. She knew she had to do something other than work in passionless jobs, and scurry back to her flat above a shop.

Melody took Rosie's silence as her signal to continue. 'Sometimes you do things, and you can't go back.'

Rosie turned once more to her sister. 'Why would I want to?'

'You do remember that time you moved to Yorkshire when you were in your *Wuthering Heights* era? You lasted three days.'

'That's because my cottage was a leaky old shack on the Yorkshire Moors. And it was haunted.'

'Rosie—'

'I'm doing this, Melody,' she said a little more firmly. It was a tone of voice she didn't use all that often with her sister, and Melody pulled back a little in surprise. 'And it's going to be great. Trust me. There has to be more out there and, if there is, I'm determined to find it.'

Chapter 1

ONE MONTH LATER

Rosie took a moment to stare at the buildings around her, taking in the architecture she'd spent so long looking at in photos and videos since making her decision to move. The sloping gambrel roofs with curving eaves, the equally portioned windows, the houses bunched together like they were squidged in shoulder to shoulder. No wonder the canal belt was a UNESCO world heritage site. It was breathtaking, screaming its history but also relaxed and calm.

The air smelt different in Amsterdam too. Rosie couldn't quite put her finger on what it was, but there was definitely something. Maybe it was the lack of pollution: the absence of dense petrol fumes that filled the city, contaminating your lungs, sitting on your skin and hair. Perhaps it was the canals. Or perhaps it was simply the freedom? Paused halfway along a bridge built of red brick with dark iron railings and old-fashioned Victorian-style street lamps, the water rushing beneath her feet, Rosie wrinkled her nose, breathing deeper. Whatever it was, she liked it.

She took another big breath and let her shoulders drop. She was here. She'd made it. Despite her sister's (albeit potentially justified) worries, she had done it and, right now, she wasn't regretting a single thing. Her worldly essentials were crammed into a large suitcase that she dragged along behind her. For some, the racket would have been annoying, but for Rosie it was like a soundtrack to a new life. Here she was, walking the Amsterdam streets with her case, not having to sidestep commuters and tourists as she would in London.

As Rosie had packed, she'd realised how few possessions she actually owned. Yes, there was the coffee machine that ground the beans and steamed the milk, and there were other utensils that kitted out her flat. But there were only a few things that actually mattered; like her jewellery, some of which came from her mum, and her photos, all of which fitted into the suitcase with her clothes. It reinforced her new-found belief that she didn't need to fill her life with needless possessions in place of actually searching out and pursuing her passion. But at least she'd identified it now and was doing everything she could to make it real.

Rosie walked along the canal side, looking for the houseboat she'd rented. It was called the *Forget-Me-Knot* and she had to admit, she'd chosen it mainly for the name.

Most had been called things like *Alternative Girlfriend* and *Captain Boaty* as well as the run-of-the-mill names of people the owners knew and loved. Not only had most of them been out of her price range, but she'd also felt an instant connection to the small boat with a flowery name. It had seemed like a good omen – a sign from above, maybe from her mum – that this was definitely the right thing to do and where she was meant to be.

The tree-lined street was quintessentially Dutch, with the relaxed vibes of a city everyone loved, while also showcasing the slight edginess of Amsterdam. As Rosie walked along, her case still making a racket behind her, she had no doubt she'd be happy here. The bright summer sun glittered off the water and dappled through the bushy branches, sending shadows dancing over the street. Ducks paddled and she even caught sight of a swan, but before she could take a photo it had passed under a bridge and out of sight. When she passed through the shadows, walking beside the bikes tied to the railings that lined the bank, the coolness swept her skin, providing a welcome break from the heat of the mid-afternoon sun. She'd worn shorts and a T-shirt, her feet clad in her most comfortable trainers. She was embracing not having to wear unflattering suits, or worse, a uniform. Some of the waitressing ones she'd had were truly awful, all itchy polyester and far too tight over her hips.

Rosie checked her phone. It was nearing three o'clock which was when she'd arranged to meet her new landlord, Piet, the man she was renting the houseboat from. She quickened her pace. Hope grew with each step as she passed gorgeous houseboats painted in all manner of colours, their decks decorated with tables and chairs and vibrant flower pots, the colourful blooms looking even more beautiful when contrasted against the dark wood. Some looked so incredibly luxurious with leather sofas and large living areas that she wondered if celebrities lived there. Rosie's list of possible new homes had been pretty small to start with, but she'd decided to go for something traditional-looking, rather than a white, shiny new boat. It had just seemed more . . . authentic, somehow – and, if she was honest, everything else was out of her price range, so she'd thought herself lucky when she'd secured a houseboat in a city known for its canals.

'Hello there!' called a man with bushy dark hair and angular features. He smiled and waved. 'You're Rosie, aren't you?'

Gosh, did she look so out of place he could tell she was a tourist already? She had hoped she'd fit in, though the giant suitcase was probably a giveaway that she was indeed the woman from England he was waiting for.

'Hello!' she called back. '*Begroeting*!' She'd been practising with Duolingo ever since she'd decided to move, but must have got something wrong with her pronunciation as the man frowned and looked decidedly confused. 'Did I get that wrong?' she asked, coming to a stop in front of him, sweat prickling the skin at her hairline in the fierce summer sun.

'Not at all,' he replied, the smile returning. 'But we don't really say that anymore. It's quite formal. We normally just say hallo.'

He'd pronounced it with an 'a' sound rather than an 'e', and she made a mental note to copy him the next time she said it.

'Right. I'll remember that. So this is the *Forget-Me-Knot*, is it?' She turned to look at the boat, and for a moment was sure the utter disappointment that flooded her system was evident on her face. Her throat tightened and her mouth went dry.

The boat still technically looked like the picture. Only now she was certain some liberties had been taken with Photoshop or one of those hide-your-flaws filters. It had the dark wood she loved, but it looked more like a garden shed, and the paint was peeling on the housey bit. (It probably had a special name but she hadn't learned that yet. She really was going to have to brush up on her nautical lingo.) The windows had condensation pooling between their double-glazed panes, which spoke to broken seals, and the little fence-type thing that ran all the way around as some kind of safety measure (a pretty useless safety measure at that) was broken in more than one place. She quickly schooled her features, though her heart sank.

'This is it,' Piet replied, gesturing like this was Buckingham Palace or The Ritz and she should be gasping in shock and awe. 'One of my favourite rentals. It's always popular. You're lucky I was able to give it to you as a longer let.'

She wasn't entirely sure about that. It was true she'd had difficulty finding others with such availability, but by the look of the *Forget-Me-Knot*, it was more likely that no one wanted this place. Rosie banished the thought as soon as it arrived. She would stay positive. For all she knew, the inside was beautiful and cosy, and she could fix up the outside. Surely it wouldn't take too long.

'Now, here are the keys,' said Piet, forcing them into her hand with such speed her fingers had no choice but to take them. 'Enjoy your stay, goodbye!'

And with that he was off, waving as he went but walking so quickly Rosie had the distinct impression something was wrong. Panic began to rise up and she forced herself to take a breath of the fresh Amsterdam air.

'Well, that was a suspiciously quick getaway,' she said, realising she'd spoken out loud.

That was the problem with living alone: she'd been talking to herself for years and didn't always realise when she did it in public. Was that the sign of a problem? Possibly. She clamped her lips shut, shook the thought away and plastered on a smile. This was a momentous occasion, and it was one that she planned to enjoy. With the keys grasped in one hand, she stepped off the safety of the pavement and onto the deck. The boat rocked with her and she let out a little squeal: a mix of pure joy and excitement. Yanking the heavy suitcase across the gap, she almost lost it between the boat and the bank, but managed to lug it across in time. 'Phew!'

She heard a low grumble from the boat next to her, called *The Rembrandt*, and peered around but couldn't see anyone. All she saw was a net curtain flying back into place. It would have been nice if they'd popped out and said hello. She gave them a moment, and when they still didn't, she decided to do it herself. There was no time like the present, and so, she left her case, and hopped back onto the pavement and around onto her neighbour's boat.

This boat was in much better condition than her own with shining, well-varnished wood and paint pots dotted around. She even spied a dog bed outside. She loved dogs and being a pet owner was always the sign of a nice person, wasn't it?

She knocked and waited for the curtain twitcher to open up but they didn't. She knocked again.

'Hello! I just popped over to introduce myself.'

A dog barked from inside, and it was told gruffly to be quiet, so there was definitely someone in there.

'Hello?' she said again, her voice uncertain. Was she living next door to some kind of weirdo shut-in?

A man's deep voice answered. 'I'm busy. You'll have to go away.'

'Oh, okay. Sorry.' Now that was incredibly rude. Or were the Dutch just a bit more blunt than Brits? She crossed her arms over her chest and made her way back to the *Forget-Me-Knot*. Well, whoever was in there was going to have to get used to her, weren't they?

It was time to explore her new home. She propped her

case against the wall and stood up some of the overturned flower pots. The plants were dead. She couldn't even tell what they'd been once upon a time. Poor things. Standing, she moved to the other end of the boat (was this the bow or the stern? she wondered) and opened the door. The keys fitted easily into the locks but as she pushed nothing moved. She tried again, a little more forcefully this time and the door moved a little, protesting as it went. The wood had clearly warped over the years and she had to throw her shoulder into it to get it to move. With another go, and a hefty thwack, it finally budged and the smell of damp and mould with an undertone of uncleaned toilet that met her made her gag.

'Urgh,' she cried, covering her nose. She heard a grumble from the boat behind but ignored it. 'Oh, that is gross.' Rosie's cheerfulness began to fade as the thought that she'd made an awful, terrible mistake began to creep in. But then she took in the layout and decided it had potential, and some of her fears vanished.

In front of her lay her new, compact home. To her right was a small kitchen area with a tiny hob and even smaller oven. Opposite it was a Barbie-doll-sized sink covered in limescale and with grimy taps. Next was the living area: a semicircular seat with a small table on one side, and on the other a built-in bench with a decent-looking seat cushion. Finally, at the end was the bed: a small double, but that was still plenty of room for her, and as she had no plans to be sharing with anyone while she concentrated on sorting her life out and making something of herself, it would be perfect. The smell would not put her off.

'No way,' she said to herself, rolling her shoulders back and removing her hand from her face. 'All it needs is a good clean and an airing. Don't be a wimp.'

The sound of something falling behind her made her spin and she saw the net curtain next door twitch again, but couldn't make out the person behind it. So they were happy to spy on her but not to actually say hello. She hoped most Amsterdammers were a lot more friendly than this one. She resisted the urge to stick her tongue out in case they were still there and stepped inside. The smell grew even more overwhelming. Rosie hurried around, casting all the windows open, and as the fresh air seeped in, she began to relax.

All the place needed was some TLC and she was more than happy to put in the work. Rosie walked through the galley (she'd picked that word up while looking through a million houseboat rentals), admiring the light pouring in through the windows. She perched on the small sofa, watching the birds that had landed on the canal float by. As if to remind her there was no time to waste, creeping damp began to edge into her shorts. She felt the cushion and realised it was cold to the touch, even a little damp. Nearly everything needed cleaning and replacing. Glancing at her bed, she decided she wasn't going to even sit on it until she'd changed all the sheets and bought a new duvet and pillows. While the houseboat wasn't as nice as she'd been hoping for (or as nice as it'd looked in the pictures) she was here and the chances of finding anywhere else within her budget were non-existent. She was going to have to make the most of it and there was only one way to do that: to clean, tidy and polish, and decorate with cushions, throws, rugs and plants until it looked and felt like a home.

After pulling her suitcase inside, she didn't bother unpacking and instead went in search of a supermarket.

The streets of Amsterdam were at least as beautiful as any other European city Rosie had ever visited. The sun bounced off the numerous windows of the buildings that towered above her on either side. But where London buildings seemed to loom over the busy streets, here it was more like a friendly giant leaning over to greet her. Flower baskets attached to the railings overflowed with bright blooms and ivy, and dense green foliage clung to walls, arched over windows and bounded from the pots and planters lining the pavement. Bikes were everywhere, as she'd expected, and the sound of people talking and chattering was punctuated now and then by the tinkling of bells as riders asked others to make way. The smell of coffee from the cafés filled her nostrils and was so strong she could almost taste it. She paused at a window, marvelling at the array of cream-filled pastries lining the display. Her stomach rumbled, and as the owner smiled and waved a greeting as they placed even more goodies into the window, Rosie's feet took her inside before she could stop herself.

'Hallo,' she said, pausing at the counter.

'Hallo,' the woman replied. She said something in Dutch and the panic must have shown on Rosie's face as the woman immediately laughed and reverted to English. 'I said you look hungry.'

'I am. Actually I'm ravenous.'

'What would you like?'

She wasn't at all sure, but her stomach gurgled again as if asking her to make up her mind quickly. She placed her hand over it, hoping the woman hadn't heard. 'What would you recommend?'

'Hmm.' After assessing all the baked goods in the window, she turned back to Rosie. 'This is your first time in Amsterdam?'

'Yes, but it's my home now. I've moved here. In fact, I've only just arrived.'

The woman's eyes widened, impressed. 'In that case, I'd recommend a local delicacy, a *tompouce*. They're filled with cream and very, very delicious. Perfect to celebrate your first day in your new city.' She pointed to a row of pink-iced oblong pastries filled with cream.

'They look delicious.'

The woman placed one in a box and Rosie paid.

'You might want to eat that in here,' the woman said. 'They're quite messy.'

'Oh, thank you, but I really need to get going. I've got a lot of cleaning to do on the houseboat I've rented and I better get started. I think it's going to take me a few days to get everything spick and span.' Rosie realised that was far more information than needed and cursed herself for being a chronic over-sharer.

She smiled and left. A little further down the street, Rosie took the pastry from the small box, eager to eat. It was hard to handle with so much cream in the centre, but she couldn't go back; she'd feel foolish. She picked it up and bit down on the corner. The two slices of pastry sunk together and a large dollop of cream escaped from the side and rolled down her chin, directly onto her T-shirt. She tried scooping it off but all that was left was a smear of pink icing she hadn't realised was stuck to her finger.

'Damn it!'

Well this was hopeless, but extremely delicious so it was worth it. She licked her finger and scraped off as much as she could from her T-shirt, not letting it go to waste. As she looked up, a man walked past her. He had long, strawberry-blond hair that curled slightly and ended on his shoulders, and a neatly trimmed beard. He scowled at her and embarrassment heated her cheeks. When their eyes met, he dropped his away and Rosie decided to admit defeat and find a park bench. She flopped down and with her back to the road, unceremoniously stuffed the rest of the *tompouce* into her mouth, enjoying every single delectable bite.

Belly full and her spirits restored, it was time to buy some cleaning products and get started on making the *Forget-Me-Knot* habitable.

After locating a shop, she managed to find all of the cleaning supplies she needed and something for dinner, including a bottle of wine for later, and paid at the till. She'd opted for one manned by a person rather than a self-service, too afraid of not understanding what it was saying. Before long, she was back at the *Forget-Me-Knot*, ready to get to work.

Later that evening, by the time she'd finished scrubbing, airing, plumping cushions and washing everything in sight while her favourite playlist rang through the tinny speakers on her phone and she sang to her heart's content, the houseboat smelled like lavender, the seats were covered in an assortment of dry, fluffy cushions and the bed was an inviting space she couldn't wait to crawl into. Her body ached from the manual work, her lower back tight and her shoulders stiff, but there was still one more thing to do before the day ended. She called her dad.

'Hey, Rosie-Roo,' he said, his usual chipper voice filling the boat as she'd put him on speaker. She could hear him pottering around in his kitchen and glanced at the new bright green clock she'd bought and hung in place of a rather dingy landscape the size of a postcard. She hadn't realised it was so late.

'Hey, Dad, how was your day?'

'Good. How's Amsterdam?'

She leaned back against the cushions, her stomach muscles protesting at the cleaning she'd done, but she couldn't stop the smile spreading over her face. 'It's wonderful, Dad. It's just the most beautiful city and the food is incredible.'

He laughed. 'I should've known you'd go straight for

the food. Your mum was the same.' There was a second's silence, and then he quickly recovered. 'She would have been so proud of you. Me and Melody are too.'

'Really? I know she's still not quite used to the idea of me doing this.'

Though her sister had been somewhat supportive, a part of her had been held back, too anxious Rosie was making a mistake.

'She just worries about you, that's all. But what's the worst that can happen? You can always come home – you know that.'

'I know, Dad, and I appreciate it. But I want to make this a success. This place—' She looked around, admiring the difference a few hours of effort had taken. 'It's already feeling like home, you know? There's just something about this city and I haven't even explored half of it – a quarter of it – yet!'

'It's good to hear you sounding so excited. So what's the plan for the rest of the evening?'

'I don't know really. I might take a walk. I definitely need a shower after all the cleaning I've done. I might just snuggle up with a good book. I've got a big day tomorrow.'

'Is that the Bloom-thingy?'

'The *Bloemenmarkt*? It sure is. I'm excited. I can't wait to start making displays and bouquets. I love seeing the look on someone's face when you hand them flowers. It's such a special gift.'

'You sound just like your mum. You know she loved

talking about flowers and plants and how they helped people.' She could hear the smile in his voice.

'What are you doing tonight?'

'I don't know. I might play guitar and watch TV.'

'You should join a band,' she declared, the idea coming so clearly, she wondered why she hadn't thought of it before. She knew he was sometimes lonely and refused to admit it to either of his daughters. He needed to do something that took him out into the wide world and she couldn't deny she felt guilty leaving him behind.

'I don't know about that, sweetheart. Maybe I'm a bit old for that sort of thing.'

'Rubbish. You should do it. It'd be good for you.'

'We'll see, we'll see.' A faint beep sounded down the line and she knew the timer on his oven was going off. 'I better get my dinner. Night night, sweetheart. Sleep tight.'

'You too, Dad. Love you.'

'Love you too.'

They hung up, and she let her phone sit on the small table, the screen turning black. For the first time she felt intimidated by the silence that surrounded her. She'd lived on her own for years but never in a new country, and suddenly the city seemed enormous and too big for her. Would she make friends? Would she need to find something to do outside of work, so she met people? For the first time, as tiredness overtook excitement, she understood her sister's concerns. This was a huge change. Something most people never did. She'd sorted out a residence and work visa, found somewhere to live, and tomorrow she'd sort out a stall at the flower market, or a job somewhere, but it was only now that the emotional impact of moving to a new country began to hit. To distract herself from sinking into fear and gloom, she peered around her new home.

Speaking out loud (after deciding it wasn't a problem; it was perfectly normal) she said to herself, 'I'm going to put a bookshelf there—' She pointed to a cosy corner. It was tight so she might have to make it herself, but she quite fancied a little reading nook. 'And I'm going to have a whole shelf of pot plants there.' This time, she nodded at a shelf that had previously been covered in nothing but dust. A smile lifted her cheeks and excitement began to fill her body once more. Tiredness always led to negativity, in her opinion. She'd feel back to normal after an easy dinner and a good night's sleep. She wouldn't let it win.

'Eeeeee!' she cried, kicking her legs in the air as a surge of pride took over.

Through the window she saw the curtain twitch once more as though angrily flung back into place. Whoever her grumpy neighbour was they better get used to her talking to herself because they were going to have to get used to a lot worse. She'd spent the day singing along to Beyoncé but she hadn't even started her Eighties ballads playlist yet. Grumpy neighbour was in for a real treat when that one began.

Chapter 2

Rosie awoke to the sun streaming in through the sparkling, newly cleaned windows of the lounge and the sound of water dripping from the tap over the tiny sink. Last night, as soon as she'd turned the light off and tried to sleep, in the quiet of the boat, she'd heard it drip, drip, dripping away and after that it was all she could hear. At about midnight, she'd got up and turned the tap as tightly as it would go and even yelled at it to stop, but after hearing a muffled shout from the boat next door, she'd given up, not wanting to disturb her clearly miserable neighbour further. She'd have to get a plumber to fix it, but the prospect of dealing with that, in Dutch, when she didn't speak a word of it yet terrified her. Perhaps a YouTube video would help. There was always advice on there.

For a second, Rosie lay in bed, appreciating the way the sun's rays shone onto her new rug through a gap in the curtains and a few dust motes danced in the light. She enjoyed the gentle sway of the boat on the water and smiled. She'd chosen this – this new life, this new adventure. And a slightly drippy tap wasn't that big a problem in the grand scheme of things. Today she had to go and try her best to land a spot at the floating flower market and that was exactly what she intended to do. If she didn't, she'd have to take whatever job she could get to pay the rent, and she hadn't come all this way to wait tables or work in a dingy office like she'd been doing back home.

Stretching luxuriously, like a cat after a particularly nice nap, she jumped out of bed and opened the curtains next to her bed, letting even more of the already warm sunshine flood into the galley. She dressed in her favourite denim shorts and T-shirt and threw on her old trainers. She'd never been one for much make-up so after applying the bare minimum and brushing her teeth, she was ready to grab a coffee and be at the *Bloemenmarkt* as early as possible. Obviously, the vendors would all be there. Florists always started early, taking their deliveries while the sky was still dark or the sun just beginning to peek over the horizon. It was one of the things she was looking forward to with her new job. She'd always loved that feeling of being awake when the rest of the world was still asleep.

Grabbing her handbag, she left the boat, enjoying the warmth on her face. As she strode through the city, smiling at the cyclists who, she was surprised to see, returned her smiles, unlike their moody London counterparts, she marvelled at the lack of traffic. Of course there were cars on some of the roads, but it was wonderful being in such a pedestrianised city after the hustle and bustle of London. People just seemed so much more content.

Rosie stared at the historic buildings in the typical style she'd come to associate with Amsterdam: five storeys tall, slim but with a facade full of windows, the old merchant-house styles that tilted at impossible angles. Down a narrow alley she saw a sofa being winched into one of the narrow houses and smiled. The modern houses didn't have that issue, but even they seemed to fit this beautiful city.

Desperate for a caffeine fix (and not the boring instant coffee she'd bought) Rosie stopped at a beautiful café on the corner of a busy street that ran alongside one of the canals. Inside, she could already smell apples and cinnamon from the famous Dutch pancakes and the deep, aromatic bitterness of coffee. Whilst she'd been busy cleaning yesterday, she hadn't yet made a shopping list of food she needed. She'd have to do that this afternoon and stock up the kitchen cupboards. Not that she could buy much given the lack of space in the houseboat, but she considered that a good thing. She'd buy fresh food and eat seasonally, support as many local business as she could find, rather than supermarkets. She sat at a table watching the boats moored in the canal and assessing the plants hanging from the baskets attached to the railings. She spotted petunias in blues, pinks and purples, the gorgeous clumps flowing over the railings in dots of colour, their sweet smell chasing away any hint of canal water.

A young waiter, about the same age as her, appeared, his blond hair tied back into a man-bun. She'd never really liked man-buns but this man wore it well. Perhaps it was his chiselled jaw and Roman nose that made it work. Rosie smiled. If this was what Amsterdam had to offer she would definitely enjoy it here. She'd been on quite a few dates in her time but hadn't ever really clicked with anyone enough to make it a long-term relationship. Perhaps that would change too now she was building a new life. Her small bed would be a squeeze but . . . it could also be fun. When talking about her dad, her mum had always said she'd met 'the one' when she'd least expected it. The memory of her smiling face leapt into Rosie's mind and she was grateful for the waiter interrupting her thoughts before the pain that always followed these memories surfaced.

Rosie smiled again, and tried once more with some of the Dutch she'd been learning on Duolingo. 'Umm . . . hallo! *Kan ik* umm . . . order the Dutch *pannen* – *pannenkoeken* and umm . . . a latte . . . please?'

He smiled and spoke in perfect English, his white teeth visible as he grinned. 'Dutch pancakes and a latte?'

Rosie beamed with pride that though her pronunciation may have been a little off, he had at least understood her. 'Yes, please. Sorry if that wasn't very good.'

'It was good! Keep trying.'

She settled back in her seat as he left and spied again the man with the beard who'd scowled at her yesterday as she had eaten her *tompouce*. He hadn't noticed her yet but just as before he was frowning, this time at his phone. What on earth was his problem? Rosie could never understand those who went through the world determined to be miserable with everything and everyone in it. She knew her happy-go-lucky personality could occasionally wind some people up, but generally she considered that a *them* problem rather than a *her* problem. There was nothing wrong with looking on the bright side and celebrating the small wins in every day. Her mum had taught her that. It was a shame though – he was really quite attractive. His hair was down as it had been before and as the sun shone through it, she could see the strawberry colour more clearly. She was pretty sure it was naturally wavy and that he hadn't styled it, and his pale blue eyes were rimmed with pale lashes.

As her breakfast arrived she couldn't help but breathe in the scent of baked apple once more. 'Hmm, it smells delicious.'

'And your latte.' He placed the coffee on the table and it smelled equally good.

'Thank you so much. I have to get a picture for my sister as it looks so beautiful.'

It really did. The apples were perfectly golden, the pancake crisping at the edges, and the whole thing had been dusted in icing sugar. Her latte had the shape of a tulip on top, which she thought was utterly adorable. She grabbed her phone and snapped some pictures hearing a tut from nearby. *Grumpy-but-gorgeous* darted his eyes away and she knew immediately it had been him tutting. She ignored him. She wanted to remember this moment: her first proper meal in Amsterdam.

It took less time than it should have for her to eat her breakfast. Unladylike it might have been, but she couldn't help demolishing the gorgeous food as quickly as possible. Once she'd eaten and paid she was ready to find the flower market and set off.

As Rosie approached from the opposite side of the canal to the *Bloemenmarkt*, she realised she was holding her breath. Against a backdrop of higgledy-piggledy merchant's houses was a row of small glass buildings, rather like greenhouses. Inside were all manner of green leaves and foliage and vibrant-coloured blooms. Some hung down from the ceiling while others overflowed from pots and tubs. What made it even more beautiful was the way it reflected on the still water of the canal: a slightly darker mirror image.

Rosie let out a slow breath. It was breathtakingly beautiful, and she quickly made her way to the correct side of the flower market to find the entrance. Again, Rosie paused and took a moment to take it all in. It was like the biggest flower stall she'd ever seen. Actually, it was the biggest flower stall she'd ever seen multiplied ten times over and then all stuck together.

It was so unlike the most iconic of London flower markets that it took her a moment to understand why. Columbia Road Flower Market in London was so tightly packed in that there was barely enough room to walk without bumping into someone. As usual, in London, everyone seemed in a rush and there was always a subconscious haste to everyone's actions. Here, there was room to walk, to see, to appreciate, and no one was bumping into you, shoving you, or huffing until you moved.

Each stall was filled with more varieties of plant than she could count. Lavender hung from the ceiling and tulips in all colours lined the floor. There were deep blue irises, white roses, purple hydrangeas and even tiny windmill ornaments that she wanted to steal and place all around her houseboat. She took video after video, determined to capture the vibrancy of the place to show Melody and her dad.

As she stepped backwards to zoom out, she landed on something unexpected.

'Ouch!'

Rosie spun around, apologising instantly. 'Oh my gosh, I'm so sorry!'

The young woman's face relaxed into a smile. 'That's all right. This place always amazes the tourists.'

Rosie could tell she was Dutch from the way she pronounced the words, even though her enunciation was perfect. 'Oh, I'm not a tourist,' Rosie clarified. 'Well I am, I suppose, but not technically and not for long.' The woman looked utterly confused. Rosie was over-sharing as usual. 'I live here now.'

'You do?'

'Yes, I just moved here.' As she was soon going to be running a stall at the flower market, Rosie thought she might as well introduce herself and stuck out her hand. 'I'm Rosie.'

'Emma,' the woman replied. She was about the same age as Rosie with striking dark red hair and emerald green eyes. Her vest top was bright yellow and her long skirt of contrasting red swished around her ankles. She looked like she'd stepped straight out of the Seventies. 'What are you doing here then, Rosie?'

'I'm going to have a pitch at the flower market and then start a shop.'

'Wow, you're doing all of that today?' Her eyes were wide with surprise and awe.

Rosie laughed. 'I would if I could but no, that's the end goal.'

'That's quite an ambition. Good for you. But you know the stalls at the flower market aren't easy to come by. Do you have a licence already?'

'A licence?'

The research she'd done hadn't covered anything about a licence. Melody's anxious voice came into her head. She wasn't a details person. Had she missed something vitally important?

In a no-nonsense fashion, Emma outlined what Rosie needed to know. 'Everyone needs a licence to trade and there's nearly always a waiting list for these spaces. They're like gold dust around here unless you know the right people.'

'Right.' Rosie's voice wavered though she tried to keep her smile intact. She had definitely missed something vitally important. Damn it.

'So you don't have a licence then?' Emma's voice was laced with sympathy.

'No. But that's okay. I'll get one.' She paused for a second. 'How do I get one?'

If Emma thought she was silly for thinking it would be that easy she didn't say anything. Instead, she just smiled. 'You need to go to the *Marktbureau* and apply for one, but I wouldn't hold out much hope if I were you.'

Rosie tried her best not to be discouraged. She'd just have to go and see what she could do. 'Well, thanks for your help, Emma.'

'No problem.' She leaned in a little closer. 'If I were you, I'd tell them that you plan to offer something a little different. They might be more likely to give you a pitch if you're doing something no one else is, or something that appeals to the tourists and the community. That's their big thing at the moment.'

Grateful for the advice, Rosie grinned widely. 'I'll definitely do that, thank you!'

She could offer talks, in English for tourists at first, then try Dutch when her language skills had improved. Her mum had often done that for WI groups and as part of her job, and she'd loved it. Her cheerfulness came from sharing her passion with people and as long as they'd had enough to pay the bills, she hadn't cared about other things.

'And here. Have some of this.' Emma moved back into her shop and picked up a plate, offering Rosie a small plate of cheese cubes. 'It's cheese.'

'Cheese?' Rosie echoed.

'Cheese,' Emma confirmed. '*Maasdammer*, to be precise. It's delicious. From a local supplier. Try some.' She nudged the plate towards her, grinning. 'Please.'

'Oh, okay. Sure.' She took a square by the small cocktail stick sticking out of it and ate.

'Isn't it delicious?'

'Delicious,' she repeated. It really was, but she wasn't quite sure of the etiquette when responding about cheese that had been gently forced on her. 'Is this what you do?' she asked, pointing at the cheese plate and the shop behind her stocked with all kinds of delicious deli items.

'Yes, this is my shop. Isn't it beautiful?'

'Absolutely.'

She grinned at Rosie's reply. 'Maybe one day you'll have one like this too.'

'I hope so,' Rosie said with a sigh. She had hoped, as stupid as it might be, that there would be a free stall and she'd be able to secure it like people did shops back home. She hadn't thought about licences and the details of starting a business here. She wouldn't admit that to Melody, though.

After saying goodbye, Rosie entered the *Marktbureau* into Google Maps and went on her way. It wasn't a long walk. Amsterdam, she was discovering, was quite a small city. The red-brick streets made her feel like she'd stepped back in time, but the increasing traffic as she moved towards the centre of the city made it clear that wasn't the case. She crossed canals, lingering over the bridges to admire the view of the water reflecting the boats and houses just as the flower market had done before. It was astonishing how one street could be busy and crowded and only a turn or two later she could be surrounded by peace and quiet, a sense of serenity encompassing her. There were pockets like this in London too, but not many and much harder to find. She loved that such quiet was easier to come by here.

Before long, she arrived at the council building. What would she say to convince them to give her a pitch over all the other hopeful people? And what would she do if there was a waiting list? She should have known this location would be popular, especially with the local vendors.

Her hopes faded even more as she approached the austere, uninspiring building. In contrast to the welcoming heritage of the city, the *Marktbureau* was a severe, stern-looking modern building. She walked inside to be met with suits and frowns, so familiar from her London office jobs. It was as if she'd been transported back there. After half an hour of pinging between floors, people and desks as she was passed off from one person to another, only to start all over again, she was finally sitting in front of the right person and her temper was fraying. But Rosie knew that a bad temper wasn't going to get her anywhere. The odds were already stacked against her. What she needed was a charm offensive.

'*Goedemorgen*,' she trilled cheerfully, not wanting to get off on the wrong foot.

The middle-aged man with thinning hair and a doughy face that made him look like he'd been moulded out of clay didn't respond.

'Umm . . . I was hoping to acquire a pitch at the flower market,' Rosie continued.

He barked out a burst of laughter so sudden and loud that it made her jump.

Rosie bit down against the temper flaring inside her and ignored him. 'I think I need a licence or something – is that right?'

'Madam, you can't just waltz up here and get a licence.' He looked at her as if she was stupid and, while she felt it, she didn't enjoy being reminded of the fact by a stranger. 'We have a long, long waiting list for spots in the *Bloemenmarkt*.'

'For all the pitches?'

'Most of them.'

'Well which one has the smallest list?' she asked, clasping her hands together in her lap. It made her feel like an old-fashioned maiden aunt but if she didn't, she'd only start wringing them together as the nerves in her stomach mounted, and she didn't want that to show.

He tapped something on his keyboard and the screen lit up. There followed a moment of huffing followed by him wiggling the mouse and some passive-aggressive loud clicking. 'The only one with a small waiting list is the *kleinste*.'

'I'm sorry, for the—'

'*Kleinste*,' he repeated. 'The tiniest pitch. Only a few people want it because it is so small. About the size of that cupboard.' He pointed to a small cupboard at the back of his office that was about the same size as one on her houseboat. 'Hardly worth selling anything from it. The current owner is about to move to a shop.'

It wasn't ideal, but still excitement surged within Rosie. It was an opportunity, and she wasn't about to turn it down. Everyone had to start somewhere. She'd lived in tiny boxrooms in bad house shares in London and made it work. She'd just need good display solutions, and a look on Pinterest later would give her lots of ideas. 'And how many people are on the waiting list for it?'

He huffed again and turned back to his computer screen, jabbing at the keys. 'Two. No, no . . . one. The other applicant has died.'

'Oh!' She hadn't expected to hear that. 'I'm so sorry,' she added, pressing a hand to her chest.

He shrugged. 'Why should I care? I didn't know them.'

Unsure what to say, Rosie mumbled, 'I suppose.' Then, steeling herself, she spoke louder. She only had one opportunity to gather all the information she needed to make this work. She wasn't going to waste it just because he was annoyed with her taking up his time. 'Can I ask, who is the other person on the list?'

'We cannot give out that information!'

'All right,' she replied, a little too harshly, but his patronising tone was beginning to irk her and she could feel the tension rising again through her body. He glared at her. So much for the charm offensive. She had to get this back on track and find some way of getting the information she needed. If she could speak to the other person on the list, she might be able to convince them to let her have the pitch. 'Sorry,' she added. 'It's just that I – I really need to get a pitch at the flower market. I've moved all the way from England to make this dream come true and I can't give up at the first problem.' Her voice suddenly filled with disappointment. This had been a lot harder than she'd anticipated and maybe it was naivety, or plain stupidity. 'You probably didn't need to know all that, did you?'

For some reason, he seemed to take pity on her and a small smile crept onto his face. 'Listen, I can't give out names and addresses, but I can tell you that the other person on the list already has a stall at the market. If you go and ask around there, someone will be able to tell you the name of the owner.' Rosie's mouth fell open. 'And,' he continued, 'if the current vendor recommended someone to take over their pitch, we would take that into account when assigning the plot, especially if the other person already had a business and you were looking to start one. We encourage diversity in Amsterdam, and especially within our small businesses.'

So whoever wanted the flower market pitch already had a business. That made her feel less guilty about trying to swipe the spot from them. And from the sounds of the pitch, maybe it was so small it wouldn't make that much difference to them, but it would make a whole lot of difference to her. Her new life was hinging on this. 'So the pitch hasn't definitely been given to anyone yet?'

'No,' he replied. 'It hasn't been confirmed yet.'

'Then can I ask where the pitch is in the flower market?'

'Just look for the smallest one.'

'Thank you. You've been really helpful.'

Smiling once more, Rosie made her way back to the flower market. When she came across the pitch, which was easy to find as it was absolutely as tiny as advertised, the owner had already boxed up most of their stock and there were only a few tubs of flowers in the space. It really was minuscule, and she wondered if the man at the council was right and that it wasn't even worth it. Would she be able to make a profit from here? But then she straightened her shoulders and told herself not to be so dismal. It was a start, and she didn't have any other ideas at the moment, apart from maybe some talks. All she needed was a base of operations. She approached the woman she assumed to be the owner.

'Hello, do you have a moment please?' The woman stopped packing her boxes. 'I understand you're moving on from this pitch?'

'That's right.'

'I wondered if there was any way I could convince you to let me have it.'

Her eyes widened in shock but her tone was kind. 'I think there's a waiting list.'

'Yes, but the man at the *Marktbureau* said there was only one name on the list and that if I could convince you, or the previous pitch owner if that's not you, to recommend me for the lot, as the other person already has a business, they'd take that into account, and it would greatly increase my chances.'

The woman, who had curly grey hair, looked around and though Rosie followed her gaze, she didn't see which vendor her eyes fell on. She suddenly crossed her arms over her chest, an inquisitive look creasing her features. 'If I'm going to annoy a fellow vendor here, I need to know why I *should* give it to you?'

'Well because I—' She remembered Emma's words of advice and though she'd meant them for the council man, they couldn't hurt here. 'I won't just be selling flowers. My mum was a botanist and I'll be giving talks on different flowers and plants too.'

'A botanist?' She cocked her head. 'That's impressive.'

'She wasn't famous, but she loved all flowers and plants. Even the ones we think are weeds. She always said every weed has a purpose, even if we haven't found it yet.'

'She sounds like a very clever woman.'

A slight sting pierced the back of her nose. Grief was on the way. She pushed it back enough to speak. 'She was.'

'Was?'

'She, umm . . . she died. It was a long time ago.' Rosie lifted her head and stopped toying with her hands. She braced herself for the look of sympathy these words normally garnered but they didn't come.

The woman studied her a moment and Rosie plastered on a smile to show she was fine. 'All right,' she declared a second later. 'It's yours.'

'Really?' She was enjoying the cultural differences already. The Dutch were far more to the point and she appreciated this woman moving the conversation away from such a sad subject. 'But won't the man at the council need to—'

'He'll still need to see your business plan, but I'm sure I can convince him.'

Rosie rolled onto her tiptoes, rocking with sheer joy. 'Thank you so much. I'm Rosie, by the way.' She leapt forwards and stuck out her hand.

'The name suits you. I'm Grietje.' Her grip was strong as she shook Rosie's hand vigorously. 'I'll call Bram at the *Marktbureau* and tell him I want the pitch to go to you, provided you can supply everything he needs. I'll be out of here by Friday and you can start from Saturday.'

'That's amazing! I – I don't know what to say! Thank you!' Unable to contain herself, she reached forward and hugged Grietje. The older woman hadn't been expecting it from the 'oomph' sound that came out of her. 'Thank you so much. I can't tell you what this means to me.'

A second later, the older woman's hand patted Rosie's back and Rosie stepped away. 'You'd better tell me your name and address. Bram will need it for the paperwork.'

Rosie grinned once more as she recited her details. She'd done it. She'd overcome two major hurdles already. She had somewhere nice to live and a stall at the flower market, as long as she got her ideas into an actual business plan and delivered it quickly.

Her new life was truly starting.

Chapter 3

Feeling both overwhelmed and overjoyed, Rosie decided there was only one thing to do: buy flowers. She stalked the market, finding the best blooms and the cutest pots to decorate the deck of her houseboat so that when she sat outside in the evenings watching the sun set, she'd be surrounded by nature and not the dead, dried-out twigs she'd been looking at since she arrived.

Loaded down with far more items than she could actually carry, she made her way back to her houseboat. A particularly tall plant (an areca palm with long frondy leaves that would look great in the corner of her living room) kept tickling her nose and blocking her view, but everything was so perfectly and precariously balanced in her arms, she hadn't been able to stop and adjust it. She was nearly there. All she had to do was get onto the deck of the *Forget-Me-Knot* and she could drop it all down. She walked along the pavement, the boats visible from the corner of her eye. This was hers, she was sure. She stepped onto the deck, feeling the slight sway of the water and . . .

'*Kijk eens waar je heen gaat!*'

She didn't understand the words but the angry tone was clear.

'Huh? Sorry, I—' Rosie peered through the fronds of the palm to be met by a man scowling. A bearded man. The handsome bearded man she'd seen before, *Grumpy-but-gorgeous*, who was perpetually tutting. *He* was her neighbour!

Great.

As these thoughts ran through Rosie's mind at breakneck speed, a tiny dog started barking excitedly and sniffing at her feet.

'Pastry girl!' Whilst not exactly angry, his tone was definitely annoyed.

'What? Don't call me pastry girl or I'll call you miserable-neighbour-who-didn't-want-to-say-hello-to-me-and-pretended-you-weren't-in.' A flicker of amusement lit his face, as she tried to get a better look through the fronds of the plant currently tickling her cheek, though his scowl remained intact. He really was very attractive, with full lips she could imagine kissing her softly, and suddenly Rosie's body began to heat from the inside. She cleared her throat and maintained her don't-mess-with-me attitude. 'What are you doing on my boat?'

'You're on *my* boat,' he said coldly, his blue eyes (quite nice pale blue eyes, she had to admit) were hard and glaring. Any amusement had vanished, as though she had imagined it.

'What?' she asked, eyes widening in concern. Rosie looked around, then, realising she'd walked past her own home and straight onto his deck. *Oh dear.*

'Oh! Whoops! I'm so sorry,' she replied brightly. 'I should've noticed, shouldn't I? Your boat's much tidier than mine. Well—' She glanced at the pots of paint, dripping brushes and sheets covering the deck. 'Sort of, anyway.' A sound emerged from him, something between a sigh and a laugh. 'Anyway, it's nicer than mine at the moment, but mine'll be spick and span before too long,' she rambled, as she nodded at the plants and pots in her hands and the areca palm flew in front of her face again, obscuring her vision. Before she could do anything, he had gently moved it to the side, his fingertip brushing her cheek and setting her skin on fire, especially when she saw him smile. She really should have asked for the plants to be delivered or made two trips. She was very aware she was sweating from carrying them in the heat and the one that had been gripped tightly in her fingertips was sliding out of her right hand. She felt herself tilting and she pressed it against her knee, hoping to hold on to it for a few seconds longer. All she needed was to get to her own deck. She tried to take a step backwards but couldn't because of the dog still sniffing her ankles and wagging its tail enthusiastically. The corner of the man's mouth lifted in amusement.

'Can you just—'

But it was no use. She felt herself leaning further and further to the right, a sense of impending doom growing. The bearded man watched her in silence, his head tilting in the same direction. She was near parallel with the floor now and . . .

'Oh no!' The pot fell from her grasp onto the deck, hitting it with a thud and rolling towards an easel with a huge canvas standing on it. The dog began to chase it and, as if in slow motion, the pot knocked into the leg of the easel near enough to the side of the deck that it could easily topple and fall into the water. The easel wobbled and her breath hitched. The canvas rocked but stayed in place, and just as she was reminding herself to breathe in, everything else in her arms came tumbling out, the finely balanced jigsaw falling apart and the pieces cascading down around her.

He jumped back, his hands in the air. '*Godverdomme!*'

'I'm really sorry, I didn't mean to—'

'You nearly knocked my painting over!'

'It is quite a stupid place to put an easel, don't you think? Right next to the side of the boat? I mean, the wind might knock it into the water.'

'What wind?' He held his hands up. Not a hair on his head moved, making the point for him.

'Well, if there was wind, I mean.' She bent down to begin gathering her plants.

He pushed his hands into his hair, gripping the strawberry blond curls, and she spotted strands of copper and sand as the light caught them. 'You – you – English people!'

'Hey!' She shot upright, ignoring the mess at her feet, poking a finger at him. 'There's no need for that. It was just an accident.'

'What did you think you were doing?'

'I was trying to brighten up my new home.' Rosie placed her hands on her hips, refusing to be intimidated. She didn't know if it was the way he was looking at her or the sun that was causing the back of her neck to prickle.

'No one can carry that much stuff,' he said crossly. 'No one. You're not an octopus!'

Well that was unexpected. She felt a smile pull at her lips and tried her best to press it down. He didn't smile in return and his eyes remained locked on hers in frustration. Unable to stop herself, she giggled.

'It's not funny.'

'I know. Sorry! It's just you saying the word "octopus".'

As if agreeing with her, the dog barked and left the pot, deciding it wasn't at all interesting and instead returned to Rosie as she tried again to gather up her things. 'Hello,' she said, stroking him as he tried to lick her face.

'You nearly ruined my painting.'

'Look . . .' she replied, standing and trying to smooth things over. The dog jumped up, leaning its front paws on her thighs, demanding attention.

'Zoon, sit.'

The tiny dog did as he was told, his tail wagging so fiercely he wiggled from side to side. Rosie couldn't tell what breed he was, perhaps a terrier, or part terrier. He had a long snout and slightly wiry hair, but his eyes were bright and lined with pale eyebrows.

'He's lovely.'

'He's a menace.'

She sensed a slight thawing and glanced again at her neighbour. His beard was a shade darker than his hair but neatly trimmed close to his strong jawline. She'd always had a weak spot for strong jaws. Her dad had always said to never trust a man without a chin, and she'd taken it to heart. There was something of the Chris Hemsworth about him, though maybe with a bit more angst and a bit less cheerfulness.

'Listen, I'm sorry about the pot. I didn't mean to step onto your boat but – wait! Did you say you're a painter?' she asked, walking towards the easel. She'd never met a real-life painter before and thought it one of the most amazing professions in the world.

He dashed in front of her, grabbing a paint-splattered sheet and throwing it over the canvas. Zoon took the opportunity to nudge himself closer to her, staring up for another fuss. She was happy to oblige. She'd always loved dogs.

'Won't that ruin it?' she asked, and he audibly sighed, pinching the bridge of his nose.

'No, it won't.'

'Can I see?'

'No.'

'Oh. Is that a thing? Do painters not show their unfinished work to people?'

'It is not a thing,' he replied, speaking slowly and coldly. 'But it is *my* thing. Zoon, leave her alone.'

Silence fell as they stared at each other. He was wearing a paint-spattered T-shirt and jeans that were also patterned with swipes and dots of paint. With his arms crossed over his chest she could see the bulge in his biceps and had to draw her attention back to his scowling face. She could just imagine his hands on her waist, hers gripping his biceps as he moved in for a kiss. She took a deep breath and thought of her old manager at the design company who had sweat patches and a sunburnt bald spot to distract herself. She had to get her mind off kissing this man because if he did actually smile, she wasn't sure her body would keep control of itself.

'Fine,' she said. It was clearly time to leave. She stepped towards him, and he watched her move closer. Something seemed to fizzle in the air between them, and his eyes locked on hers. Then she bent down to retrieve the pot lying at his feet. 'I'll just clear my stuff.'

'Yes, thank you. Then I might be able to get on with my work.'

There didn't seem any point in trying to smooth things over, so she gathered up a few more bits and stepped onto the pavement, walking around to her boat and placing a large pot and the areca palm on the deck. When she turned to go back for more, she was surprised to see he was right behind her, carrying her remaining items onto her boat. Zoon was, for once, doing as he was told and had remained on *The Rembrandt*.

'Here,' he said a little more gently. 'Nothing seems to be broken.'

'Except this.' She held up one of the green-gold trunks of the areca palm. 'Poor thing. I'll have to snip it and hope it grows back.'

'You like plants, don't you?' He gestured at the flowers and pots she'd lugged back with her.

'Yep. Some people are crazy cat ladies; I'm a crazy plant lady.' That small flicker of amusement flashed again over his features, and she stood up, straightening her T-shirt. 'I'm a florist. That's why I wanted to come here to work in the floating flower market.' She braced herself, ready for him to tell her off for not getting it all delivered. To her surprise, he nodded but didn't say anything else. 'Listen, I am honestly sorry for disturbing you. I didn't mean to. Can we, maybe, start again? I'm Rosie.' She held out her hand and, for a second, he stared at it like it might be a red-hot poker or covered in some kind of dangerous poison and this was all an elaborate assassination attempt. After glancing at her face, his eyes assessing her features in a way that made her heartbeat skitter, he shook it.

'Max,' he replied. The warmth and strength of his hand sent goose bumps up her arm despite the heat from the sun.

It had been a long time since she'd felt an attraction like this. The men she'd dated back home had been nice and many of them handsome in that put-together way that some women liked. But she quite liked a man who was a little rougher around the edges.

'I moved in yesterday,' she said, forcing her brain to focus on the conversation rather than staring at Max.

'I know. You were singing very loudly and shouting at taps in the night.'

She hadn't realised her Beyoncé concert while cleaning had been quite that loud. Her cheeks reddened. 'I—'

'I have to go.'

He turned and walked quickly to his boat, never once looking back. She heard him say something to his dog in Dutch and a second later, the door to the galley slammed shut and Rosie was left with the chaos at her feet, wondering why she had to have the rudest, but also most attractive man in the whole of Amsterdam as her neighbour.

Chapter 4

'Honestly, Mels, I've never met anyone so moody. Like, I get I did something wrong stepping onto his boat, but did he really have to act like that?' Rosie told herself to calm down as she nearly bent the stalks of the flowers she was pushing into the empty wine bottle from yesterday she was using as a vase (minus the label, of course). She was kneeling on the floor in her favourite old T-shirt. It had once been a bright, vibrant red, but was now washed out to a pale pink. With holes in the armpits and tears in the hem, she should really throw it out, but wearing it gave her comfort. It was like a link to home.

Not only was she growing angrier at the way he'd spoken to her, but she was also growing angry with herself because each time she thought about grumpy neighbour Max, she couldn't help picturing him clutching his hair, his biceps tensing, his neck lengthening and her mind went to kissing him, the hairs of his beard tickling her lips.

'He could have been a bit more welcoming,' her sister said, but Rosie could hear the amusement in her voice and picture her at home, grinning at Rosie's misfortune.

'Why're you smiling?'

'I'm not.'

'You are – I can hear it. Have you googled handsome men with washboard abs again?'

'No. I'm on my lunchbreak actually. I'm on lates today.'

'Oh, I'm sorry. I should have checked instead of just calling and ranting at you.'

'It's okay, I like your ranting. You're funny.'

'Thanks,' Rosie said, in mock annoyance.

'So what does he look like – this miserable neighbour?' On the other end of the line, she heard a packet of crisps being torn open. Her sister only ate salt and vinegar crisps, and Rosie could almost smell them as if they were sitting face to face. They'd often met for lunch – or dinner, in Rosie's case, if her sister was on lates at the hospital and she missed her, but this was the next best thing.

'He's all right, I suppose.'

Melody chuckled. 'Come on, I can hear it in your voice. He's a looker, isn't he?'

'Oh my God, he's gorgeous!' She gave up trying to push a second stem into the wine bottle and stood up. Max was out on his deck, so she lowered her voice. She didn't need another Beyoncé concert being overheard. 'He's got this gorgeous hair and a nice beard that makes me want to run my fingertips over it and—'

'Wow, you've got it bad.'

'It'll pass,' Rosie said, more to convince herself than Melody. 'You know I can never date someone who's miserable and hates laughing. How's the ward, anyway?' She desperately needed to move the conversation on before she started imagining kissing him again.

'Chaos. But I've got lovely patients so I don't mind. Listen, just ignore his crankiness and be your normal irritatingly cheerful self. You'll bring him round eventually.'

'I don't think I will. I've never met anyone more determined to be unhappy. I can see him now, actually.' She peered through the window to see Max back on his deck, smacking paint onto the canvas with a huge brush.

'Ooh . . . what's he doing?'

He was frowning, as per usual. His brows were drawn together in concentration, or consternation; she wasn't quite sure which. Yet again, his broad shoulders tensed as he wielded the brush and Rosie grew hot.

'Being a brooding artist.'

'He does sounds sexy. Like Byron or Shelley.'

'They were poets.'

'So . . . ? Fine. Like Caravaggio or something.'

'Better, but this isn't the eighteen hundreds, and didn't they all die of syphilis or something?'

'Do you think he has syphilis?'

'No.' She glanced again at the biceps. 'Have I ever had a thing for arms before?'

'Arms?' Her sister burst out laughing. 'I don't think so. Shoulders yes, arms no. Has he got good ones?'

'Mm-hmm. Oh, hey, have you asked that hot doctor out yet?'

Her sister groaned. 'No.'

'Why not?' Rosie heard the phone adjust, which meant Melody was calling from the staffroom and someone else was there. She'd been lusting after her work crush, Dr Marsh, for at least eight months but hadn't done anything about it. Rosie, on the other hand, was always happy to ask guys out if she wanted to. The worst that happened was they said no, and she always figured nothing ventured, nothing gained. Blokes did it all the time, getting knocked back more often than not, she presumed, so why shouldn't a woman in the twenty-first century? But even though she could do that, she hadn't met anyone who'd made it past date three. She glanced at Max. She wouldn't be asking him out anytime soon even if her hormones did go into overdrive when she looked at him. She wasn't willing to make room for negativity in her life.

'You'd wait forever for a man to ask you out. You should just do it yourself. Don't be scared to make the first move.'

'I just can't, okay. Don't bug me about it.'

'I'm not bugging you, but you need to do something. I know how much you like this guy.' Rosie swapped over two of the flowers and placed the bottle-cum-vase on the tiny windowsill behind the sofa. The light shone off the bright yellow petals, making her smile. 'Just walk up to him and say, "Hey, would you like to have a coffee tomorrow?" Job done.'

'I can't do that!' Melody squealed.

'Yes, you can – and by the end of this week, please.'

'Why the end of this week?'

Unable to stand still, Rosie moved one of the small plants she'd bought earlier, now in a vibrant, blue-glazed pot, and turned it so the long, ivy-like leaves trailed down over the edge of the tiny shelf. 'Because you've been putting it off for long enough. I'm giving you a deadline.'

'That's not much of a threat. You're in Amsterdam; you can't do anything about it if I don't.'

'I can. I can ring you up all hours of the day and night singing, "just ask him out, just ask him out".' Rosie stood up and began dancing around the tiny galley, repeating the phrase over and over again. Her sister started to giggle, and she began to sing louder. Max's voice penetrated her good mood like a knife jabbed into a balloon.

'Can you keep it down in there!'

'Oh my God, was that him?' Melody asked.

Rosie peered out of the window to where Max was standing, paintbrush in hand, his feet planted. Annoyance had hardened his features into a scowl. She ducked down onto the sofa and lowered her voice. 'See how grumpy he is! You could you hear him down the phone and I wasn't even singing that loud.'

'You were a bit loud. Everyone could hear you here in the staffroom.'

'Oh. Sorry. Sorry, Melody's colleagues!'

'That's all right,' came a muffled reply, followed by laughter.

'They think you're mad.'

Rosie ignored this. 'I told you, though: the grumpiest man in the world.'

Max was back to slapping paint onto the canvas as though it owed him money. The sun was setting now, the sky glowing with golden strands, the water of the canal calm except for the birds speaking to each other as they floated along. All of a sudden, Max threw down the paintbrush and went and sat on a chair, his head in his hands. A pang of sympathy nudged her. Whatever he was doing, it didn't seem to be going very well.

'He does sound quite cross. Good luck with him, Rosie-Roo.' She heard Melody stand and gather the empty packets from her lunch. 'Maybe it's best to avoid him in future.'

She thought about taking him a cup of tea, knowing how someone making her one always cheered her up when she was feeling low, but she wasn't sure what greeting she'd get. Actually, she was sure. She was one hundred per cent certain he'd tell her to go away and maybe even not that kindly. No, she'd stay here and let him get over himself. It wasn't her job to fix everyone else's life.

'I'll do my best.'

She drew her eyes away. She had some work to do before

she opened her pitch on Saturday, like finding suppliers for one and checking her bank balance to see what she could actually afford to spend. She'd already clocked the prices the competition was charging so she knew what sort of margins she'd be making and it was going to form the basis of her business plan, which she really needed to get started on if she was going to take it to the *Marktbureau* tomorrow. It wouldn't be much for now, but it would be enough to live on if she didn't go partying every night, and hopefully the talks would prove popular and give her a little extra too.

'I better go,' her sister said.

'Yeah, me too. I've still got a lot to sort out before I open my stall. I need to come up with a name, too. What do you think to Rosie's Blooms?'

'It's sweet. I like it.'

'You don't think it's a little boring?'

'Maybe a little,' Melody conceded. 'But you'll think of something. I know you will.'

'Thanks. I love you.'

'Love you too.'

'And ask Dr Marsh out by the end of the week, okay? And I won't take no for an answer!'

'Fine,' her sister huffed, but then Rosie heard her blow her a kiss into the phone as they said goodbye.

Rosie, with one last look at Max who still had his head in his hands, went back to organising her plants and flowers. The *Forget-Me-Knot* was looking more and more like a home with each passing day. What had begun as a drab, tatty boat was now blooming with new life and colour. There was still the drippy tap she needed to sort out, but she'd found a hammer in the cupboard under the sink and was going to give it a whack with that if it carried on dripping. For now, though, she had to write her business plan, ready for her grand opening on Saturday. She resisted the urge to squeal in excitement for fear of disturbing Max and settled down with her phone and a to-do list, even though her eyes kept wandering to the window and the sexy, brooding artist living next door.

Chapter 5

Many of the larger florists, especially the chains, purchased their flowers at *Bloemenveiling Aalsmeer* – a flower auction in a town about half an hour away, just outside Amsterdam. It was housed in one of the largest buildings in the world, and she wanted to go to see it full to the brim of flowers, but with such a small pitch there didn't seem much point. Also, she didn't have a car – not even a bike – so unless she rented one, she wasn't going to get them back intact. No. It would be much more efficient to source her flowers locally. But from which vendor? She decided the best way to find out was to visit the floating flower market again and talk to some of the other stall owners to find out who they preferred to work with. There was nothing quite like local knowledge and making new friends in the process.

On another glorious day, she dressed in her usual denim

shorts and T-shirt, her hair in a messy bun, and went about the next phase of starting her dream life. As she left the houseboat, she couldn't help but glance over at *The Rembrandt* to see if Max was awake. The memory of him with his head in his hands looking so distraught preyed on her mind. Not that she should care. He was incredibly rude and curt, but she didn't like to see anyone suffering. The galley curtains were closed and there were no signs of life. As tempted as she was to peek at the easel still sitting on the deck covered in a cloth, she resisted, knowing that if she were caught, Max would probably never speak to her again, and there was no need to make things even more awkward than they were already.

A cool breeze swept her face, refreshing her skin. While she loved the houseboat, it did get a little stuffy, even with all the windows open. With the weather so wonderful, Rosie decided that this time she'd take a different route through the city. Unlike London, where she had to rush through miserable commuters to get to work in a carbon-copy office block, today, there was no need to rush, and as the sun was already brightening the sky with its warm glow and only a few puffy clouds drifted lazily above her head, she wandered this way and that enjoying the hidden canals lined with houseboats, some as big as the flat she'd lived in in London. They must have been worth a fortune with their shining dark wooden decks, the galleys painted bright colours with the names written on. Maybe one day her little boat would be like that. Piet, the owner, had already said she could do what she liked with the place after she'd messaged to say she needed to make it feel more homely. He just seemed happy someone was living there.

Strolling down the tree-lined streets of shops filled with couples and families chatting and eating, Rosie tried to make out what they were saying, attempting to improve her Dutch. Amsterdam had a wonderful vibrancy and was full of energy. London had been too, but that energy had seemed frenetic and never-ending, whether it was the middle of the day or the middle of the night. Amsterdam's energy was different, motivating and animated, but tempered somewhat by the pedestrianised streets and the water flowing through the city, which made it seem somehow more settled. It was almost as if it was older and more mature, though she knew that wasn't technically the case. Rosie smiled to herself, knowing she was being fanciful and happy to indulge herself as she followed the streets aimlessly.

When she looked up again, she realised she was outside the Rijksmuseum and paused to take in one of the most famous galleries in the world.

'Wow,' Rosie muttered under her breath. A passer-by heard and smiled at her. The red-brick building was enormous with a central section flanked by two towers connected to two recessed wings and then further blocks that jutted back out. With sandstone windows and blocks running in vertical lines across its frontage it was both Gothic and Renaissance in style. The dark grey roof rose into peaks, punctuating the clear blue sky. It was breathtaking: a beautiful building to house the amazing works of art inside. Her mind flew to Max and she wondered what style of work he painted. She shook him from her mind. She'd have to make time to go in and look around. After all, it was one of the most well-known museums in the world. She'd be an idiot not to go, and it would be one of the first questions her dad would ask. But for now, she needed to find her way back to the flower market.

After a few wrong turns (map reading had never been Rosie's strong point, even when it was all on Google Maps), she made it back to the Singel canal and stepped inside the gorgeous floral-scented space. As soon as she entered, the different colours spread like a Van Gogh painting before her and the smell was almost overpowering. There was a strong aroma of pollen from the different types of lilies, and the earthy scents of peat and mud mixed with that of the canal. Some stalls stocked seed packets, garden ornaments and bird baths, others more novelty items like windmills and gnomes. Noise and chatter already filled the air with vendors speaking to each other in Dutch and others conversing in English. There were other stalls nearby too: a cheesemonger, a coffee shop, all welcoming some of the earliest customers.

Rosie made her way to her small pitch. The space measured about the same as the galley of her houseboat, tiny compared to some of the other stalls but bigger than the cupboard Bram at the council had described it as, and being here, in this historic place, was worth it. The pitch was reasonably well kitted out, although like her houseboat it was a little tatty in places. It could do with a lick of paint and though she usually preferred brighter colours, something pastel and muted would make the beautiful flowers stand out. She made a note on her phone and snapped some photos for a before-and-after shot for Melody and her dad.

Rosie began calculating how many bunches of flowers and what different varieties she wanted to stock, when a woman's voice called over her shoulder.

'It's you again!'

Rosie turned to see Emma, dressed in another colourful skirt, her apron tied tightly around her waist, showing off her hourglass figure. Her pillar-box red hair was tied back away from her face, and she was slicing an enormous ham by hand, cutting thin strips of it with a dangerously sharp knife, then arranging them on a plate. From the cocktail sticks sticking out of some of the pieces, these were more samples for those visiting the market. They were in for a treat if the cheese Rosie had tasted before was anything to go by. It'd been delicious, and she planned to buy some more while she was there. Maybe she could get some of this ham too and have a relaxed dinner when she got back to the boat tonight. She might even sit out on her deck now she'd re-potted the plants.

'Hello again,' Rosie replied. 'Emma, wasn't it?'

'It was. Well remembered.' Emma pointed the knife at her and Rosie instinctively took a step back.

'Whoa! You having a bad morning?'

Emma laughed, suddenly realising she was brandishing the knife like a weapon. 'Oops, sorry.' She went back to carving. 'Actually, it's been quite good so far.' She glanced towards another shop, but Rosie couldn't tell which one. 'So, I heard you got your pitch.'

'You did?'

She nodded. 'Everyone talks here. Nothing is a secret in the flower market.' She was flourishing the knife again as she spoke.

'Should you be doing that?'

'Doing what?'

'That.' Rosie made stabbing motions with her hand.

'Of course, I've done this a million times.'

'While talking?'

'Sometimes. Grietje said she was happy you were taking over her pitch. Though Finn won't be.'

'Who's Finn?' Rosie asked, worry bringing frown lines to her forehead.

'He was next on the waiting list, and is one of the most unpleasant people in the market.'

'Oh.' Rosie bit her lip.

'Don't worry, no one likes him all that much. And as he already has one of the biggest pitches here at the *Bloemenmarkt* and two shops, he doesn't really need another outlet. Look—'

She pointed with the knife to where a man with one of the largest stalls was standing. He had some of the most beautiful flowers Rosie had ever seen and three staff scurried behind him. Rosie hoped one day that might be her, though she wouldn't be standing with her arms crossed over her chest, looking angry like he was. He surveyed the scene before him like he owned the place.

'We were all quite worried about him taking over everything,' Emma continued, done with the knife and laying it down. Rosie felt herself relax a little. 'We all want there to be diversity here and lots of different shops offering different things. Yes, it's the flower market and that's what it's famous for, but that doesn't mean the same person should own all the flower stalls. Lucky for us Grietje said she liked you and she's a very good judge of character. I'm so pleased to welcome you.'

Emma loaded the meat onto the cocktail sticks and arranged them on an elegant platter. 'There,' she said, peeling off the thin rubber gloves she'd been wearing and putting them in a small bin behind the counter.

'Do you know who he buys his flowers from?' Rosie asked. 'They're beautiful.'

Emma shook her head. 'Sorry, but you can ask Fenna. She has another flower stall further down that way—' She pointed along the canal. 'She always has lovely flowers and unlike Finn, will be happy to talk to you.'

Emma gave her a description of the stall and some easy-to-follow directions.

'Thanks. So, have you been here long?'

'Two years. I used to sell from a small cart in the city centre, but when this place became available I couldn't say no.' She lifted a wooden tray stacked high with treats and placed it behind her.

Rosie took a second to look around the rest of her shop. Jars full of everything from pickled fish to olives, vegetables and sweet jams lined the shelves. Intermixed were boxes of crackers, bags of *stroopwafels*, and cured sausages. Just looking at it all made her incredibly hungry, and she realised she hadn't yet had breakfast.

'Can I buy a bag of *stroopwafels*, please?'

'No, but I'll give you one as a welcome present.' Emma took one from the nearest shelf and handed it over.

'No, I couldn't!' Rosie protested, but Emma was not to be deterred.

'I insist. Please.'

As she was handing them over, a tall handsome man with thick horn-rimmed glasses passed them by and Emma pulled back, leaving Rosie's hands dangling in the air.

'Hi, Noah,' Emma called out and the man smiled and raised his hand in greeting.

'Hi, Emma.' A blush began to colour his cheeks, and he turned away and walked on.

Before Emma could say any more, he'd gone, and her shoulders fell.

'Everything all right?' Rosie asked, reaching out for the *stroopwafels* again, and this time Emma let them go. Rosie knew she was being nosy but couldn't help asking. 'Does he work here too? Is he not very nice or something?'

'Noah? No, he's the nicest man I ever met – I mean—'

Emma began to blush too, and she dropped her eyes. Was he the one she'd been looking at earlier? 'He's normally very polite. He must just be busy. He was talking to me this morning.'

'He did look in a rush.' Rosie could tell there was something more going on but didn't want to press too much, given that they hardly knew each other. Perhaps when she'd been working here for a week or two she'd be able to ask more about it. Rosie offered Emma one of her *stroopwafels* from the open packet and she took one.

'Thank you. So, when will you open and what's your shop called?'

'Saturday. I'm just about to deliver my business plan to the *Marktbureau* and then I need to source some flowers, and the truth is, I don't know what my shop will be called. I had thought something like *Rosie's Blooms* but that's boring.'

'It is a little. No offence.'

Rosie chuckled. 'None taken. I know I need to come up with something else.'

'I'm sure you will. If you're selling flowers then Fenna is definitely the person to talk to. And she's really kind and always happy to offer advice. She's been here for years and helped me when I first arrived. She helped me make friends here.'

'I can't wait to speak to her then.' Rosie gave a huge grin. 'This is delicious, by the way. I'll definitely be back later to buy some bits for my dinner. Your stall looks amazing.'

'Thank you.' Emma beamed. 'It's my pride and joy. And the market is the most wonderful place to work. You'll love it here.'

'I'm sure I will. See you later.'

The thought that she'd made a friend, or at least knew someone friendly at a neighbouring stall, lifted Rosie's spirits as she made her way down to Fenna and introduced herself. Fenna was probably in her mid-fifties, her long blonde hair highlighted with strands of silver. She had rosy cheeks and wide, bright grey eyes. She also had two members of staff working for her and a stall equal in size to Finn's. As there was a coffee shop nearby, Rosie treated them both to a drink as a thank you to Fenna for sharing all the details of her suppliers.

'Get your order in quickly though,' the older woman advised. 'The flower auctions, where they get their flowers from, always sell out quickly, so if you don't get your request in on time, you might miss out. Always call the day before for the next day's flowers and be specific. And don't let them tempt you to go over budget.'

'Thank you so much for all your help. Everyone here's so nice.'

'Not everyone,' Fenna said in an off-hand way. Rosie knew she was speaking of Finn and apprehension made her chest tight. She doubted he was going to be exactly friendly when he realised she had stolen the stall from him, even though he had more than enough premises already. Perhaps she should bite the bullet and go and meet him? Maybe take him a coffee as an apology? Surely being a businessman, he'd understand that she'd had to do it. She had to make this work. A member of staff called out to Fenna and with a quick thank you for the coffee she was forced to say her goodbyes.

Rosie took a moment to finish her drink and decide what flowers she was going to order for her first day's trading. Looking around, she saw that everyone was selling tulips, which could either mean they were a sure bet, or that she'd end up with lots left over at the end of the day as everyone else, who the locals knew and trusted, would sell out first. It was a conundrum. Then she struck on an idea. As she'd walked through, she'd noticed that there were far fewer herbs on sale and, as a botanist, her mum had always championed the healing properties of plants. What if she sold a mixture of flowers and gorgeous herbs people could use for their cooking and homeopathic remedies? That would make her stand out from the crowd. But what flowers and what herbs? That was the next thing she needed to figure out.

After half an hour, Rosie had made a list of everything she wanted to stock and made her flower order with the help of a translation app. After some difficult negotiations between the man on the other end and his limited English, and her pretty much non-existent Dutch, she was ninety-nine per cent sure she'd ordered everything she needed, and it would be delivered bright and early in two days' time.

Rosie puffed with pride. Another hurdle had been

overcome and she was now ready for her first day's trading. All she had to do was rinse and repeat until she had enough money for a larger pitch and from there, she'd move to selling flowers on her boat and even having a shop in the centre of Amsterdam. Rosie's Blooms would be everywhere. She scowled. That name was definitely boring. She'd absolutely have to come up with something more attention-grabbing, and soon.

Chapter 6

When Rosie opened the door of the *Forget-Me-Knot*, the first thing she did was shriek. It wasn't a quiet, ladylike exclamation of surprise; it was a loud, echoing, 'What the fuuuuuudge . . . ?'

Her stomach shrank, tightening into a knot as she stepped down into the boat to see a thin film of water covering the floor. The new rug she'd purchased in a startling but gorgeous pink hue was drenched and the sink, where the tap had been dripping, was overflowing, with water pouring out of it from the base of the tap.

She rushed forwards, muttering expletives as she went, tripping over the step and falling to her hands and knees. The water seeped into her trainers and shorts as she stumbled forwards.

'Oh no, oh no, oh no!'

She splashed towards the cupboard under the sink to try and find the stopcock. Surely there must be one. She pushed aside the cleaning products and cloths she'd recently bought, wailing and cursing as she did so.

'Why me? Why is this happening now?'

Relief flooded her as she saw the shiny tap and reached forward. The water was freezing cold and though the day had been warm, she wasn't particularly enjoying cooling down this way. She'd much rather have sat on the deck with a cold, crisp glass of wine. She tried to turn it, but it wouldn't move.

'Crap!' She stood up, water dripping down her shins. There must be something she could turn it with. She grabbed the tea towel, wrapping it around the tap for extra purchase, but still it didn't budge. Throwing open cupboards and drawers, she searched for tools but the only thing she could find was the hammer and screwdriver left by Piet or the previous owners. She wasn't entirely sure who. She stood and looked around, her heart hammering in her chest. Would the boat sink if she didn't stop the water?

'No!' she screamed, tears stinging her eyes and frustration closing her throat as she gripped the short hair of her pixie crop. Everything she'd purchased was being ruined. She grabbed some towels, trying to soak the water up off the floor, but with more of it spilling over the sink, it did no good. She had to find a way to turn off the water and began scrambling around trying to find something to help her turn the stopcock.

'What have you done?' asked Max, his broad shoulders filling the open doorway, Zoon once more at his feet.

'Me? Nothing! This wasn't my fault!'

He dived in, straight to the stopcock, struggling for a moment (which made her feel less like a wimp) then turning it in his strong hands. The water slowed, trickling to a halt a second later. Relief flooded through Rosie even though her trainers were under water and her toes were ice cold.

'What happened?' he demanded, his hands on his hips.

'I – I don't know. I went to work this morning and when I came back it was like this. I mean, it's been dripping for a few days, and I did—' She stopped herself, realising now what a stupid thing it was she'd done and how he was going to be even more annoyed at the situation when he found out.

'You did what?'

'Hmm? Nothing.' She shook her head and reached down into the water, collecting a towel that was about to float towards Zoon.

'Oh no.' He crossed his arms over his chest, his biceps tensing in his tight T-shirt. Where had this obsession come from? She'd never even noticed any of her ex-boyfriends' arms. Did Max wear his tops so tight on purpose? She didn't think so. He didn't seem to be aware of how attractive he was. His beard was trimmed but not groomed to perfection like some men's were and she wasn't sure his hair had even been brushed. His eyes were pinned on hers, the pale blue sharpening to an icy brightness. Rosie swallowed, turning her gaze away to the devastation in her home. 'You said,' Max began, 'it's been dripping for a few days and you . . . what did you do?'

Rosie grew hot. She'd never felt so foolish, but she was going to have to tell the truth, wasn't she? She kept her voice calm even though humiliation crept over her skin. 'Look, I didn't know it was going to end up like this.'

'Rosie, what did you do?'

The use of her name, the way it rolled out of his mouth, sent a shiver down her spine. 'I might have . . . hit it with the hammer.'

Max's eyes widened and she could see the shock turning to anger, building inside him like a volcano that was preparing to erupt. 'You did what? Why? Why would you do that?'

'It'd been dripping for days, and it was driving me crazy.' It was a stupid reason, even to her own ears. 'It was all I could hear every time I tried to sleep. I just . . . got a bit cross in the middle of the night and I . . .'

'Hit a tap with a hammer?' He said the words slowly, trying to comprehend the logic.

'It seemed like a good idea at the time,' she replied quietly, averting her gaze again.

Zoon took this opportunity to hop down into the galley, padding in the water and sniffing at her furniture, clearly not bothered by the cold creeping up his body. He started lapping at it.

'Zoon, don't do that!' she said, picking him up and putting him back on the top step, in the dry.

'You could have asked me. I have tools. I live on a houseboat. I could have helped you.' She was more than a little surprised by his offer, especially given the last thing he'd said to her was a warning to stop singing so loudly. She glanced at him, and this time, he was the one to avoid her gaze as he surveyed the damage. 'If you're going to live on a houseboat, you should have tools too.'

'Well Piet didn't leave me any and I haven't had a chance to buy some because I've been trying to build a new life myself and start a business and get to know this new city I'm living in.'

Their eyes locked, and neither looked away. As usual, he looked grumpy and annoyed, even a little angry. She refused to cry in front of him, or to be beaten, and she lifted her chin. The water was off and there was no point in standing here feeling sorry for herself. She had to clean this entire place – no one else was going to do it for her – and if she didn't start bailing out the water soon, who knows how much more damage would be done.

'I need to sort this out and call a plumber.'

'Don't do that,' Max said as she moved to grab her phone. 'It will cost a lot of money, and I can probably fix it for you. I'll fetch my tools and have a look first. You start to clear up. Soak up the water with towels if you can. I'll bring some over. It's clean water so if we get things dry soon, they shouldn't smell. Clear some space on the deck. It's so hot, the sun will dry most of it and you can even put some things on the street. No one will mind.'

'You sound like you've done this before,' she said with a small smile which, surprisingly, he returned.

'You're not a true houseboat owner until you've dealt with some kind of flood.'

'Is that right? So I'm now officially in the houseboat-owning club?' He nodded. 'Cool. I've never been in a club before, unless you count the Brownies, but I got kicked out because I refused to take down the tent I'd made.'

'Why did you refuse?'

'Because I'd decorated it and filled it with pillows. I was going to live there when I got older.'

A slight laugh escaped Max's lips, or it could have been a huff of frustration. She wasn't entirely sure. After a second, he said, 'I'll get my tools,' and left, leaving Rosie wondering where the kind side of her grumpy neighbour had come from and worrying at how insanely attractive it made him.

'Well, Zoon,' she said, seeing the dog's tail wag at the use of his name. 'What are we going to do, hey?' He barked in response and then grumbled at a duck passing by the window. Max's advice made sense, and she cleared some space on the deck, removing the damp rug and laying it in the sunshine.

Max reappeared, placing a large toolbox down at his feet. 'Did you wring it out?' He nodded towards the rug. She shook her head. He picked it up and began coiling it. 'Here, take the other end.' They moved so it was over the side of the boat and he twisted it. The water ran out in increasing volume and then, when he had it as tight as he could, he squeezed it so fiercely, his shoulders and arms bulged with the effort. Rosie forced herself away, back inside to find towels and a bucket or saucepan to collect some of the water, worried she'd start drooling if she stared any longer at his plain, dark green T-shirt, watching the muscles of his chest work with the effort.

Max followed her and began working in the cupboard as she bailed out water and eventually started mopping up the remaining mess with all the towels she owned. He began tutting, offering little conversation except with himself, in Dutch. She could tell he wasn't saying complimentary things about her, and the atmosphere grew uncomfortable. As usual, Rosie felt the need to fill it.

'So,' she began, as she stood in the doorway after wringing out another towel. 'What type of things do you paint?'

'Can you hand me the wrench?'

She glanced at the toolbox, picked up what looked to be the most wrench-like thing and handed it to him.

He looked at the metal object and then her face. 'They're pliers.'

'Oh. Is this the wrench?' She picked up another thing from the toolbox and waved it at him.

Max sighed. 'Never mind. I'll get it.' He grabbed it, glancing at her and then wriggling back under the sink.

'So . . . painting? What do you do? Portraits? Landscapes? Abstracty-type stuff?'

'If you're going to live on a houseboat, you need to learn about basic maintenance. This stopcock turns the water off. I've oiled it so it should be easier to move next time.'

'Hopefully there won't be a next time,' she added, looking around at the mess. The floor was dry but would need a good clean, and she was more than a little worried all the wooden furniture, including the built-in sofa and bench, would warp. 'Will the floorboards rot?'

'Not from that.' He pulled his head out of the tiny cupboard and stood up, drying his hands on the only dry towel she still owned. 'They need to be varnished, though. Piet hasn't been keeping the place as well as he should.'

'He said I was lucky to have it.'

Max scoffed. 'No one's lived here for a while, and he hasn't maintained the boat as a good owner should.'

'That's what I thought,' Rosie admitted, her cheerful tone faltering. Had she been done? Was she just another gullible tourist? Max's words confirmed it, and she felt even more stupid than she had earlier for hitting the pipe.

Surprisingly, he seemed to see that she was uncomfortable, and his tone softened. 'It won't take much to fix up. As this dries out, you need to keep the windows open. Houseboats can get very damp with condensation and general moisture. You don't want mould and mildew forming. There is some already under there.'

'Where?' She dived forwards onto her knees, sticking her

head in the cupboard. She didn't like the idea of breathing in mould spores. Max knelt down and leaned in too.

'There.' He pointed to the back corner of the cupboard where a line of blue-black splotches rose up the wall. 'It's not that serious.'

'It is,' she replied, turning towards him, suddenly realising how close together they were, barely centimetres apart. She watched his pupils dilate as he focused on her then scanned her face, down to her lips. Was she imagining the way the air had tightened between them? The way it sat so heavily around them as if charged with expectation? Her own eyes fell to his mouth, and she couldn't help but wonder what it would be like to kiss him. As her eyes rose back to his, he pulled back out of the cupboard, whacking his head in his haste.

'Ow! *Godverdomme!*'

'What does that mean?' she asked, repressing a giggle as he rubbed the back of his head.

'God damn it, you English and Americans would say.'

'Are you all right?'

'I'm fine,' he replied brusquely, dropping his hand. 'So why is it so serious?'

She jumped up too, concern ringing through her. 'Because mould spores get into the air and then you breathe them in, and they get into your lungs. It's gross and not very good for you.'

He looked around, studying the galley, seeing her shelves covered in plants. 'Is this what you do? Plants and things?'

'Plants and things?'

'You know what I mean.'

'Yes, I'm a florist, and technically spores aren't plants, they're fungi but – yeah – I love plants.'

His expression had softened but before she could carry on the conversation, he suddenly picked up a tool and tightened the tap itself. Before she could think of anything else to say, he said, 'That's all fixed,' and began to collect his things.

'Really?' As confused as she was by Max's hot and cold nature, a huge grin spread across her face and some of the tension melted away. Things were back on track. 'Thank you. I really do appreciate your help. I better get cleaning that mould and airing everything out.'

He stopped on the top step of the galley, the sunshine lighting him from behind. 'Are you always this happy at cleaning up mess?'

'No, but there's no point in moaning about it, is there? It has to be done and at least I can put some music on while I work – as long as you don't mind me having a singalong, that is.'

'Given what's just happened I think that's fair enough.'

'Thank you.'

'I'll put on my noise-cancelling headphones.'

'Hey!' He didn't exactly smile, but the corner of his mouth lifted. Had that been a joke? Was he teasing her? The thought sent a thrill through her. 'Anyway, I didn't have anything else to do this afternoon, so I might as well be useful. I might even paint the cupboards. That dark wood is nice outside but in here it makes everything feel gloomy.'

Max watched on, shaking his head in bafflement. 'Give them a few days to dry out first.'

'Oh, all right.' He turned to leave and without thinking, Rosie said, 'Can I make you dinner or something to say thank you?'

His features closed again, the veil of indifference coming down over his eyes and his jaw hardening. 'No, thanks. I – I have stuff to do.'

'Stuff?' Why did she say that? It was clear he wasn't interested, and she was just making a fool of herself by prolonging the conversation. 'Stuff, right – yeah, sure. Of course.'

'Maybe another time,' he added, turning and walking away. 'Zoon, come.' He stepped onto the pavement and back around to his own boat, the little dog following behind.

Another time my foot, she thought and for the first time a slight tinge of embarrassment shot up her spine that she'd been knocked back. She hadn't cared whenever she'd been rejected before but for some reason this stung. Maybe it was because they were neighbours or perhaps it was because she was clearly more attracted to him than he was to her. Rosie sighed, placed her hands on her hips for a moment and thought about what colour she'd paint the cupboards. She shouldn't care what Max thought about her, she reminded herself. He was clearly allergic to fun and laughter and having friends. A small voice in her head told her she was being unkind. That there was something more to him or he wouldn't have helped her today. He'd have let her pay for a plumber. And what was that moment in the cupboard? Remembering it sent a shiver of heat through her.

Rosie glanced behind her, but Max was now out of sight. Why did his rejection sting so much?

Chapter 7

The *Bloemenmarkt* looked even more beautiful as Rosie arrived bright and early on Saturday morning. She was filled with excitement. She'd tied a 1940s-style headscarf around her head and had taken a bit more time over her make-up, wanting to look and feel her best. Grietje had met her to hand over the keys and wish her luck but had soon disappeared with her own new store to open. Now Rosie was ready for the flower delivery. Nearly all the stall owners were there opening their stores and the place buzzed with energy and enthusiasm. Rosie couldn't stop smiling. She hovered around, rearranging the buckets she'd purchased for the flowers to go in, eager for her first ever delivery to arrive.

Before long, men and women carrying flowers, crates of bulbs, pots and boxes of garden accessories were scurrying backwards and forwards between the different stalls. A young man arrived and turned on the spot a few times.

'Harper?' he called out, looking between the piece of paper in his hand and staring at the stallholders in the market. 'Harper?'

'That's me!' Rosie cried, leaping forwards in response to her surname and waving to get his attention. 'Over here.'

With a nod of acknowledgement, he marched forwards, deposited the first bunch of flowers he'd been holding and then went off to collect more. Rosie looked down at what he'd left on the ground in front of her and frowned. A horrible sinking sensation climbed up from her stomach, gripping her throat. These weren't the flowers she'd ordered.

For some reason, she lifted them up and moved them around as if magically the ones she'd requested would be hidden underneath. They weren't. The man appeared again with more flowers she hadn't asked for. He tried to place them down but Rosie grabbed them and forced them back into his arms.

'*Tjongejongejonge!*' he exclaimed, pulling away from her as if she was about to hit him.

'I have no idea what that means, but—' He started backing away, looking absolutely terrified. 'No! Wait! I'm sorry but these – these aren't the flowers I ordered.'

He stared at her wearily, clearly not understanding her English.

She tried again, frantically loading up her translation app on her phone and trying to type it in. He edged forwards and tried putting the flowers down. Rosie leapt in to stop him.

'No, no, no—' She picked them up and gave them back to him. He shook his head and moved backwards. Rosie held up her phone trying to show him the screen, but her hands were shaking so much all she did was wave her phone in front of his face. The poor boy looked even more confused.

'Is everything all right?' Emma asked, coming to her side.

Rosie could have wept with relief, but only for a second as she recited what was happening. 'No, there's been some mistake. These aren't the flowers I ordered.'

'What did you order?'

'Roses, carnations . . .' She listed a few more and Emma began to translate for her.

The young man responded but Rosie couldn't make out anything he'd said. He showed Emma the screen of his small handheld tracker and Emma took it, showing it to Rosie.

'This is what they have down for you.'

Rosie shook her head. 'I don't know what's happened, but I didn't ask for these—' She signalled to the arum lilies at her feet.

'Could you have maybe . . .' Emma didn't finish, but her meaning was clear.

Rosie thought for a moment. 'I said the Latin names of some of them, maybe they didn't catch them.' Rosie raised her eyes to the sky, urging her brain to start working. There had to be a solution to this but if there was, she had no idea what it was. Emma was staring at her worriedly. 'Between Latin, English and Dutch, it looks like there's been some mistake.'

The young man took his device back and spoke again. Emma translated.

'He said he's sorry, but he has other deliveries to make. Do you want the flowers or not? There won't be a refund though.'

'But this isn't what I wanted.' This couldn't be happening on her first day of trading. Everything was supposed to be perfect, but just like the other jobs she'd had through the years, everything was going wrong. Like when she'd started at a temp job in the city and the fire alarm had gone off while she was in the loo. By the time she'd yanked up her knickers and made it out into the corridor there was no else around, and she'd got so lost trying to find her way out that she was the last one to leave and everyone had given her a round of applause.

Other vendors were beginning to stare at her, wondering what was going on. She didn't want to make a spectacle of herself on her first day. All she wanted was to sell some flowers.

'I guess I'll have to take them,' Rosie replied, her shoulders falling and tears stinging the backs of her eyes.

Emma gave the man the message and he quickly delivered the rest of her unusual order. Instead of the beautiful array of blooms she'd been hoping for, launching her stall along the lines of an English country garden to stand out from the crowd, she was left with a mishmash of plants and flowers that didn't really go together.

'It'll be all right,' Emma said, rubbing her shoulder. 'Can you make some flower arrangements or something? I don't really know much about flowers.'

Rosie swiped at an escaping tear and sniffed, forcing the others back. 'And you work in the world's only floating flower market?'

'It's bad, I know.'

'I might be able to make a couple but there's so much to consider when making an arrangement, like the different scents and how they complement each other, the balance of colours and the size of the flowers, the vase life and weight of the blooms, the—'

'I get it,' Emma said gently, rubbing her shoulder again. 'So what can we do?'

That she'd said *we* made Rosie feel a little less alone.

'There's got to be a solution,' Rosie replied. She just had to calm down and think straight. She still had time before they opened to the public to do something. But what? Perhaps someone in the market would swap with her?

She tried Fenna first, who kindly swapped a small bunch of lilies for some tulips, but couldn't really do much more. Rosie then approached a number of other stallholders who either pretended they couldn't understand her English, or just said no and scurried back into their much bigger stalls. She looked around and spied Finn, the man she'd stolen the pitch from, who was clearly as miserable as Max. He had such a large pitch, full to the brim of flowers, and with such huge variety, he could surely swap a few bunches with her, or perhaps she could pay for some of his. Not that she could really afford to. Rosie rolled her shoulders back to brace herself and began walking.

Seeing the direction she was headed in, Emma sprang in front of her. 'No, Rosie, I—'

'I need to, Em. I haven't got much choice.'

'Rosie—' she hissed. But Rosie kept on walking.

'Hi,' she said to the man who everyone seemed to dislike. Obviously, he had reason to dislike her most of all, but she ignored that and carried on regardless. 'I'm Rosie, I've just taken over Grietje's stall.'

Finn was older than she'd thought from a distance, clearly in his mid-forties from the gentle lines around his eyes and on his forehead. His hair was greying at the temples, silver strands taking over from a soft, sandy blond. He was tanned from days working in the sun and, she suspected, possibly the odd sunbed or two. There was a slight discolouration around his eyes where the goggles went, and his skin had a thick, worn look about it. Most people at the market were dressed in jeans or shorts, but Finn was clad in a fitted beige suit and crisp white shirt.

Rosie thrust her hand out and smiled. They were going to be working alongside each other for the foreseeable and there was no better time to start things off on the right foot. Finn's lip curled. He didn't take her hand and after a second of it hanging in the air, she withdrew it.

'Umm, so . . . hi – I've already said that, haven't I? Sorry. So, I'm Rosie – I said that too, didn't I? Sorry . . . again! Look, I know we've just met and it's incredibly cheeky of me, but I've had a bit of a disaster, and I was wondering if you could help me. I don't really know what happened, but none of the flowers I requested have been delivered, apart from some lavender, and well, this is a bit of a mad request but—' She was babbling and had to rapidly draw in a breath. He watched her, cold eyes staring mercilessly. 'I was wondering if we can possibly swap some flowers.'

'You want to swap flowers?' His English was perfect, and she blew out a breath, relieved he'd understood her, and she hadn't had to attempt all that again using the translation app. An app she was beginning to mistrust intensely. He laughed and then instantly stopped. 'You stole my stall!'

'I didn't mean to steal it,' she replied. She totally had but didn't think saying so was going to help at that moment.

'I don't believe you.'

'I know you're probably cross but if I can just explain. You see—'

'I don't care.'

'Wow! At least you're honest, I suppose. But you've already got a shop—'

'Two shops.' His smug smile made her want to punch him.

'There you go! Two shops. And this—' She motioned behind him. 'This huge, amazing, gorgeous stall here. You don't need that tiny pitch, but for me – this is the start of my life, of me making something of myself and—'

She was over-sharing again, and he clearly didn't care for it. 'You want to swap some flowers?'

'Yes!' Hope began to rise, lifting her spirits, perhaps her over-sharing had shown him she wasn't here to try and sabotage his business, but simply start her own. 'Just a few bunches. Or I could buy some.'

'Look around you.' He gestured to the width of his stall and the breadth of his displays. 'I already have all the flowers you have and more. Why would I want extra?'

Rosie felt herself shrinking. Heat burned her cheeks, and she knew she was turning pinker with every passing second. 'I know you don't *need* them but—'

'You want me to take more flowers than I need – flowers I already have – just to help you out when it won't actually help me at all?'

She couldn't answer. He'd summed up exactly what she was asking for and though it sounded cold and selfish (especially given he was already cross she'd taken the pitch he'd been after, even though he already had this one and shops as well), she was just desperately trying to make her first day a success. If today was a failure, what would that mean for the rest of her future here? She couldn't help but feel as though what happened today would set the tone for the rest of her time here. She didn't want this to end as all her other crappy jobs had. She didn't want to prove Melody right and let her mum's memory down.

Rosie cleared her throat and drew herself up taller. 'I just – I just really need some help. I know you've no reason to help me but we're both people and—' He scoffed, and her eyes shot up to his face. All the embarrassment she'd felt fled, to be replaced with anger. She'd politely reached out and he'd actually laughed in her face. 'There's no need to be so rude, you know. You could have said—'

'What? Should I have made up a lie as to why I won't help you? What's the point in that?'

She tried to calm herself, but her body was buzzing with adrenalin. The fight-or-flight response was kicking in and she'd always been one to fight rather than fly. 'I just thought as we're both florists—'

'That we should stick together? This is a business. *I'm* running a business.'

The way he stressed the *I'm* annoyed her even more. She was running a business too, or at least trying to, and though today hadn't gotten off to a very good start, she was going to do her best to make it work. She didn't have any other option.

'And you stole my pitch!' he finished, jabbing a finger at her.

Rosie glowered at him. 'Well, thank you for your time, Mr . . .' He didn't answer. 'Fine. Thank you for your time, Mr Miserable. I'll remember not to bother you again.' She spun on her heel and walked away. Emma was waiting for her when she returned to her stall.

'I could have told you that was what would happen,' she said sympathetically, if also a little unhelpfully.

'I thought I had to try.'

'I understand. It's not you, though. He's a horrible man. No one likes him. And you gave as good as you got, which is pretty impressive actually.'

'You think so?'

'Definitely.'

Rosie thought about trying some of the other stalls again, but it was already opening time, and people were beginning to flood into the market. Locals and tourists were swarming everywhere, examining the flowers, taking videos and photos. There was no time. She had no option to but open with what she had.

'I'm so sorry, Rosie,' Emma said. 'But I have to go.'

'Yes, of course. Thank you for being there for me. I really appreciate it.'

Emma placed a kiss on her cheek. 'Come and find me later, okay?'

She hurried away to where customers were lining up outside her stall, searching for the vendor to pay for the goods already piled in their arms.

How Rosie wished that was her, but everyone was walking past her stall frowning in dismay at the state of it compared to the other beautiful, colourful works of art. Rosie quickly got to work displaying the flowers she'd had delivered: a strange assortment of the potted herbs she'd requested and anemones, irises, lilies and chrysanthemums, none of which really went that well together according to the rules of floristry. Feeling dejected, she did her best to display them as decoratively as she could and put on her apron, tying it tightly around her waist. Her stall looked like it was filled with everyone's cast-offs. With a cheery smile and a quick tighten of her headscarf, she stepped in front of her stall, smiling at the customers and hoping her jolly 'good morning's might tempt them in. The day could only get better from here, right?

It didn't.

The few customers who entered her stall went away again without buying, or even touching, anything and all the time she was aware of Finn, whose staff did all the work while he stood out front welcoming his customers like long-lost members of his family. He was laughing at her. And that wasn't just her being paranoid. Several times she caught him speaking to people, pointing in her direction and then laughing so hard he had to hold his stomach. The tears Rosie had been fighting all morning threatened to spring from her eyes again, but she took a deep breath and stared at the sun shining radiantly in the sky, willing them to disappear. Why did some people have to be cruel?

She hoped against hope that the afternoon would get better. In her opinion, it couldn't get much worse. As she couldn't afford to close for lunch, Rosie worked through, her stomach rumbling, but she ignored it and continued her attempts to tempt people into her shop. At one point, she found herself actually beckoning people inside, but all that did was make them scoot past in a strange kind of waddle or out-and-out run. The real question then became could she stand this humiliation much longer? Her positive attitude waned but the steely backbone her mum had blessed her with straightened inside her. Perhaps if she cut her prices or offered three for two on the plants, she might make some sales. It was worth a try and she had the rest of the afternoon to get through.

As the day neared its end, and all the other stalls were packed with last-minute shoppers, hers remained empty. Feeling utterly defeated, Rosie made the decision to close up and head home.

The day had been an absolute disaster from start to finish. First the boat flooding the other day and now this. She couldn't help but feel that if this was a sign of things to come, moving to Amsterdam might not have been the best idea she'd ever had. It might actually be the worst. And instead of making something of herself, she was in danger of damaging her financial and career prospects to a point she'd never recover from.

Emma had asked her to call by, but Rosie couldn't face talking to anyone right now. She felt completely humiliated, stupid beyond measure and so worried she felt physically sick. All she wanted was to hide under her duvet and pretend the day had never happened and after a quick stop for a bottle of wine (possibly two), that was exactly what she intended to do.

Chapter 8

As Rosie approached the *Forget-Me-Knot*, her heart heavy, she noticed something on the deck. She hadn't ordered anything to be delivered and from a distance couldn't make out exactly what it was. It was only as she approached she saw it was a small toolbox with a note attached. She opened it and read quickly.

> Don't get excited. These are extra tools I don't need but they might be useful for you. You don't owe me anything. Just don't hit anything else with hammers, please.
> Max

Well, that was unexpected. For a second, a small smile spread across her face, but as nice a gesture as it was, it didn't make up for the absolute write-off of a day she'd had. Picking it up, she headed inside.

The door to the *Forget-Me-Knot* was still sticking and Rosie had to shove her shoulder into it harder than a rugby player tackling his opponent to get it open. She managed it with a grunt of effort, and threw her keys onto the counter, placing the bag full of shopping on the floor. She took out a bottle of wine and opened it, filling a glass with a hefty measure, and for a moment stared around her.

'What are you even doing?' she asked herself, picking up one of the new bright cushions she'd bought to cheer herself up and throwing it across the room. 'This was such a stupid idea.'

Rosie caught her reflection in the mirror she'd taken from the tiny toilet and hung instead on the galley wall. Her short hair was beginning to need a trim, and she tucked a few strands behind her ears. Worst of all, she looked tired with unflattering smudges under her eyes.

'Why did you ever think you could do this?' she said to herself, before returning to her shopping and beginning to unpack. 'I mean, you've never even held down a job longer than a year and you thought this was going to be easy? You're an idiot, Rosie Harper. A complete and utter idiot. Like an A-plus idiot. An idiot with bells on. The Queen of Idiot Kingdom and all the idiots who dwell within it.'

After putting away the scant supplies she'd bought

for her dinner, she flopped onto the sofa and this time, didn't bother to stop the tears that came to her eyes. For a second, the release as they fell down her cheeks made her feel better, but then she found she couldn't stop. For a few minutes, she let herself sob until there was nothing more to give.

Rosie wiped her nose and her eyes, smudging mascara across her cheeks. The water that had flooded the boat had all dried, as had the rug and the towels. It was almost as if it had never happened. She'd added some colourful throws to the small sofa and it was now a lot more comfortable. Her plants were flourishing, both inside and out, and she had to admit she liked it here. Much more than she had any of her tiny flats in London. But that wasn't enough to stay. If she couldn't make the business work, she'd have no choice but to return home with her tail between her legs. Yet again failing at getting her life in order.

There was only ever one person Rosie wanted to speak to when she felt like this: her dad. She quickly called him, keeping it to a phone call rather than a video chat so he didn't see the state she was in. She didn't want to worry him. He'd worried enough about both her and her sister in place of their mum. But she needed to hear his voice and know he was there.

'Hello, my Rosie-Roo. How was your first big day?'

To think she'd been so excited about it when she'd spoken to him last made the back of her nose sting with more tears, but she refused to let them come.

'It was fine,' she replied, overly breezily, and the silence that met her on the other end of the line told her he hadn't bought it for a second.

'What's happened?' His tone was sharp and perceptive, and she could imagine the narrowing of his eyes behind his blue-framed glasses. 'Something has. I can tell by your voice. What is it? That grumpy neighbour been griping at you again?'

Rosie had already given her dad the low-down on Max, though she'd left out how insanely attractive he was and how her body seemed to fizz with sexual tension whenever he was around. That wasn't generally the type of thing you talked to your dad about. Rosie considered lying but despite her best efforts the tears had started again and there was no holding them back. 'Oh, Dad,' she sobbed, taking in a shaky breath. 'It's all going horribly wrong already.'

'No, come on, Rosie-Roo, that's not like you. Where's my little ray of sunshine gone? Now, what's going wrong?'

'The supplier sent me the wrong flowers and I didn't sell a single thing.'

'Oh, I'm sorry, rose petal. But come on, that's not going to happen every day. Was it just a mix-up?'

'I think so, but I feel like I've made the biggest mistake of my life.'

'What? Even bigger than when you cut your own hair?'

A slight giggle bubbled in her throat. 'Even worse than that.' At the age of twelve, when she'd first decided she wanted short hair, she'd thought she could cut it herself. Unsurprisingly, she couldn't. Her dad had to taken her to an emergency hairdressing appointment to fix the bald spot and uneven clumps sticking up here, there and everywhere. She grabbed a tissue and blew her nose. 'I just don't think this is going to work, Dad. Maybe I should stop now and come home before I land myself in debt and end up homeless.'

'But is that the only thing that's gone wrong? Because it's not like you to get knocked back by one little mix-up.'

'There've been other things too. My boat flooded.' She didn't add why. 'I haven't done half as much research as I should have and—'

'Now you listen to me, rose petal. Things going wrong – that's life! Nothing goes smoothly. If it did, we'd all be walking around whistling show tunes and bursting into song all the time. Life is full of problems and obstacles; that's just how it is. I don't think I've ever seen you as excited as when you said you wanted to move there and start a flower shop. I saw a spark in your eyes that reminded me of your mum whenever she talked about plants and botany. You've got the same passion she had, and you owe it to yourself to explore it – to do what makes you happy. It's taken you a while to figure out what makes you tick and now you've found it, you're just going to give up? What would your mum say?'

She sat in silence for a moment and glanced at one of the few photos she had of her mum and dad on their wedding day, which sat in a frame on the narrow windowsill. The memory of her mum's voice, the way she always encouraged them, sent a familiar raft of pain, and now confusingly, hope, through her. 'She'd want me to keep trying.'

'Of course she would. Do you know she was the first woman in her family to go to university? Her parents worked night and day to be able to send her and support her while she studied, and when she said she wanted to do a PhD, she worked every hour she could to afford it – we both did. We didn't do that so you could take a job that didn't make you happy. If you came home, what would you do?'

'I don't know. Go back to the design firm maybe.'

'You hated that job. You said the person you sat next to smelled of tuna and onions.'

They had. It'd been gross – even worse than the damp and mildew had been when she'd first arrived. 'So you think I should stay?'

There was no hesitation in her dad's reply. 'I do. You'll work everything out; I know you will. You've got your mum's gumption and my stubbornness. That's a lethal combination. Why don't you give it to the end of the summer? And if you still feel things aren't working out, you can come home then.'

That wasn't a bad idea. Rosie took a sip of her wine, almost spilling it as the glass was so full.

'You just need to have some faith in yourself, Rosie-Roo. You've always held yourself back, well now's the time to grow your wings and fly.'

'But what if I crash and burn?'

'I don't think you will.'

She stared out of the window at the setting sun. It had sent the sky a beautiful orangey-yellow and reflected in the canal as a delicious peach. Birds bobbed along, occasionally speaking to each other. She liked it here. Was she really going to give it all up after only a few days? Leaving her decision to the end of the summer was a much better plan.

'There's a lovely saying, you know,' her dad continued. 'And I can't remember who said it, but it was one of your mum's favourites. It went: "Shoot for the moon, because even if you fall, you'll land among the stars".' A great racking sob emerged from her as she couldn't hold it in any longer, only to be met with her dad's laughter. 'There now, my rose petal. You can do this; I know you can.' Emotion choked his voice, and he cleared his throat, putting on a much brighter tone. 'So, what do you need to do to make tomorrow better than today?'

'Get drunk?'

'That'll just give you a hangover and make tomorrow even worse. Come on, tell me one practical thing you can do right now to make tomorrow a good day?'

Rosie thought for a moment, biting her fingernails and watching the ducks float past on the canal. Nearly all the blooms would be good for the next day, but what good was that when she still had nothing to pair them with? Was it worth placing another order for delivery tomorrow morning? Could she even afford to? She'd have to. She definitely wasn't going to make any sales if she didn't.

'I can order some more flowers that'll complement the ones I have from today. It's more expense but with any luck I'll make it all back tomorrow and then some.'

'Brilliant! Now, stop yapping to me and place that order. You can call me again later when it's done.'

'Thanks, Dad,' she said, the familiar feeling of comfort he gave emanating from the phone. 'I shouldn't still need my dad to give me a pep talk, should I?'

'Of course you should. You and your sister have given me a few over the years. I only started going out again because you two nagged me into getting a life once you'd left home.'

'We didn't nag!' she replied, pretending to be cross. 'We were just looking out for you.'

'Yeah, I know.'

'Speaking of which, have you thought any more about joining a band or something?'

'No, I haven't. Now go, make that call. That's an order.'

'Yes, Dad,' she replied. 'Love you.'

'Love you too, rose petal.'

Rosie placed her glass to the side and made a quick list of the flowers she wanted, then called the supplier. This time in plain English, and ensuring the guy on the other end read the list back to her, she placed her order. Things like this were bound to happen, she told herself, some of her normal positivity returning. There were always going to be problems. That wouldn't make her a failure, unless she let it.

She stood and took a swig of her wine, staring at her reflection once more and spotting the toolbox from Max, which lifted her spirits further. 'Right, Queen of the Idiots, you've got till the end of the summer. If things don't go right by then, you can call it quits and go home with your head held high. After all, it's not like you've bought a house or anything; you're renting a houseboat and have a tiny pitch at the flower market. That's not much to give up. Got it?'

She nodded to herself, just as Max's grumpy voice pierced the silence.

'Will you stop talking to yourself! You sound like a crazy person and I'm trying to paint!'

Rosie watched her reflection as her eyes widened and her jaw dropped. She peered out of the window to see him on the deck of his boat, standing at an easel, paintbrush in hand and glaring at her. Had he heard all that?

Oh no!

'Sorry!' she called. 'I'm done now.'

'Good!'

'Thanks for the tools, by the way.'

There was a moment's silence before he said, 'You're welcome.'

A swarm of butterflies were swirling in her stomach at the sound of his voice, and she pressed down the smile forcing its way onto her face. Taking a deep breath, she took a big gulp of wine and began to plan the arrangements she'd make tomorrow and the offers she could give to shift some of the stock. No matter how much Evil Finn laughed at her, she wasn't going to give up that easily. Rosie's Blooms needed a chance to shine.

Rosie's Blooms? It really did sound basic. She still wasn't convinced by that name but that was a problem for another day.

Chapter 9

The next day, the sun had barely risen in the sky as Rosie was one of the first to arrive at the flower market. Bright-eyed and with much of her usual cheer returned, she tidied her stall, waiting for the delivery of flowers, keeping busy as nerves grew in her stomach.

Other vendors began to arrive, including Finn who reluctantly nodded his head in her direction when she smiled and waved a greeting. She wouldn't let him see that anxiety was biting at her, sending her morning coffee swilling around her tummy and threatening to reappear.

When the young deliveryman appeared, and she saw the correct blooms in his hands, Rosie couldn't help but hop onto her toes and clap her hands together. Her dad had been right: things were going to get better if she hung in there. Yesterday had been such a disaster, the only way was up.

She hoped. She tried not to count her chickens and instead went to meet him, helping him with the bulky load.

'Thank you! Thank you! Or should that be *bedankt*.' He smiled and as he placed the load down, Rosie held out her hand. 'I'm Rosie, by the way. Rosie Harper.'

He seemed surprised. Perhaps he couldn't understand her English, or perhaps not many of the stallholders bothered getting to know the delivery people. She was sure Finn wouldn't. He probably thought himself above all that.

'Err, my name is Bas.' His English was stuttering, the words spaced out as he had to think about the pronunciation.

'Bas. Hallo!'

His smile grew wider, and he signalled behind him, ready to go and collect the rest of her order. Rosie let him go and began sorting out her flowers. She made some arrangements using the new delivery of hydrangeas and salvia, including the stock from yesterday, and as the market began to hum with activity, she felt ready for the day. Her stall no longer looked a mess, now full to the brim with small green pots containing the herbs she'd ordered and brightly coloured flowers to tempt customers over. Rosie stepped back with pride. She also wrote a sign in the prettiest handwriting she could manage, promising talks on the medicinal value of mint and the uses of basil and myrtle, an old Victorian plant her mum had always loved.

'Wow!' Emma said, coming over. 'Just look at this place. I can't believe it's the same stall as yesterday.' She admired two of the large arrangements Rosie had made. 'These are beautiful.' She leaned in and inhaled the scent of the roses. 'So gorgeous. I can't believe you made these too. What time did you get here?'

'Pretty early,' Rosie replied. 'But it was worth it.'

'It certainly was.' Emma turned her attention back to Rosie. Her bright red hair was down, spilling around her shoulders, though she would tie it back when she began work. Her long skirts had been replaced with blue harem-style pants decorated with a peacock-feather pattern. 'Why didn't you come and see me last night? I came over after closing but you were gone.'

Rosie could see the look of hurt on Emma's face and knew she'd been selfish disappearing. She should at least have popped over to say goodbye and explain. 'I'm sorry about that. I shut early. The day had been such a disaster, it didn't seem worth staying till the end and, to be honest, I was quite upset so I went home and had a good cry and called my family.'

'Did it make you feel better?'

'It did. But I promise to make it up to you. If all goes well today, how do you fancy going for a drink after closing? I think by the time 5.30 p.m. comes I'll need one.'

Emma's face instantly brightened. 'Me too. That sounds great. See you later. And good luck.' Emma hugged her and Rosie squeezed her in return.

'You too! Hope you sell lots of cheese and . . . meat!'

Emma giggled and headed on her way as Rosie checked her card reader was set up to take payments. Everything was working as it should, and she was ready to face whatever the day was going to throw at her.

Though it started slowly, and her nerves mounted with every customer who walked past, eventually one stopped and bought one of her displays. After that, it seemed that as more people browsed, others were attracted too and eventually Rosie's stall was heaving. She had to squeeze past people in the tiny space to see if they needed any help, and struggled to keep up with the demand for her attention. Every time she put down the card reader she had to pick it up again as there was always another customer to serve.

As the time for her first talk drew near, Rosie's confidence began to wane. She'd never particularly minded public speaking, but speaking to people in another country, who spoke another language, was daunting. What if they didn't understand her? What if they asked her to speak in Dutch and she couldn't oblige? She really needed to double down on her efforts to learn Dutch, but for now she had no option but to speak in English. As the small crowd gathered, eager to learn about mint and all the uses it had other than for cooking, Rosie relaxed. The talk went well, even though she'd noticed Finn frowning at her group and watching her intently. Afterwards, several of the small potted herbs she'd had delivered were sold.

The day continued in the same vein and, thanking her lucky stars, Rosie raised her eyes to the sky as she tallied up her takings and closed her stall. It had been a good day. Better than she could have hoped for. Another bad one would have most definitely sent her home, despite promising her dad she'd stay until the end of the summer. Now there seemed a chance she could actually make something of herself. A chance she could make this work.

Rosie quickly placed her order for the next day and made her way around to Emma, who was waiting for the final few customers to leave.

'I hate forcing them out,' she confided in a whisper. 'But it's past closing and you can get into lots of trouble if you stay open after other vendors. People don't like it.'

'Would you like me to help?'

'Sure, but what can you do?'

'Just you wait and see!' Rosie walked over to a jar, picked it up and then looked dramatically at her phone. 'Oh my gosh, I can't believe it's already past closing time. They'll be kicking us out soon!' Her acting was more hammy than the smoked meat Emma was selling but suddenly everyone rushed to the till. When Rosie had worked in restaurants, she'd learned a few tricks of the trade – like beginning to loudly clean, turning the lights up high and even sweeping and mopping the floor to give customers the hint.

Emma mouthed a subtle 'thank you' and worked quickly through the queue and before long, the last of the customers had been served and she could close the metal grille on her shop.

'What a day!' she declared, as she too cashed up her takings. 'How about you?'

'I was so busy – it was brilliant!'

'That's wonderful. Oh no—' She suddenly frowned. 'I lost count. Let me start again.'

Rosie quietened down while Emma finished off. Browsing the range of foods and treats, she decided that if the rest of the week went well, she'd get herself something to enjoy on her day off. Though she'd likely be working a seven-day week until she was more established in the market. In which case, she might have to treat herself to something sooner.

'There. All done,' Emma declared. 'I just need to drop this off at the bank.' She held up a secure cash wallet. 'I really need to go card only.'

'I'll come with you,' Rosie said. 'We can find a bar afterwards. What do you prefer – red or white?'

'Anything after the day I've had. I haven't sat down, and my feet are killing me. I know a great place and I'm sure you're going to love it.'

They exited the flower market and luckily the bank was only a few streets away. With the cash deposited, Emma led them to a local bar on the banks of one of the canals. The seats outside were full, the sound of people talking and laughing filling the air. Inside, upturned wine glasses hung from a central bar like a glorious chandelier and all around was a mix of tall bar stools with high tables and more comfy chairs with low tables. Rosie could just make out some pop music playing in the background, but she couldn't distinguish the song. They grabbed the only two vacant seats at the bar and ordered a bottle of white wine to share.

After taking a sip, Rosie sighed. 'I needed that.'

'Me too. You know, I was worried you wouldn't be coming back.'

'Really?' She shouldn't have been surprised; she had felt the lowest she'd ever felt the day before. 'To be honest, I thought about it, but I decided I had to give it another try.' She thought about adding *for my mum* but didn't want to bring the mood down.

'What made you move to Amsterdam? Don't get me wrong, I love my city, but it's not everyone's first choice if they're relocating.'

'Honestly, the flower market drew me here.'

She explained about seeing it on her phone, how it was a last-minute decision and how she hadn't felt that she'd had much to lose.

'That's so brave!'

'Is it? I wonder if it was stupid, but either way, today was a good day and I intend to celebrate it.'

Rosie watched as Emma took a sip of her wine and glanced around. Her eyes lit up and Rosie followed her gaze to see Noah, the cheesemonger, walking past.

'Hi, Noah,' Emma said, spinning round so he spotted her.

'Oh, hi.' An awkward silence descended.

So, thought Rosie, there was definitely something going on between these two. Emma's feelings were clear, but she wasn't sure about Noah's. Was he just shy? There was only one way to find out.

'Did you want to join us for a drink?' Rosie asked, seeing from the corner of her eye Emma's face freeze in shock.

'Yeah, do,' Emma added, recovering quickly. 'Sit down, take a load off.' Noah glanced around but there were no other chairs. 'Oh, you can sit here if you like, I can get another.' She hopped off her stool as Noah held his hands out, palms up, to stop her.

'No, no, no, that's fine. I'm here with some friends anyway. Thanks, though.' He turned to Rosie, and she quickly introduced herself. 'Nice to meet you, Rosie. I'll, umm . . . see you tomorrow, Emma.'

He headed off in the direction of the toilets and Emma climbed back onto her stool and lowered her head onto the bar. 'What was that? Why? Why do I act like an idiot around him?'

'I take it you like him?' Rosie asked, sipping her wine to hide her smile.

'He's gorgeous! Don't you think he's gorgeous? And he makes the best cheese. I LOVE cheese.'

'Everyone loves cheese. He seems sweet. Very quiet, though.'

'I know. That's why I always try and start conversations but half the time he says no and backs away from me like I'm crazy. I know I can be too much sometimes—'

'You're not too much. But I know the feeling. I'm a chronic over-sharer and sometimes other people don't like that.' She remembered Max shouting at her not to talk to herself. It was the absolute worst that she found him so attractive when he clearly wasn't interested.

'Maybe I should just leave him alone,' Emma said. She'd let her long red hair down after work and with a flick of her hand tossed it back over her shoulder.

'Let's swap places,' Rosie said.

'Why?'

'So I can watch him and see if he's interested or not.'

'Have you done this a lot, then?'

'I've been on a lot of dates, yes, but never found anything that lasted more than a few months. Some of the guys I've dated have been nice – some better than nice – but . . . I don't know. I just haven't ever fallen head over heels in love.'

They shuffled about and Rosie watched as Noah returned. He smiled at Emma as he passed and as the evening went on, it was clear he had a thing for her too. Every time he could, he glanced over, especially when Emma laughed or stood up to go to the ladies'.

'He's definitely into you,' Rosie declared.

'Really? Are you sure?'

Rosie nodded.

'What if he's been watching you and not me?'

'He hasn't. Look.' She pretended to sneeze incredibly loudly. So loudly, in fact, that nearly everyone else in their immediate vicinity turned to look at her. Everyone except Noah. He carried on his conversation and didn't even flinch.

'Why did you do that?' Emma hissed. 'You sounded like a cartoon character.'

'I wanted to test something. And I've got one more thing to try to be sure. Give me your earring.'

'What?'

'Give me your earring. I promise, this is a great test.' Emma handed it over and Rosie leaned forwards as if to speak to her and dropped it on the floor at her feet.

'Rosie!' Emma jumped off her stool and knelt down to find it. Just as she put her hand on it, Noah appeared. 'Is everything all right, Emma? Do you need some help?'

She stood up, her face flushing as red as her hair. 'My earring – it fell – I dropped it – I've got it now. Thanks.'

'Oh, okay. Cool.' He gave her a shy smile and stepped away.

'See! He's totally into you,' Rosie confirmed. 'Totally.'

Emma grinned, her smile lighting her eyes and filling her face with joy. 'He's into me! He's into me!' They jiggled about in their seats. 'But what do I do? Every time I try and ask him for a drink or something, he says no.'

'Well, he's clearly shy. You need to get him on his own, flirt with him a bit, break down his barriers, let him know you're definitely interested and not just being polite. Then, if he hasn't asked you out within a few days, you ask him. When he feels more comfortable with you, he'll definitely say yes.'

'You're my hero, you know that?' Emma said and Rosie laughed. 'Will you help me?'

'Help you? With Noah?'

'Yeah. Help me get my man.' Emma emphasised each word. 'Sorry, I'll calm down.'

'I mean, I'll do what I can.'

Emma held her wine glass up in a toast and they clinked them gently together. 'That calls for another bottle.'

Before she could protest, Emma had stuck her hand in the air and ordered another one, and all Rosie could do was sit back and relax.

Chapter 10

Still pleasantly tipsy, Rosie returned to the *Forget-Me-Knot*, humming to herself as she wandered the streets of Amsterdam, admiring the city at night. Some of the bridges had lights around the semicircular arches that shone in the sapphire blue night sky. The glow of the street lamps was mirrored on the water, making the city sparkle.

She approached as quietly as she could, careful not to disturb her neighbours. One cranky neighbour in particular. She wasn't entirely sure anyone lived on the other side of her; she hadn't seen hide nor hair of them.

Hide nor hair. That was a funny phrase. She started giggling to herself and as she stepped onto the deck, forgetting it was a boat, she squealed as it rocked. Hurriedly shooshing herself, she pushed the key into the lock and braced herself to open the door. Just as she was ramming her shoulder into it, knowing it would stick and need a good shove, a voice over her shoulder called: 'Don't do that, I've—'

But it was too late.

Rosie shrieked as the door gave way easily and she fell through with alarming speed. Luckily, she kept her balance and leapt down the steps. 'Aargh!'

The voice sounded again, and she looked over to see Max watching her, a look of alarm on his face.

'It's okay. I'm all right. Did you . . . ?'

'Yes. You left it unlocked this morning when you went out. I assumed you'd only be gone a few minutes but then you didn't come back so I stayed in to keep an eye on the place and I decided to plane the top where it was sticking. I was going to tell you, but you found out for yourself before I could.'

She must have been so nervous she'd forgotten to lock it in her haste to get to the flower market.

'Don't worry, I didn't go inside or snoop around. All the colours made my eyes hurt.'

She looked over to see him retake the seat on his deck, a steaming mug in hand. A small lantern and a few tealights lit the darkness around him. He looked like a work of art himself, like a statue of a Roman or Greek warrior. His body was just so strong-looking it made her want to stroke his chest and grip his arms. Gosh, she really was drunk if her mind was going there so quickly.

Straightening her hair and clothes, she walked back out onto the deck. 'Good evening,' she replied, knowing she sounded ridiculously formal. For some reason, she gave a small bow. 'Sorry if I was noisy.'

'You're always noisy.'

'And you're always grumpy!' She clapped a hand over her mouth. 'Sorry! Sorry, I shouldn't have said that.' To her surprise, Max's beard twitched as though he was smiling. 'Right, well it was very kind of you to fix my door. Thank you and . . . night, night.'

'You could do with a coffee. He stood and walked to the edge of his boat. 'Come and sit down. I'll make you one.'

For a moment she didn't move as her brain, slow to contemplate his offer, didn't send any signals to her mouth.

'Well?' he asked, swiping his hand out towards the chairs. 'Are you coming?'

'Sure.' She stepped back off her own boat and down a few paces onto his. Zoon was asleep in his dog basket, placed out on the deck in the cool evening air. She gasped as her eyes fell on the painting that had previously been covered with a cloth. It was an abstract of blue and grey swipes and blocks of paint.

'I knew you painted abstracty stuff!' she declared as he came back with two cups of coffee.

'It's called abstract.'

'That's what I said. Abstracty.'

He sighed.

She wasn't sure if it was the wine, but something about it made her think of sadness and grief. The black slashes made with a smaller, slimmer brush, made her think of anger and frustration. She'd never had that sort of response to a painting before. Perhaps it was the colours. Perhaps it was just the wine.

Max, who had gone back into the galley for milk, came out and picked up the cloth to cover it.

'Please don't,' Rosie said, her voice quiet. 'It's beautiful. Wonderful. What does it mean?'

Surprised, he didn't move for a second but studied her as though she'd been teasing him. Then he dropped the cloth. 'It means whatever you want it to mean.'

'But what did it mean to you when you were painting it?'

'I—' He stopped mid-sentence as though checking himself. 'I'll get some sugar.'

She wondered why he wouldn't answer her question but knew better than to push. She let the subject drop. Rosie sat on one of the low camping chairs on his deck. In the dim light she could see splashes of paint on the fabric of the armrest and ran her hand over it to make sure it was dry. The cool night air brushed her face, and she closed her eyes, listening intently to the gentle lapping of the water against the hull.

'You're smiling,' he said a moment later.

Was she? She hadn't realised it. Contentment flooded her body, calming her mind after the last few days.

'You're always smiling,' he clarified.

'I try to.'

'And talking to yourself?'

'Don't you?'

'Not really.' He took the mug in both hands. 'Sometimes, I suppose.'

'There then. We're not so different after all.'

'Most of the time I talk to Zoon.' He signalled to the dog, who opened one eye, noticed Rosie and wagged his tail but was obviously too tired to move.

A number of other, smaller paintings were stacked against the side of his boat. They were similar in design – all abstract – but in various colours and shapes. Some blocky, some with gentle, curving arches that reminded her of the canal bridges. 'Do you display your work anywhere?'

He shook his head and didn't elaborate. Rosie sipped her coffee, feeling the tipsiness of earlier subside. After her walk in the fresh air, the alcohol was working its way out of her system. 'Have you lived here long?'

'A few years.'

Did he always answer with such short, sharp phrases or was it just with her? 'Do you like it?'

He cocked his head. 'Yes.'

'Jesus, this is like pulling teeth.'

He didn't laugh and instead, stared down into his mug.

Feeling slightly guilty for being so blunt, she tried once more to start a conversation. 'Did you have a good day?'

'Why are you asking?'

'Oh, forget it.' She stood up and placed her mug down on the table with such force that some of the coffee sloshed out over the side. 'Look, if you don't want to talk that's fine. We can sit here in silence, or I can take this coffee and drink it on my own on my boat. You didn't have to offer it to me.'

Max looked shocked, his eyes wide, catching the moonlight. Then he laughed. A loud, booming sound that filled the quiet night more than anything Rosie had said or done.

'You might be all sunshine and rainbows but you're steely too, aren't you?'

'I am. I like being cheerful. I like singing and talking to myself. I like dancing around while I clean and looking on the bright side – most of the time – but that doesn't mean I'm a pushover or that I'll put up with someone being rude to me.'

'Okay,' he said with a firm nod. 'Point taken.' Max gestured to the seat, and she took it again. 'I'm sorry. Nothing exciting happened in my day, but yours must have been better. I'm assuming so as you've been out all evening, or are you drowning your sorrows?'

'You heard all that yesterday, did you?' she asked, referring to her conversation with her dad.

'I tried not to, but you had your door open, you were on speakerphone, and you are quite loud sometimes. Queen of the Idiots.'

It was her turn to laugh. 'That's me. But today was a lot better, thank you for asking. And tomorrow will be just as good. Which makes me think I should probably go to bed. I've got another early start, and I might have a bit of a sore head if I don't get some sleep.' She stood, leaving her half-empty cup.

'Drink some water first and take two painkillers now. It'll help.'

She hid her surprise at his helpful, almost kind advice. 'Okay, thank you.'

'Goodnight then.'

She walked away, swaying slightly, and as she went to step onto the dock, she suddenly felt the weight and warmth of his hand in hers as he steadied her. Rosie's breath stilled in her body. It was very Mr Darcy, impossibly romantic, and the rush of emotion it started forced every thought from her head. She turned to look at him as she stepped over the gap, trying to catch his expression to see if he'd meant the gesture to be as gallant as it had felt. But as his hand fell away, all she saw was the back of Max's head, his thick hair parting as he pushed a hand through it and stepped back into the galley.

Rosie continued on unsteady feet; sure it wasn't the wine making her so wobbly. She filled a glass of water and took two painkillers, her hand still tingling at his touch as her head hit the pillow and sleep overcame her, her last thought of his skin touching hers.

Chapter 11

Life became everything Rosie had ever dreamed of over the next two weeks. She developed a new work routine that seemed to suit her body and mind more than any job she'd had before, even though she was working longer hours. She preferred to be up early and at the flower market before many of the vendors arrived and worked till the very last second, then she'd often join Emma for a drink after work. Rosie's relationship with Bas, the delivery guy, was becoming more and more friendly and he was teaching her odds words of Dutch while she taught him a few words of English. She was beginning to feel settled into her new life quite nicely.

Every day she added different flowers to her stall and whilst it wasn't as big as Finn's, it was almost as colourful. Her talks were proving popular too as people seemed to love learning about the different properties of herbs and flowers. Word seemed to be spreading and every day different faces appeared in the crowd. She'd had to expand her repertoire and was glad she'd brought her mum's books with her. Finn always watched with unveiled disgust as people gathered at her stall and she couldn't help but feel slightly triumphant given how rude he'd been to her.

The more content Rosie felt, the more new ideas sprang into her head. She'd begun to consider teaching some of the basics of flower arranging. No one else in the market seemed to do that. Maybe the vendors worried it would stop people buying premade arrangements, but Rosie loved to empower people with knowledge and wanted to encourage them to play with flowers and plants as she had as a child. Her mum would often watch on and suggest other plants she could gather to make her displays. It was where her love stemmed from and she wanted to share that with other people.

The next morning, as Rosie stepped off the *Forget-Me-Knot* ready for another day, she spied Max having breakfast on the deck of *The Rembrandt*. Since the night they'd chatted she hadn't seen much of him, unsure whether he was away on holiday or business, or simply hiding from her every time she came near. Taking the hint, she'd forced herself not to bother him, no matter how much she was tempted, but today he glanced up and though he didn't smile (she was learning he hardly ever smiled), he did at least make eye contact.

'Morning,' Rosie trilled happily. Max looked up from

reading something on his phone. The deck was clear of canvases, and she took a tentative step towards him. 'Have you sold your paintings?'

His brow furrowed, deep lines etching their way across his forehead. 'No. I've put them away in case it rains.'

She looked up at the clear blue sky. The sun was already blazing and her weather app had said it was going to be another warm, sunny day. There wasn't even a single lonely cloud to spoil the view.

'It doesn't look like rain,' she replied. 'Do you have a garage or something where you store them?'

He let his phone drop to his lap. 'You are very nosy.'

'I am,' she replied, ignoring his snippy tone. She secretly suspected Max wasn't quite as miserable as he liked to make out, and thinking of the way he'd taken her hand still sent chills down her spine. 'But if I didn't ask you questions, I don't think we'd speak at all. And that's not very neighbourly,' she added, not wanting to sound like talking to him was something she actually liked doing.

Zoon appeared from the galley and ran towards her, leaping up and again resting his paws on her thighs so she could scratch his head. She leaned down to speak to him and his tongue popped out as he tried to lick her cheek.

'Hello, you, are you being a good boy?'

'Mostly. He tried to eat some ham I'd left out, so he's been told off.'

'Have you?' she said to the dog. 'Poor boy. I meant to ask, what does "Zoon" mean?'

'It means son.'

'Aww, that's cute.' Max rolled his eyes. Rosie shooed the dog back towards his owner and took a step backwards. 'Right, well—'

'How are things at the flower market?' he asked, surprising her.

'Good. I'm starting to build a decent customer base and people like my talks.' She explained briefly what they were about, and did her best to tame the grin spreading over her face that he'd asked her a question in return.

'You like teaching?'

She hadn't thought of it in that way, but maybe that's what it was. She had once worked as a teaching assistant at a primary school but being surrounded by small, noisy children had turned out not to be for her after all. Teaching adults, though, that she was enjoying. 'I do.'

He mumbled something that sounded like, 'Interesting,' and she waited for him to say more. When he didn't, she said goodbye and went on her way.

Why did he find that interesting? She pondered it all the way to the flower market, enjoying once more the feel of the vibrant city around her. She walked down one particular street that was fast becoming a favourite. Instead of the merchant houses, tall and narrow, and a mass of windows, the houses and shops had three floors ending in a single windowed room at the top. The roof either side curved away, with white decorative gable tops. Perhaps one day she'd be buying a house like that and she'd look out of that top window at the people passing by. But then, she'd miss being on the canal. She liked waking up to the gentle swaying of the boat. She loved sitting out on the deck in the evenings. Her next purchase was going to be a comfortable chair so she could sit and read as the sun set. Though there was still some maintenance to do first. The deck needed a good varnish, as did the floor of the galley, especially after the leak. She hadn't got round to doing that yet, and knew she should soon.

When she arrived at the flower market, Emma greeted her with a worried expression, her downcast eyes a contrast to the bright green skirt and yellow vest top she was wearing.

'What is it?' Rosie asked, genuinely concerned to see her normally happy-go-lucky friend so worried.

'I think Noah has a girlfriend.'

'What? Why?'

'He's brought some girl to the flower market with him this morning and he had his arm around her shoulders. Then she hugged him and went off. I think they spent the night together.' She slumped on the small stoll Rosie used when there weren't any customers around. 'I've left it too late and now he's found someone else.'

Rosie hated to admit it, but it did sound like her friend might have, but that didn't chime with the Noah she'd seen a week or so before, who'd definitely been interested in Emma. Life was strange sometimes though and it was quite possible someone new had crossed his path. She'd need to scope them out for herself to be sure though. There was no point in upsetting her friend by agreeing when it could still be nothing. 'Did either of them say anything?'

'I didn't hear what they were saying when they arrived. They had their heads together speaking quietly and then when she hugged him to say goodbye, she said, "See you tonight." Urgh.' Emma leaned forwards and rubbed her hands over her face. 'I always leave it too long, afraid to do anything, waiting for men to make the first move, and now I've missed my chance with the nicest man I've met in years.'

'Listen . . .' Rosie placed her hands on Emma's shoulders, and she lifted her head. 'How about a little light espionage after work?'

Her eyes widened. 'You want to follow them?'

'Yeah, but not in a creepy, stalkerish way, just in a let's-see-where-they-go-and-what-they-do kind of way. We can check it out after work.'

'Isn't that . . . a bit . . . the literal definition of stalking?'

'I like to think of it more as proactive. Don't you want to know what the situation is?' Emma nodded. 'Then I'll meet you at five-thirty and we'll just happen to leave at the same time he does, so make sure you're cashed up and ready to go.'

'I will. I—' Suddenly, Emma's arms were wrapped around Rosie. 'Thank you.'

Rosie returned the squeeze, wondering if Emma had been in a similar situation to her when it came to friends. She'd have to ask. 'Now go. I have work to do and so do you.'

Rosie wrote up the poster for her talks. She'd have to get some professionally printed but there wasn't much point until she was sure of her business name. At the moment, Rosie's Blooms seemed to be the best bet. She'd also been considering Rosie's Floating Flower Shop, though that seemed too strong a name for her little pitch, and she didn't want to tempt fate by getting ahead of herself.

Fenna had kindly said she could place a poster near her shop and Rosie swiftly took one round.

'Rosie, wasn't it?' Finn said, stepping out in front of her, stopping her in her tracks. He was dressed in another suit, making her feel untidy and slobbish in her jeans and vest top. His tan was even deeper and the contrast around his eyes even stronger. The thought that he'd been at the sunbeds again almost made her laugh. He was the same colour her deck should be – would be, once she'd varnished it.

'That's right. How are you, Finn?'

'I'm very good.' The deep lines on his forehead intensified as he glanced at the poster. 'So, these are the famous talks I've been hearing so much about.' He pointed to her hastily made sign.

'That's right.'

'Can I see?'

Reluctantly, she handed it over, feeling the need to defend herself as his lip curled. 'I know it's not very professional at the moment, but I'll get some printed soon. I'm just so thrilled people are coming and talking about them.'

'You're right,' he replied, handing it back.

'People have been talking about them?' She couldn't conceal the hope and pride in her voice.

'No, I mean that this doesn't look very professional. Make sure you take them down at the end of each day or I'll report you for littering.'

Finn turned on his heel and walked back inside his shop, leaving Rosie speechless. Her cheeks burned but she refused to be browbeaten by a man who was the same colour as her dad's garden fence. He was just jealous she'd thought of doing something he hadn't. Rosie continued on her way to Fenna's, regaining her smile and eager for another great day to begin.

Everything was going well, until the time for the first talk came. The usual, albeit small, crowd that she'd had almost every day was nowhere to be seen. She stepped out to the front of her tiny pitch, looking around. Her own small poster was still visible, but she relied on the one at Fenna's as it was nearer the main thoroughfare to drive traffic to her. She quickly ran around to see it wasn't there.

Damn it. The income from the flowers and herbs people bought after her talks was proving not just helpful but also necessary. What could have happened?

Then she saw it: a huge crowd gathering at Finn's stall as he stood on a small, sturdy box, holding forth and gesticulating as he spoke. Anger began to rise inside her, heating her further on this already warm day. Beads of sweat began to form on the back of her neck and her hands grew clammy. He wasn't! He couldn't have, could he?

As his words began to pierce her ears she listened intently. He was speaking Dutch, and she quickly grabbed her phone from her bag, recording what he was saying and reading the translation. According to the screen, he was saying:

'The common tulip, known as *tulipa* in Latin, grown extensively here in the Netherlands, has been used for many years to treat several conditions. The petals can be used to relieve inflammation and burning from bee stings, rashes and bites, and other parts of the plant have been known to treat headaches and migraines.'

Rosie's mouth fell open, and she could feel her eyes widening with shock. That two-faced, idea-stealing, mahogany-coloured cheater! The talks were her idea! She'd started them first! How could he do this? Surely there was some law against stealing people's ideas like this.

In that second, Rosie nearly marched over to Finn and interrupted him, but what could she say? Not only was he speaking in Dutch, and she only knew English, but deep down Rosie knew that giving talks on plants wasn't exactly a new idea. She was pretty sure he hadn't bothered doing it until she had, but that didn't mean she could stop him.

Silently seething, she watched as more and more people gathered to hear Finn speak. He was better at it than her, more confident and charismatic. Rosie had a habit of stuttering, even when she'd tried to plan what she was going to say. And of course, she couldn't speak Dutch, which meant she was relying on people knowing at least some English. Her muscles taut with anger, she trudged back to her tiny pitch, feeling tears welling in her eyes.

'Rosie,' Fenna said, rushing up to her. 'I'm so sorry! I just noticed what he's doing. It isn't fair.'

'No, it's not, but there isn't much I can do about it, is there?' She slumped onto the stool, taking the opportunity to sit down as her tiny pitch was completely empty of customers.

'There isn't really, I'm afraid. But that doesn't make it okay. I'm so sorry. It's an underhanded trick. Just please know, no one else in the market would behave like that. The rest of us have more integrity than him.'

'I don't understand why he hates me so much. Is it because I'm English?'

Fenna shook her head, her eyes widening. 'No! Not at all. His husband is English. He likes English people. Well, as much as he likes anyone.'

'Just not me then,' she said, attempting a smile but knowing it looked sad and dismal. Perhaps she should have spoken to him and asked him to withdraw his request for the pitch rather than going to Grietje, but even if she had, she knew what the answer would have been. She thought about explaining to him how much this meant to her, telling him about her mum. But she couldn't bear to be so open just to have him laugh or scoff at her, which was exactly what he'd do. 'I guess I'll have to find another way of bringing in the crowds.'

'I heard from Grietje that your mother was a botanist,' Fenna said.

'That's right.'

'Is there some knowledge she passed on to you that you can share?'

'That's what I was doing, talking about herbs and not just flowers but Finn's stolen that idea now.'

'Hopefully it will help you think of something else. You must have knowledge that Finn doesn't.'

'Does he make his own arrangements?' Rosie asked as the idea that had started earlier began to form more solidly in her mind.

'I don't think so. I've never seen him make one, but then he has so many staff they tend to do that for him. Why? What are you thinking?'

'I'm not really sure yet. I'll need to work it through in my head.'

'If I can help at all, let me know. I know lots of people in the market who hate Finn and would be happy to see him taken down a little. It's like he wants to turn the entire market into a big Finn Meijer shop. He's a megalomaniac. It's a shame, though. He hasn't always been like this.'

Was that a bit strong? Rosie wasn't sure, but it was nice to know other people disliked him as much as she did.

When Finn finished and the crowd dispersed, Rosie tried to corral a few into a talk on marjoram, an underrated herb in her opinion, which could be turned into an essential oil and used to treat stomach cramps. But as most had come straight from Finn's talk, no one was interested in sticking around for another. Clearly, they'd stood still for long enough as Finn had talked on and on, enjoying the sound of his own voice and the captive audience.

Great, she was going to have to work twice as hard to sell these plants tomorrow, especially given the delivery she was planning. The idea from earlier was seeding in her mind growing shoots and leaves, getting bigger. If Finn's particular skill set didn't extend to flower arranging, which had been a key part of her course, she would try leaning into this tomorrow, implementing her idea of teaching people how to arrange flowers and some of the things to consider when choosing and making a display themselves. It was worth a shot.

The day's takings were meagre and Rosie joined Emma at her shop, hoping her friend had had a better day. Emma had cleared most of her customers and was just serving the last one when Rosie arrived.

'Sorry, I had a last-minute rush.'

'Lucky you.'

Emma frowned. 'I heard what happened. I'm sorry. I'll just add everything up and then I'll be ready.'

She peered at Noah's stall. 'You better be quick; he's just closing up.'

Emma worked like the wind and was soon ready. They lingered in the shop and as soon as Noah exited, closing the metal grille behind him, Rosie and Emma followed suit.

They chatted loudly about the day, but waited a second before following so he didn't get suspicious.

'So what does this woman look like?' Rosie asked.

'She's gorgeous. Blonde, beautiful, tall. Wait—' She grabbed Rosie's arm, tugging her backwards as they exited the market. 'There she is.'

Rosie followed Emma's gaze. The woman was indeed beautiful with long blonde hair that shimmered in the evening sunlight. 'She is pretty, but not as pretty as you,' Rosie added quickly, wanting to show her support, and besides, it was true. Emma was equally as pretty and vibrant too. Her personality shone through her green eyes.

They kept them in sight as they walked behind them.

'She must be a girlfriend, don't you think?' Emma asked.

'Let's not jump to conclusions.'

'I'm such an idiot,' Emma declared a little too loudly and Noah turned as her voice frightened some pigeons into flight. Rosie bundled Emma into a doorway.

'Shh! He'll see us.'

'Oww!' She rubbed her arm.

'Sorry,' Rosie replied, grimacing. 'He was going to see us.'

'I've never been a spy before. Not sure I'm cut out for it.'

'Me neither. And we're not spying, we're fact-finding.'

Emma giggled as Noah and his friend stopped at the closest bar and grabbed a table. 'What do we do now?'

'We have a drink. Come on.' Rosie chose a table away

from them, but from where she could keep an eye on what they were doing.

'Won't he suspect?'

'Why should he? Look . . .' She pointed to her right where Fenna waved back. 'Other stallholders are here. It's natural to come here for a drink after work as it's the closest bar.'

'I wish I had a newspaper to hide behind,' Emma said.

'Do you ever read newspapers?'

'No. Who does these days?'

'Then that might look even more suspicious.' Rosie nodded to the bar. 'Come on, what will you have?'

'White wine, please.'

'Large?'

'Definitely.'

Rosie tried to listen as she passed Noah on her way to the bar, but couldn't hear anything. A few minutes later she returned to their table with two cold, delicious glasses of wine. 'Here, get this down you. Did you hear anything while I was gone?'

Emma shook her head. 'No, nothing. She rubbed his elbow though. That's got to mean something, hasn't it?'

'Not necessarily.' Rosie turned the conversation to the day's events to distract her friend.

'I don't understand what's wrong with that man,' Emma replied, referring to Finn. 'Why does he hate everyone? We're all in it together. He really doesn't need to be so aggressive. I know he was originally lined up to have your pitch but that doesn't mean he can be so nasty.'

'Fenna said he hasn't always been like this.'

Emma sipped her wine and thought. 'No. I suppose he hasn't. He was always focused but never so . . . mean.'

'Do you think he's determined to ruin me?' Emma looked up, catching Rosie's eye, and they both fell into fits of laughter. 'Sorry, that sounded quite dramatic, didn't it?'

'Considering we're on a stakeout, no, not really.'

'I've been meaning to say,' Rosie began nervously, 'thank you for being there for me. The friendship you've shown me since the day I arrived – well – it's meant a lot to me. I don't keep in touch with many of my friends. They all seemed to move on with their lives while I've been sort of . . . stuck.'

'I know exactly what you mean,' Emma replied. 'All the friends I've had have seemed to disappear lately. I get it – their lives are moving on as they get into long-term relationships, buy houses and have kids but I'm just—'

'Not ready for that yet?'

Emma smiled softly as their eyes connected in mutual understanding. 'I'd quite like the long-term relationship thing and maybe the house with someone, but I'm not ready to change my life so much just yet.'

'I feel like I'm only just getting to live the life I was supposed to. Moving here and opening the flower stall, it's the first time I've ever felt like my life was finally moving in the direction it should.'

Just then, Noah and his friend rose from their seats.

Rosie and Emma weren't anywhere near finished with their wine. They'd have to abandon their drinks to follow them, which would look overly suspicious to the other stallholders still enjoying theirs, or they'd have to glug them as quickly as possible. Both looked at each other in panic, then Noah glanced shyly in their direction and Emma gasped.

'He's coming over.'

His friend confidently led the way, Noah following behind. Rosie couldn't help but hold her breath. They stopped just in front of their table, the woman staring expectantly not at them, but at Noah. As his cheeks coloured and his eyes dropped, she gave a tiny shake of her head.

'Hallo. It's Emma and Rosie, right?'

They glanced at each other before Rosie answered, 'Yes, that's right.'

Noah received a sharp elbow from the woman, surprising Rosie. He adjusted his glasses, pushing them up the bridge of his nose with his forefinger. 'Can we join you? This is my sister Brechtje.'

'Your sister?' Emma declared, her gaze flitting between them both. For a second, a strange silence descended, and Rosie quickly saved them.

'I can see the resemblance now you say it.'

'Can you?' Brechtje asked with a worried expression. 'Oh dear.'

'Only in the eyes,' Rosie added with a cheeky smile. 'Sit down, please!'

Emma gestured to the two empty chairs at their table.

'Are you visiting, Brechtje? I don't think I've seen you before.'

'Yes. I live in Rotterdam. That's where our family are. Noah's always so busy he doesn't make it home often. If I want to see him, I have to come here and kidnap him, but I was glad to hear he has friends.'

She was clearly referring to them, and Rosie glanced at Emma, who was unsure how to read the comment. Did that mean she was in the friend zone?

'He's so shy,' Brechtje continued. 'I always worry he's doing nothing but staying at home.'

'I promise you,' Emma replied, 'he does have friends. I've seen him out for a drink lots of times.'

'Well that's good to know.'

'It's hard to find the time, though,' Noah suddenly said. 'To go out. It is hard running a business yourself.'

Emma nodded her agreement. 'We don't often get days off.'

'Especially in the summer. I have to take advantage of the tourists. Well—' His cheeks began to turn pink. 'You know what I mean.'

'I do,' Emma replied and for a moment, they caught each other's eye before looking away self-consciously.

Rosie, who had been on plenty of dates, loved this part of a relationship: the flirting, the getting to know each other. Her mind ran to Max and his grumpy, uncommunicative ways. The way he'd taken her hand like Mr Darcy. If only he was more her type. She drew her mind away from his thick hair and sturdy frame, swallowing heavily.

'I didn't realise how difficult it would be to get a day off,' Rosie said. 'I thought being my own boss would be fun – and it is – but—'

'You feel guilty when you do,' Noah added, and Rosie nodded her agreement.

'But you should see the city.' Emma took Rosie's hand. 'You've hardly had the chance to sight-see since you arrived. You started work within days.'

'I could take a half-day Wednesday, couldn't I? Then I don't have to feel wholly guilty.' Everyone around the table agreed with nods and smiles. 'But how long are you here for, Brechtje?'

'Only a few more days, then I have to get back to work.'

Conversation turned to Brechtje's job and Rosie watched as Emma visibly relaxed. It was clear to her that Noah fancied her friend. Why else would he have introduced her to his sister? He'd obviously wanted to join them for a drink and introducing her was the best way to sit with Emma. They fell into discussion of their shared love of artisan products, Emma through her deli and Noah through his cheese. Rosie spoke with Brechtje and she was just as charming as her brother, though clearly less shy.

The evening was a perfect end to a terrible day. She felt surrounded by friends and allowed her eyes to wander to the canal, to the bikes tied to the railings that ran alongside it. As the sky darkened and stomachs began to rumble, Brechtje and Noah excused themselves for dinner. Noah had already booked them a table and though he asked Emma and Rosie to join them, both refused, realising that family time was so sacred to Brechtje and Noah it would be rude to interrupt it.

After they'd gone, Emma and Rosie finished their drinks and left. They walked a little way together, stopping by a lamppost, the Victorian-style light casting shadows around them. 'See, I told you it would be all right.' Rosie nudged her friend's shoulder.

'You did. Thank you.'

'But you really should just ask him out. He's clearly into you.'

'I've tried, but every time I open my mouth, I just can't get the words out. I'm so scared of being rejected I just stand there like a fish, my mouth opening and closing. It's incredibly embarrassing for a thirty-year-old woman. You know, when I was little, I thought I wouldn't have any insecurities at all when I got older. Now I think I have more.'

Rosie laughed. 'I know the feeling. But you'll do it when the time's right,' she reassured her.

'And you—' Emma started, rubbing her friend's arm. 'The market will be all right, I promise. We'll help keep Finn off your back.'

The disappointment she'd felt earlier came flooding back. 'I need to come up with something special, something to make me stand out from everyone else. My pitch is so small I'll be overlooked if I don't keep doing something a little bit different. The talks were doing that, but now I don't know what to do. I had thought about flower arranging, but I worry that's been done.'

'You'll think of something,' Emma reassured her. 'Now, we've both got an early start again tomorrow and I need some sleep. It'll do you good to rest your brain too. Let the ideas come to you when they're ready.'

Emma kissed her on the cheek, and they said their goodbyes. Rosie wished she felt as confident as Emma that she'd think of something, but every time she tried, her mind went blank. Perhaps some rest and relaxation were what she needed. Tomorrow, she'd take that half-day and explore the city. She hadn't come all this way to only see the inside of the market and her houseboat.

Chapter 12

The next day, Rosie closed the market stall at lunchtime, determined to stick to her word and explore the city.

Finn had given another talk that morning, though the crowd was slightly smaller, she'd been pleased to see. As he'd finished, a flash of something strange had flittered across his face. If she'd been feeling sympathetic, she might have called it shame, but she quickly decided it couldn't be, given that he hated her so much. A few people had turned up at her shop, having heard about her herb talks, and she spoke to them for far longer than she would have if she'd had to speak in front of twenty people. It had been lovely, a special one-to-one conversation. They'd asked questions that she'd been able to answer thanks to her mum's books. It had been incredibly rewarding in a way her previous jobs never had been, and this raised her spirits. She felt guilty taking the afternoon off when she really should have been working every hour she could to try and up her takings, but something about the conversation she'd had with Emma, Brechtje and Noah had rung true for her. She'd worked hard to get here and deserved to enjoy the city for a few hours. What's more, she definitely had to think of a way of driving more business down to her tiny stall and her best ideas always came when she was least expecting them.

Ignoring Finn's gleeful face as he watched her close up early, she left the market and put on her shades as the sun's warm, bright rays hit her eyes. Where to start?

She began with the Rijksmuseum; after all, it was a major tourist attraction and from there she'd wander and see what she found. The museum didn't disappoint and after staring at the Vermeers and Rembrandts, she felt like she'd ticked something off her bucket list. As she hadn't yet had lunch, she decided to visit the De Pijp neighbourhood, home to some of the best food shops around, according to Emma.

Rosie wandered the narrow paved streets in awe, passing cafés, restaurants, food stalls and more. Different nationalities and backgrounds mixed here with such a vibrant energy that the place itself felt alive, as if every street had its own personality. London had a similar feel, but the vibe was always more frenetic, as if everyone was searching for the next thing to do, or see, or feel. It was exhausting. Devoid of canals, this area of Amsterdam felt entirely different to the one she'd grown used to. As she exited a shop, she saw Max at the window of an art gallery, staring at the large canvas displayed in the window. It was a painting of a tulip in an Andy Warhol style and if Rosie could afford to, she would have bought it for the *Forget-Me-Knot*. She marched over and stopped at his side.

'I like that piece, don't you?'

Max turned to her in surprise before looking back at the window. 'What are you doing here? Are you following me?'

If he'd said this when they'd first met, she wouldn't have been able to identify the slight teasing tone to his voice, but as she'd had a few conversations with him now, she caught the intonation.

'You wish,' she joked. 'Actually, I'm having an afternoon off and exploring Amsterdam.'

'Yeah? Good.' He seemed to approve. 'Where have you been?'

'Only the Rijksmuseum so far and—'

'Pfft.'

'What? What's that noise for? Surely you approve of me seeing the Rembrandts and the beautiful art the Dutch are famous for.'

'I do, but it's so . . . so—'

'So what?' She crossed her arms over her chest, looking him in the eye. She caught the way his gaze flittered down to her vest top and a bolt of electricity flew to her toes.

'So touristy.' He shrugged. 'There are many more exciting places to go.'

'Like where?' He could give her a list if he was that clever.

'Like the Houseboat Museum, some of the art galleries here and across town, *De Koffieschenkerij*.'

'What's that?'

'It's a café in the cloister gardens of the *Oude Kerk*. That means Old Church. It's one of the most beautiful and peaceful places in the whole of Amsterdam. And . . .' A mischievous glint came into his eye. 'There's definitely somewhere else you should go too.'

'Oh yeah? Where's that?'

'It's the—' He paused as if catching himself or considering what to say next. He glanced around, and then said, 'Actually, I can show you if you want?'

'You?'

'Yes, me.' He rolled his eyes, his tone cross. 'Do you want me to show you or not?'

A wide grin spread across her face as the sun glinted in his eyes, making them sparkle.

'Go on then. Where do we start?'

He took a breath in, taking in the city as though mapping the best route. 'There is somewhere I think you'll love. Come on. Where's your bike?'

'My . . . ?'

'Bike. Two wheels? You ride it around the city. Looks like that—' He turned her by the shoulders to look at someone cycling past.

The feel of his hands on her bare skin sucked the air from her lungs, but she spun back to face him and suddenly they were closer together than she'd realised, face to face.

Electricity filled the air as neither of them pulled away. Her mind had gone blank, but she recalled quickly the remark she'd planned in response to his sarky comment. 'I know what a bike is, thank you very much. The truth is, I prefer walking. I've never been that great on two wheels.'

She'd tried riding once in London and had nearly been murdered by half a dozen taxis, two London busses and even a couple of pedestrians. By the time she'd got to work, her life had flashed in front of her eyes in cinema-quality detail and she'd hadn't been that impressed by what she'd seen. All that added to her racing heartbeat, as she was woefully unfit, had put her off the two-wheeled contraptions for life.

'Cycling is the only way to get around Amsterdam. It's not a huge city but if you want to see the best bits in the next—' He checked his watch. 'Three hours, you better get one.'

'How?'

He rolled his eyes again, but Rosie could tell he wasn't really annoyed. 'From a rental shop. This way – there's one around the corner.'

Of course there was. And though the thought filled her with dread, Max was right. Everyone in Amsterdam rode a bike, so she followed him to the shop and was soon wearing a cycling helmet and mounting a cute dark red bike with a small basket on the front.

'Ready?' he asked, sitting astride his.

'No, not really.'

'Just try it. Go up and down a little first.'

With a huff she pushed off and wobbled a bit before careening to the side and narrowly missing a pedestrian who ran out of her way.

'Sorry! Sorry!' she called out while trying to stand upright and righting the bicycle.

'What was that?' Max asked, stroking his beard in an attempt to hide his laughter.

'It was me riding my bike,' she replied, readjusting her helmet. 'My hat's too big and it distracted me.'

Max propped his bike against a lamppost and went to her. 'It's a helmet, not a hat.' He adjusted the strap, his fingers brushing her skin, his eyes flicking to hers then back to the strap. 'Is that better?' She nodded, unable to speak. 'Try again.'

Rosie cast off again, screeching as she did so. After a second, the wobbling subsided, and she got the hang of riding up and down the street, turning and even ringing the little bell just for fun. 'I'm doing it!' she declared with a giggle. 'I'm actually riding and not dying!'

'I'll ride beside you,' Max replied, and she could hear the amusement in his voice. 'So you aren't next to the traffic. That's it, you're doing great.'

A second later he was by her side, slightly ahead as he led the way. Rosie smiled. She was actually beginning to enjoy herself. The pace was much more sedate than in London and as so many areas were marked out for bikes only, she felt perfectly safe. She followed Max's directions and fifteen minutes later they pulled in at their first stop.

'Where are we?' she asked, staring up at another typical canal house with its tall narrow windows and gabled roof.

'This is Museum Van Loon.'

'Oh,' Rosie replied, trying to hide the disappointment in her voice. The building was gorgeous, but she was hoping to see more than just museums. She wanted to see the spots the locals went to.

'This is a must-see in Amsterdam. It was a palace built in 1672 and inside it has remained the same since the seventeenth century.'

Well, that was quite impressive. 'We'd better go in and have a look then.'

If Max was being kind enough to show her some of the best things Amsterdam had to offer, it would be childish to argue, and the locals she'd met were certainly proud of their history.

She had to admit the house was stunning and they wandered around admiring the furniture, the architecture and the ornaments decorating each room. A couple of times, when Rosie and Max found themselves in a small room along with other people, he scowled and tutted.

'What's the matter?' Rosie asked.

'Tourists,' he said through gritted teeth.

'What about them?'

'I hate them. They're everywhere, with their large backpacks, hitting everything and everyone.'

'I'm sure they don't mean to.' She tried to hide the laugh in her voice.

'Why is that funny?'

'Because it's just so grumpy. I'm a tourist too, technically.'

'Yes, but you're slightly less annoying than they are, but only because you don't have a backpack.'

'I'm starting to wish I did, just so I could hit you with it.'

'Ha ha.' They edged out into the corridor. 'Actually,' Max said, 'this isn't the best bit. Not for someone like you, anyway.'

'Someone like me?' Rosie raised her eyebrows. 'What does that mean?'

'You'll see.'

He led her through the house and as she stepped back into the sunlight, she had to shield her eyes so she could see the beautiful garden stretching out before her. Because the canal houses were tall and narrow, squidged in together, the gardens too were long and slender.

'Wow,' she breathed, taking in the beautiful space.

Rosie glanced behind to see Max watching her, an intoxicating smile on his face. She cleared her throat. That he'd brought her to this beautiful garden because of her love of plants made her cells tingle. The garden that lay before her was surrounded by a gable wall that ran down to another building.

'What's that?' she asked, pointing at the classical-style building with blue-painted alcoves and bright ornamental statues.

'That's the coach house. This is the only museum to still

have the canal house, garden and coach house all together. That's why it's worth visiting. You can really see how people used to live. And a pupil of Rembrandt's lived here.'

'Is that why you like it?' she asked.

He nodded.

'I'd have thought you'd like something more contemporary given the abstracty stuff you paint.'

'Abstract,' he corrected, but this time he was smiling slightly. 'You cannot be Dutch and not love Rembrandt. He was a genius. I wish I had half his skill.'

'I'm sure you do.' He looked up and Rosie realised it might have seemed like she thought him less talented. 'I mean, I'm sure you have just as much skill as he does. I didn't mean that—' She shrugged apologetically. 'I loved your painting when I saw it.'

'Let's walk down,' he said, gesturing to the garden and Rosie cursed her stupidity. A mask had come down on Max's face again and the carefree version she'd enjoyed moments before had disappeared. She'd have to bring it back.

The formal garden was beautifully symmetrical with a circle of small, neat hedges brimming with pale pink roses. In the centre was a sundial on a small plinth, its gold rings reflecting the sun. All around were shrubs and plants blooming in the summer sunshine. Tall, leafy trees towered overhead, creating welcome shade. Whoever looked after the garden did a wonderful job: every path was clear with not a leaf out of place on the topiarised hedges.

'This is amazing.' Rosie leaned down to smell one of the roses. 'Gruss an Aachen roses,' she said. 'Gorgeous.'

'Do you know the name of all plants and flowers?' Max asked.

'Not all, no. Some. I've learned them from when I was tiny. My mum . . . she was a botanist, and I was always fascinated by her books. She'd show me pictures and tell me the names. For some reason they stuck with me when things like maths equations and literary quotes never did.'

She could smell the damp mud from where they'd been watered, and it filled her with joy. She caught Max watching her again from the corner of his eye, though he turned away quickly when she looked at him. After a short time, when Rosie had just finished walking around the garden for the third time, he said: 'So are you ready to move on?'

'You've got somewhere else in mind?'

'Of course. Come on.'

He led the way out, and as she caught up with him, he placed his hand gently on her lower back to guide her forwards. She could barely feel the weight of it and couldn't decide if he was trying not to touch her on purpose, but then his warmth spread through the fabric of her vest top and heat radiated across her skin.

Outside, she took her helmet and, after checking she was ready, Max led the way through the streets to their next stop. Her cycling was getting better and Rosie found herself smiling and enjoying the ride. This was why Amsterdam was known to be one of the happiest cities in the world. Cycling to work kept you fit and was enjoyable. The culture of the place was a strange mix of vibrant energy, but also relaxation and respite. The people were friendly and accepting and it just felt like home.

Max pulled up and before he'd even dismounted, he turned to her, smiling.

'You look very pleased with yourself,' she said as she climbed off her bike and secured it to a rack.

'I am.' He gestured to the building they were here to see, and Rosie finally read the sign. She'd been so busy concentrating on not falling off her bike or hitting a pedestrian, she hadn't noticed it before.

'*Hortus?*' Rosie read and then realisation dawned as some of the words her mum had taught her came to the fore. 'The garden.'

'Welcome to Hortus Botanicus, Amsterdam.'

'A botanical garden?' she asked excitedly, springing a little.

Max's grin widened again, lighting his eyes. 'Come on.'

He insisted on paying their entrance fee despite Rosie's protestations.

'Then how about I buy dinner?' She had wondered if he'd immediately revert to his grumpy, closed-in ways, but to her surprise he agreed.

'Okay. But maybe we can get something on the way home and eat at the boat. I don't want to leave Zoon for too long.'

'Sure. That makes sense.' She bit the inside of her cheek to stop from grinning. Max was definitely beginning to warm up to her, but was he as interested in her as she was in him? Hope that he was lightened her steps.

The next hour passed so quickly Rosie couldn't believe there was still so much to see. They'd barely been around half the botanical gardens, and she knew this would be a place she'd be spending more and more time. Even Max seemed to enjoy himself as Rosie pointed out interesting things about the plants she recognised. He even teased her when there were some she didn't know.

As they returned their bikes with moments to spare before the shop closed, she thanked Max for a wonderful day.

'It's been amazing.'

'There's still a lot more to see. Amsterdam is the best city in the world.'

'Maybe you can take me?' She held his gaze, and he chewed his lower lip.

'Yes . . . maybe. Now, we should grab some food and head back. Zoon will need his dinner and some fresh air.'

They stopped in some of his favourite shops and gathered enough for a light supper: delicious bread, meats and cheeses and some traditional *appeltaart* – Dutch apple cake – for dessert. She couldn't wait to sink her teeth into the sweet treat. The pastry was flaky and topped with icing sugar, and the apple poking out of the sides smelled of delicious cinnamon. Her mouth was already watering.

Zoon greeted them enthusiastically as they approached the galley door, charging out, ignoring his owner and heading straight for Rosie. He almost knocked her over in his enthusiasm and responded when she commanded him to get down in her firmest voice.

'Zoon, sit.'

Max stopped from unpacking the shopping. 'That's the most serious I've ever heard you be.'

'Hey, just because I'm not all doom and gloom like you, doesn't mean I'm not serious, or that I'm stupid.'

'You think I'm doom and gloom?' He seemed genuinely shocked that that was what she thought of him.

Her cheeks burned. 'Maybe a little serious, sometimes.'

He walked out onto the deck carrying two glasses and a bottle of wine. He signalled to a chair, and she sat down. 'I don't think you're stupid, by the way. Not at all.'

'Good.' She looked at him from under her eyelashes, giving him her most flirty look. The compliment filled her with joy.

'How did you become a painter?' she asked, eager to learn more about him.

'I never wanted to do anything else. Even as a kid it was all I wanted, but it doesn't pay very well, and some people find that hard to deal with.'

Was he talking about himself or someone else? Rosie decided not to press. He was so prickly he'd probably shut down and the evening would be ruined: an evening she didn't want to end anytime soon.

'What about you?' he asked. 'Have you always wanted to be a florist.'

'Yes and no,' she replied. Was she going to talk about her mum again? Normally she tried not to. It brought up such pain and the grief could still catch her unawares even after all these years. 'I've had so many jobs I don't think I could name them all. This is the only one that's felt right for me. My mum, she—' She took a breath, feeling the familiar well of sorrow. 'She died about twenty years ago, which sounds a long time, but it's not really.'

He looked up. 'I'm so sorry.' The gentleness of his voice was like a warm hug and his eyes were dulled with emotion.

'I made the move to do something that made me happy, something with flowers like she did. Maybe it was to feel close to her.' She briefly closed her eyes. 'I've never said that out loud before.'

Max gave her a smile that could melt an iceberg, but didn't speak. Somehow, she knew that it wasn't that he didn't know what to say, more that he was giving her space to continue.

'She would have loved the flower market. It was a spur-of-the-moment thing deciding to work here. My sister's always nervous of my spur-of-the-moment decisions. They don't always work out.'

'But this one has?'

'I think so. If I can keep Finn off my back.'

'Finn?' She explained who he was. 'Ah, I think I know who you mean. I know someone who owns a gallery next to one of his flower shops and they say he is a very difficult man. Very territorial.'

'Territorial's right. He's got it in for me as he was hoping to get the pitch I got. I don't know why he's so bothered; it's so tiny and it sounds like he's doing absolutely fine without it.'

'Some people just like to have all the toys.'

Zoon tapped her leg with his paw and rested his head on her knee. His doleful eyes were so wide and sad-looking he was like a cartoon character.

'He wants to come up,' Max said. 'But you don't have to let him.'

'I don't mind.' She patted her lap, and the dog wagged his tail. After wiggling his back legs he then jumped up, turning on the spot before settling down like a cat. 'He really is very sweet.'

'So what will you do about Finn?'

'I don't know. I need something to set me apart from the rest.'

'What about talks or a workshop?'

'I tried talks but now Finn is doing the same thing. Workshops might work,' she replied, the idea fizzing in her mind. 'I don't know what I'd do them on yet, but that's definitely an idea.' She made a note on her phone. 'I think I'd like to do something that celebrates this city.'

'But everyone will already sell our famous flowers and those awful, tiny windmills you see in souvenir shops.'

It was true: she'd seen plenty of them. Then suddenly the idea crystallised. 'I think I know what I'm going to do.'

'What?'

'I'm going to make arrangements inspired by Amsterdam itself. Its food, its culture, its places. I can promote the different attractions and places I visit. I know what it's like when you live somewhere – you take it for granted. You don't see it the same way a tourist does. I'm going to turn being a tourist into my superpower and use it to show the locals how amazing their city is.'

Max grinned, shaking his head a little.

'What?'

'Nothing. It's just . . . it sounds like you have a plan.'

'I do. And now, I'm hungry.'

To her surprise, he laughed as he stood and said, 'I'll make us some food.'

Rosie would have leapt to her feet too had it not been for the dog. 'No, no, no. You paid for us to go into the botanical garden. I'll make it – that's if you don't mind me going into your boat.'

For a second, something passed over his face. It wasn't concern or annoyance, more like remembrance; a memory that he had to force down. 'Not at all,' he replied, signalling the way. 'But I'll come too. I need to feed Zoon.'

Over dinner they discussed life on the canals and things she needed to do before the summer was over to prepare the boat for winter. That's if she was still here then. She hoped desperately that she would be. Her world was growing, widening as she embraced this new place and all it had to offer. She wasn't ready to let that go. Max didn't tell her much about himself, only that his parents lived on the other side of the city. He clearly didn't have a girlfriend and valued his own space, his privacy. She wondered when that privacy had become the walls he'd built around himself.

'So where should I . . . or we, visit next?' she asked as they finished their meal and cleared away their plates.

'I know just the thing,' he said with a mischievous grin on his face.

Chapter 13

'Where are we going?' Rosie asked Max as they met on the dock by their boats three days later. It was late morning and though she'd been loath to miss a day's trading, Max had insisted it was the only time to see what he had in mind.

'You'll see,' he replied with a grin. He was wearing a T-shirt and jeans despite the heat of the day and Rosie forced herself to look away from his chest. The way the T-shirt clung to the ridges and grooves of muscle made her heart flutter. He'd trimmed his beard, she noticed. It was cut closer than before, hinting at the strong jawline underneath. Had he done that for her? The idea filled her with excitement.

'Well, am I dressed okay?' she asked, signalling to her denim shorts (black this time) and a simple white vest top. She'd also worn her favourite trainers, unsure of what they'd be doing, but pretty certain they'd be a good fit no matter what.

Though she hadn't been fishing for compliments, the way he glanced at her, his eyes running up her legs and the curves of her waist, to her chest and face, sent a thrill into her tightening muscles. His eyes widened as if seeing her properly for the first time.

He cleared his throat. 'You look fine.'

Okay, that wasn't quite what she was hoping for based on his reaction, but that was all right. She was beginning to learn that Max was a man of very few words and didn't enthuse about anything.

He made a sound in the base of his throat. 'Let's get going.'

'Wait! I have something for you.' He paused, clearly surprised and she spun back into the depths of the galley to grab his gift. 'Here.' She handed over a plant in a bright blue pot. 'This is Mandy.'

He frowned. 'Mandy?'

'Mandy. She's a *Haworthia fasciata alba*. I wanted to thank you for the other afternoon – and for today – and . . . her leaves reminded me of your painting.' They were thick, striped and pointed, like the swipes of colour on the canvas. 'And she's non-toxic so you don't have to worry about Zoon.' She studied him as he stared at the plant, turning the pot in his hands to study it from all angles. 'You don't like it.'

His eyes suddenly lifted to hers. 'No, I do. I know just where I can put her but . . . Mandy?'

She giggled. 'All right, you can rename her if you like, but it has to be a woman's name. She's definitely a girl. You can leave her here till later.'

She took the plant back and closed the door behind her.

They began to walk through the city, and once again Rosie took a moment to appreciate the gorgeous houseboats lining the canal. It was becoming a familiar sight now but one she knew she could never tire of. Not like the tower blocks and glass offices of London. Seeing the other houseboats, she knew she needed to do some more work on the *Forget-Me-Knot*, prettying it up so it looked as good as the others. She quite fancied having a giant forget-me-not flower painted on the side. As they turned off the canal, the houseboats were replaced by the architecture she'd grown used to: merchants' houses calling back to times gone by, but it was so typically Dutch she couldn't help but smile when she saw it.

'What are you grinning at?' Max asked.

'The houses. They look so lovely.'

'Do they?'

'See! This is exactly why I want to make arrangements that showcase the colours and feel of the city. You live here so you've stopped seeing how beautiful it is.'

'Maybe I just see beauty differently.'

She frowned, her brow creasing 'How so?'

'Well, I don't necessarily see the details, like you do, but I see the beauty in the shapes and colours.'

'Is that why you paint abstracty work?' she asked,

genuinely interested. She'd never met an artist before and had always wondered what inspired them.

He tutted but didn't bother correcting her. She'd only said it to annoy him anyway. 'Correct. For me it's the feel of something, the emotions it induces, and it doesn't have to be an object or place either. Sometimes I paint feelings – I know that sounds silly.'

'No, it doesn't at all. When I saw that painting on your deck, the one with the blue slashes, I felt . . .' She paused and noticed him watching her from the corner of his eye. 'Sort of . . .'

When she didn't finish, he said, 'Sort of what?' His tone gentle but eager.

'Sad, but also angry. It made me think of my mum and how sad I was she wasn't here anymore and how I used to be so angry at the world that it had taken her from me.'

'You still miss her a lot,' Max replied, and it was a statement not a question.

Rosie nodded. 'Is that the way I was supposed to feel when I saw it?'

'You should feel whatever is right for you to feel. Art doesn't tell people what to think or how to act. It should encourage them to connect with it however they want. I'm glad you connected with it somehow.'

'I'd love to see more of your work. Do you display anywhere?'

'Not at the moment. It's been . . . difficult to get my work into galleries for a while.'

'Why's that?'

'Do you mind if we talk about something else?' His tone was a little sharp, as she'd grown accustomed to, but without malice or anger.

'Sure. Are you going to give me any hints as to where you're taking me?'

It felt like they'd been walking for only a few minutes, but she'd lost track of where she was.

'Nope, but if you didn't come, you'd be the only person in Amsterdam not there.'

'Sounds intriguing.'

They carried on to Westerpark and as they walked towards the large gate with the legend *Milkshake Festival* written over the top, Rosie felt her smile widen.

'What's this?'

'It's the biggest dance festival in Amsterdam, but it's not just that. It's about encouraging love, courtesy, respect and tolerance.'

'A dance festival?' she exclaimed. 'Like club music?'

'Listen—' Max pointed to his ear and through the chattering crowds she could make out a deep rhythmic bass note. She burst out laughing. 'What?'

'This just didn't strike me as your type of thing.'

'Why not?' His face was a picture of indignation, which only made her laugh more.

'Because dance music is all about letting go, feeling the rhythm, throwing some shapes.' She started showcasing her best dance moves. 'And you don't strike me as a dancer.

You strike me as a sitting at the side of a wedding reception doing this.' She mimed him drinking from a cup and saucer with shaking, old man hands.

'Please don't do that again,' he replied, deadpan. 'This festival isn't just about the music. And don't be so judgemental – I can dance.'

'I'm not!' It truly wasn't that she was being judgemental, more that he was always so serious that she imagined him liking classical music or something highbrow like that. As a shyness crept into his gaze, she softened. 'So where do we start?'

'Hungry?' he asked, that mischievous look back in his eyes.

Rosie melted once more. When Max relaxed, there was something magnetic about him, something that drew her in. She didn't know what it was and normally, if a man had been as grumpy with her as Max had been, she wouldn't have bothered sticking around. But the flashes of kindness, the way he'd helped fix the leak and given her some tools, the way he was with Zoon, the way he'd fixed her door without her asking and listened about her mum, told her there was more to him than met the eye. And, of course, he wasn't bad to look at either.

'I'm always hungry,' she joked.

'Then let's start with the food.' He held out his hand and she took it, enjoying the sensation of his warm palm against her own. 'Everything is vegetarian or vegan.'

'Really?'

'It's all part of the ethos.'

They browsed the different vendors and settled on black bean tacos that were so delicious she could have eaten them every day for the rest of her life and never grown bored. They then stopped off for mini Dutch pancakes covered in icing sugar. As she placed the first bite in her mouth she made a noise of appreciation. Max's eyes were on her in a second and his Adam's apple bobbed as he swallowed. She felt her cheeks heating under his gaze.

'Good?' he asked, his voice a little huskier than usual.

'Very.' She held his gaze for as long as she could and it sent her body tingling, but when it came time to place another spoonful in her mouth, she had to look away. The intensity of his gaze, the way he watched her face, made her heart race and she wasn't sure how she managed to eat while it was pounding so hard in her chest.

After they'd finished their food, they moved through the crowd, Rosie adoring the smiling faces all around her. The way everyone dressed was outlandish: some people wearing next to nothing, others in intricate, unusual, brightly coloured costumes. Feathered headdresses, bikinis – anything and everything – and most with glittery make-up. The festival reminded her of a smaller Glastonbury. She'd been a few times in her youth and always loved the friendly vibe but the Milkshake Festival had it in spades. Perhaps because it was in a smaller area, the feeling was so much more concentrated. Everyone was out to have a good time.

From the corner of her eye she saw Emma, dressed in a blue cowboy hat, cowboy boots, a short bright red skirt and a white T-shirt with a giant pink heart on it. She also had a pink feather boa around her shoulders and pink star-shaped sunglasses. Rosie waved and called out to her.

'What are you doing here?' she asked as Emma enthusiastically approached. 'And what's with the outfit?'

'Everyone dresses up for Milkshake. Well, nearly everyone. Who's this?' She eyed Max approvingly and Rosie cleared her throat.

'This is Max. He's my neighbour and has been helping me to see the sights.'

'Has he now?' Rosie flushed as a Cheshire-cat grin spread over Emma's face.

'Who are you here with?'

'You'll never guess,' she declared happily. 'Noah! He's just gone to the bathroom.'

'When did this happen?' Rosie was so pleased he'd finally plucked up the courage to ask her out.

'Last night.' She turned to Max. 'Noah works in the flower market with us. He's a cheesemonger and I've had the biggest crush on him for ages, but I've never got anywhere. Not until Rosie came along, that is.' Max chuckled at her honesty as Emma grabbed Rosie's wrists. 'It's all down to you.'

'It's not really. He was already mad about you; you just hadn't seen it. That's brilliant, though. Wait, here he comes.'

Noah greeted them both warmly, his shy eyes darting downwards. Rosie introduced Max who, to her surprise, instead of being quiet and insular, instantly struck up a conversation.

'Nice to meet you, Noah,' he said. 'We were just on our way to the Ferris wheel; would you like to join us?'

Emma slipped her hand into Noah's and bounced on her toes. 'Definitely! We'd love to, wouldn't we?'

'Umm . . . sure.'

As they walked, Noah and Max moved slightly ahead, Max asking questions about the cheese stall and how he found working at the flower market. Rosie walked behind with Emma, suddenly noticing the difference in her and Noah's outfits.

'I take it Noah isn't the dressing-up type?'

'Too early to say,' Emma replied mischievously and then burst out laughing. 'Actually, I was mortified when he turned up. I'd said about dressing up – everyone does it – but turns out when I thought he'd agreed, he actually hadn't.'

'What did you do?' asked Rosie, who remembered the embarrassment of once turning up to a party in fancy dress not realising it wasn't. She'd never been so embarrassed in her life.

'What could I do? I laughed. I did offer to change, but he said I looked great as I was.'

'You do,' Rosie agreed. 'Definitely.'

'So I thought I'd just go with it. They seem to be getting

on well.' She nodded at Max and Noah. 'You've never mentioned Max before, though. Why's that? Keeping him all to yourself?'

'It's more that he's normally so grumpy I didn't want to risk it. And to be honest, we're still getting to know each other.'

'Well, he clearly likes you.'

'I don't know.'

'What?' Emma paused. 'I thought you were the expert! Surely you can see the way he looks at you.'

'If he looks at me like anything it's with annoyance. He gets annoyed by everything.'

By now they were near the Ferris wheel and one of the smaller tents. Dance music blasted from the speakers. The strong beat pulsed through the ground, the bass thumping through Rosie's muscles. The fast, upbeat tempo made her want to smile and move.

Emma, still nervous, was chattering at Noah, who as usual was fairly silent.

'Are you ready to go up?' Emma asked Noah. 'Or would you prefer to go down?' She lowered her voice, attempting to be sultry.

Noah coloured to the tips of his ears. 'I think we better, umm . . .' He stepped forwards in the queue, leaving Emma's face turning crimson. He began speaking with Max and Emma edged back towards Rosie.

'Oh my God,' Rosie whispered as Emma turned despairingly to her. 'What the hell was that?'

'I don't know,' Emma murmured, pressing her hand to her forehead. 'I was trying to be sexy and coy.'

'Why? We're in the middle of a field.'

'Because that's what men like, isn't it? And I'm not. I'm brash and loud. I was just trying to flirt a bit. Bring him out of his shell.'

'You're brilliant just as you are. Just be you and he'll relax and chat more.'

'This was such a mistake. I've blown it, haven't I? Now he thinks I'm some sex-craved madwoman.'

'Absolutely not,' Rosie replied, encouragingly. 'He's still here, isn't he?'

'Only because he's in a queue and can't escape. He looks a bit . . . shell-shocked.'

'Only because that came a bit out of nowhere.'

'I'm so out of practice it's embarrassing.'

Rosie took her hand. 'Just forget about it, okay, and pretend it never happened. But no more innuendos out of nowhere, all right? Just be yourself and let the conversation flow naturally.'

'All right.'

'You've got this.'

Emma moved back to Noah's side and when his conversation with Max naturally ended, he returned to Rosie.

'So,' Max began, grinning. 'What was all that about?'

'Never you mind. Some of us are just better at flirting than others.'

'Is that so? You're sharing your wisdom with Emma, are you?'

'Just being a friend.'

'You've never flirted with me.'

Her whole body grew instantly hot. 'Maybe I have, and you haven't noticed.'

He stared at her, his eyes pinning her to the spot with an intensity that set her chest on fire. 'I'd have noticed.' With a grin that melted her into a puddle, they moved along the queue for the Ferris wheel, and the tension of that moment eased. But Rosie was left bemused at this glimpse of another side of Max: a side that was flirty and fun. Not to mention downright hot. 'Ready to go up?' he asked. 'This gives the best view of Amsterdam. If this doesn't inspire you, nothing will.'

'Maybe it'll inspire you? Not that you need any inspiring, I'm sure.' She was babbling now, her stomach a net full of butterflies all flying around each other.

The carefree Max began to fade. 'Oh no, I do.' She looked at him quizzically, tilting her head to one side. Suddenly, they were forced forwards by the crowd, and into the seats. It was far more snug than she'd thought it would be. Their thighs were touching and though he had jeans on, seeing and feeling his body so close to hers made her heart rate climb. The safety bar came down, and he sighed. 'The fact is, I could use all the inspiration I can get right now. The reason my paintings haven't been displayed anywhere for a while is because I haven't been able to paint.'

'Why?'

'It doesn't matter. But the life of a penniless painter isn't as romantic as it sounds. Things are pretty dire really.'

'Dire how?'

'Creatively and professionally. Not to mention personally and financially.'

'I'm so sorry – I had no idea.'

They were at the peak of the wheel, the Amsterdam skyline before them. The wheel paused, giving those at the top a chance to enjoy the view. Rosie noted the canals snaking through the city, the muted colours of the houses and the bright white gabling so typical of Dutch architecture. Trees punctuated the view with bright clusters of green, as though a painter had dabbed his brush here, there and everywhere. She could already picture a display she might make. Something in a small, flat basket with rivers of tiny blue flowers to represent the canals and larger white ones for the houses. She'd add leatherleaf fern for the bushy trees lining nearly every street. Max leaned a little forward, studying the view.

'Does it make you want to paint?' she asked hopefully.

'I'm afraid not.'

'Perhaps your creativity works differently to mine. Maybe something will come to you later.'

'Yes, maybe.'

The wheel began to move, and they enjoyed the rest of the ride in a comfortable silence, each content to ponder their own thoughts. As they got off, Emma and Noah, who had been in the seat behind them, suggested a drink.

They made their way to a stall selling Dutch beer and though not usually a fan, Rosie gamely tried some. It was quite enjoyable, the slightly bitter, hoppy taste different to her normal choice of wine.

'Excuse me,' Max said, during a break in conversation. 'I just need to use the restroom.'

He excused himself and Rosie and Emma wandered to a nearby tent. A DJ danced behind his decks, enormous headphones over his ears. People were jumping and moving as if the music gave them life and Rosie found herself wriggling along.

'Max has been gone a while,' Emma said. 'Noah and I were going to head out before the crazy evening crowd gets here. They're the real party animals. Do you want us to wait with you till he comes back?'

'No, it's fine,' Rosie replied. 'I'll take a wander back towards the beer tent in case he went there.'

'Okay, see you tomorrow?' Rosie nodded. Emma kissed her on each cheek and as Noah approached, gave her a tight squeeze as well, whispering, 'Thank you.'

Rosie took another sip of beer and made her way back to the tent. As she rounded the corner, she heard her name spoken loudly over the dull thud of the music. She edged forwards, not wanting to disturb the speaker, who she was sure was Max. She tipped her head around just enough to see who was speaking. Max was standing with someone she'd never seen before. He was about the same age as Max, holding a beer and wearing a baseball cap. His American accent seemed out of place as he spoke to Max, and she wondered if her British one did too.

'She's just a neighbour,' Max said. 'And an annoying one at that.' Rosie immediately pulled back out of sight as her heart twisted. 'She lives on the boat next to me.'

Unable to stop herself, she peeked around the side of the tent again.

'Hey,' said the man, holding up his hands in surrender. 'I was just saying you look happy, that's all. And I—' Rosie waited for him to speak again. He seemed to take years, but it could only have been a second or two. 'I know I haven't been in touch since you and Johanna split up. I should have. I was trying not to take sides, but I ended up losing one of my closest friends here. I'm sorry.'

As if her ears were tuned in to Max and only him, she could hear his heavy intake of breath. 'Thanks, Dan. I appreciate that. I know it was hard for you too. It's good to see you again as well, but there's nothing going on with Rosie, and even if there was, it wouldn't be any of Johanna's business.'

'Max, cool it. It's fine. I'm not judging. I think it's about time you moved on.'

'I'm not moving on,' he said again, the tension in his jaw clear from where she was. 'There's nothing going on between the English girl and me.'

Wow. She'd been rejected before but this was harsh. Brutal. *The English girl*. Was that all she was? And yet, today, she'd thought there was something growing between them. She tried to ignore the ripping feeling in her chest. The way her heart felt like a deflating balloon.

Who was Johanna? Max had never mentioned her. She was clearly an ex, but for how long and why had they broken up? Rosie bit her lip. Whoever she was, she was causing quite a reaction from Max, and for some reason, that thought hit her heart like a hammer, hurting it even more than the words he'd just said. Words that were still echoing in her brain, taunting her.

Chapter 14

She hadn't come to Amsterdam looking for a relationship, but hearing this about Max was definitely stirring something within her heart and it felt a lot like jealousy. What's more, the pain at being referred to so coldly was definitely out of proportion with what she should be feeling for her grumpy neighbour.

The other man, Dan, continued. 'I just thought she seemed nice, and you looked happy for the first time in ages. It's been a long time since I saw you smile like that.'

'It's been a long time since you saw me.'

An awkward silence descended. The music in the background seemed to fade and Rosie continued to listen, hoping to hear Max say something nice about her. Something to undo the cold comments he'd made moments before.

A moment later, he seemed to calm and she chanced

another glance. His hands rested on his hips, then he pushed one through his hair. 'I'm sorry, Dan. I shouldn't have reacted like that.'

'It's okay,' his friend said. 'I know how difficult it was when . . .' He didn't finish, but he didn't need to. Rosie knew what he was going to say, *when Johanna left*. Instead, Dan changed the subject. 'So how long is she staying?'

'Permanently, I think. But she's only just moved here. That's why I'm showing her the sights. She's just a . . . friend. Just a neighbour.'

Another twist of the knife. She shouldn't care that he only thought of her as a friend or neighbour. She'd been pretty sure that's what he thought of her anyway. They'd only known each other a few weeks and it had been clear from the start she was more attracted to him than he was to her. But hearing him saying it so starkly when she'd begun to think he was thawing towards her, maybe even liking her a little, felt almost insulting.

'We should have a beer sometime,' Dan said, trying to lighten the mood.

'Yes, I'd like that. I'll call.'

'Okay, good. But until then, maybe you should think about being more than friends with that English girl. A smile like that normally only means one thing.'

'That's one thing I'm never going back to.'

'You can't swear off love forever,' Dan joked.

'Watch me,' Max replied grimly, his grumpy, closed-off demeanour firmly back in place.

Rosie bit her lip and spun back around, edging back a few paces. For the want of something to do, she ran her fingers through her newly trimmed, short pixie crop, tucking the fine flyaway hairs behind her ears. All the while, she told herself that what she'd just heard didn't change anything. Max hadn't shown any real inclination towards her, except for the Mr Darcy hand-holding, so it didn't change anything. There was nothing *to* change. Yet she couldn't shake the thought that this Johanna was responsible for Max's insularity. He'd clearly closed down his life to new people and she was pretty sure this woman was the cause.

'There you are,' Max said when he rounded the corner of the tent and spotted her.

'I was just coming to find you,' She forced a bright smile onto her face.

'Sorry, I got held up. Are you okay?'

'Fine,' she replied, smiling wider to prove it. He stared at her. She clearly looked manic.

'Are you sure?'

How could he tell? Given everything she'd just heard, that he could read her so well shouldn't affect her the way it did. 'So where to next?'

'Time for a dance?'

That was not what she'd been expecting. Hearing his voice and seeing his face as he spoke to Dan, she'd been convinced he'd want to leave as soon as possible.

'You dance?' The shock was clearly evident in her voice and on her face.

'You haven't seen anything yet.'

They edged into the nearest tent, the music pounding in her body as soon as she drew close. Though feeling self-conscious, she began dancing. Her movements were gentle at first, rocking from side to side. Then she began to move her feet, watching Max do the same and smiling. To her surprise, Max was the first to start dancing with real freedom, enjoying the rhythm of the music. She copied, letting all thoughts and worries leave her mind, and they danced the afternoon away, growing closer, the flirty Max of earlier coming to the surface again, before others would force them apart. She loved seeing this side of him. It was proof to her that underneath his harsh exterior there was someone fun-loving trying to get out.

Again, her mind flew to this Johanna person, and what might have happened between her and Max, surer than ever that she was responsible. Every time they separated, she felt herself drawn towards him, and she was sure Max felt the same pull towards her. But then her mind would go to the words he'd said and to the mysterious ex who was still clearly in his heart, and she would pull back. When the set ended, despite everything, Rosie felt a rush of disappointment, compounded further when Max said: 'We should head back. I don't like leaving Zoon for too long.'

'Of course.'

'You can always stay if you like. I don't mind heading back on my own.'

She shook her head. 'It's been wonderful to see but I'm up early tomorrow for the market, so . . .'

'Shall we get something for dinner?' he asked, his voice rising a little with hope. Her heart gave a double beat. 'That's if you can manage anything else.'

'Of course I can! I can always manage more food.'

He smiled, warm and wide, and they decided on a curry to take away and share when they got back to the boat.

The walk back was punctuated by longer, lengthier silences than the stroll they'd taken in. Something had shifted again in Max's mood and though he'd tried to hide, the ghost of Johanna was obviously still haunting his thoughts. Rosie wanted to ask him about it, be her normal direct self and find out what she wanted to know, but that approach wasn't going to work with Max. Not ever. He was the type to talk about things when he was ready. Asking about her would also make clear Rosie had overheard his conversation – every word – and she didn't want his pity, his awkward apologies and excuses for being so brutal about the state of their relationship – their friendship, she glumly corrected herself.

They decided to have dinner on her boat rather than his, sitting on the deck in the evening sunshine, as the sun turned the sky a deep, rich orange. Clouds, tinged with grey and mauve, were beginning to gather and the air felt hot and heavy, as if a storm was brewing. The night carried that feeling of electricity that always came before thunder, but perhaps that was just her feeling on edge.

Max had let Zoon out and after a run around the deck and up and down the street, he'd settled in the shade on Rosie's boat.

'I would need sunglasses to live on your boat.'

'What?' She laughed and turned, following his gaze inside to the colourful throws, cushions and decorations she'd added. 'It's nice. Don't you like colour?'

'On canvas. And you need to varnish the deck,' Max said after taking a sip of beer.

'All right, all right! Sorry, I didn't realise you were a trained interior designer, and the deck's on my to-do list. I'm hoping to get it done one evening this week.'

'You must definitely do it before autumn. Piet should have taken much better care of this boat.'

'Well, he didn't so that's that. The *Forget-Me-Knot*'s got me now, and I don't mind getting my hands dirty.'

'Always with the cheerfulness.'

'Yes,' she replied, laughing. 'What else should I do?'

'Some people don't find it as easy to climb out of a bad mood.'

'No?'

This was the first time he'd ever mentioned his feelings and she didn't want to put him off.

'Sometimes . . .' He didn't continue and Rosie waited, her breath stuck in her lungs, unable to let it out for fear any noise would frighten him back into silence. He took a deep pull on his beer and tried again. 'Sometimes it's like trying to climb out of a dark hole or wade through mud.

It can seem like almost too much effort to pull yourself out.'

She'd felt like that after her mum had died, but she hadn't been able to say anything to Melody or her dad, wanting to be strong for them, knowing that they were all suffering and that her grief – her feelings – were no less severe than theirs. Her dad had encouraged her to talk about it, but she'd always found it difficult, not wanting to burden anyone else. She shifted in her chair and Max seemed to sense the change in her. He was watching her but didn't push her to respond. For the first time Rosie found that she wanted to.

'Grief gets you like that. Are you grieving someone . . . or . . . something?'

'I suppose I am in a way.'

Would he mention Johanna? Her muscles tightened.

'I think I'm mourning my career.'

'Your career?' Surprised again, she couldn't help but glance around at the covered canvases and paintings. 'But I thought—'

'Being an artist is not the same as being a *successful* artist. I know I mentioned it before but—' He took a deep breath. 'That creative block I've had . . . it's been there for a while now. It often seems too hard to get over.'

'I'm so sorry. I can't imagine what that's like. How does it feel?'

'Imagine if I told you that you couldn't ever be cheerful again. You couldn't ever look on the bright side. Painting is in my nature. Not painting feels like fighting who I am, but no matter how much I want to do it, I stare at the canvas, and nothing happens.'

'What about the painting I saw?' She pointed to where it had stood on his deck.

'An old one. I'd been trying to add to it, hoping it would help me, but it didn't. Every time I look at it, I feel nothing but sadness that it isn't good enough.'

'Good enough for what?'

'For me, for a gallery, for someone to spend their hard-earned money on.'

'How do you get by?' From the way his head shot up, she worried she'd overstepped.

'I have some money from previous sales, and I teach – well, I used to teach.'

'But you don't anymore?'

'Not for a while.'

'Why not?'

'Have you ever heard that saying those who can't do, teach?' She nodded. 'Teaching more than painting? It feels like giving in. Admitting that I'll never paint again.'

'I'm sure that's not true and it's not giving in. There's nothing wrong with having multiple strings to your bow.'

'There you go again, being positive.' She didn't know whether it was a compliment or not and dropped her eyes. 'The truth is if I don't get back to painting or teaching soon, I won't be able to afford this place.' He sighed heavily, and Zoon, attuned to his owner's sounds, lifted his head, his ears flicking about as he listened. After a moment, sensing everything was fine, he lay back down and closed his eyes.

'Then how do we get you back on track?'

Max barked out an unexpected laugh Rosie had no idea how to take. 'How do you do it?'

'Do what?'

'Just tackle everything head on, trusting that it can be solved?' His question was genuine, as if he was asking for help.

'It's a habit, I guess. Like brushing your teeth. You have to keep doing it until it becomes second nature.' She took a sip of her own drink for courage, feeling the soft, citrusy wine slide down her throat. 'I think some of it is nature. I was always quite easy-going but after my mum died, I – I lost it for a while.'

'I'm sorry you lost someone so important to you. That must have been incredibly hard.'

'It was.' She swallowed. 'My mum, she – she was the type of person who made everything better just by being around. She got down sometimes, and upset, like everyone, but she'd always encourage us to think positively. To make things happen for ourselves instead of sitting back and letting the world pass us by. She was all about being happy with the simple things in life. Enjoying a bright blue sky or a simple meal. But, after she'd gone, I felt so lost and . . .' She couldn't finish. 'Then I realised I had to be strong for everyone else – my dad and sister – so I started every day thinking of three things to be grateful for and at night I'd list three things that went well that day. I've been doing it ever since, so my brain automatically thinks of the things to look forward to.'

'And when something goes wrong?'

'There's always someone worse off than ourselves. I try and remember that a problem to me could be something someone could only dream of dealing with because everything in their life is so much harder.'

'Interesting,' he said, his eyebrows pinching together.

'I don't mean to sound preachy.'

'You don't,' he assured her, holding her gaze. 'My mother, she . . . isn't like that at all. She was proud of me being an artist but she tried to run my career for me, acting as my agent. It was . . . too much. It pretty much ruined our relationship. And when the sales started slowing down, she decided she'd had enough of playing agent and went back to her own life.'

'I'm so sorry,' she replied, appreciating how honest he'd been with her, and feeling even more grateful for the mum she'd had. Even if she hadn't had her for long. 'So, what can we do to help you get out of this creative rut?'

He gave a wry smile. 'To the point as always.'

'I'm here to help,' she teased.

'The honest answer is, I don't know.'

'Why don't you come to the flower market with me tomorrow? You can advise me while I make some displays inspired by today.'

'Maybe. We'll see.'

Rosie let out a disappointed breath as quietly as she could. She shouldn't want him to come as badly as she did, and she still didn't know anything about this Johanna. She opened her mouth to ask him, her nosiness getting the better of her, when he stood up.

'I better take Zoon for a walk before bed.' Hearing his name, the dog rose and stretched. He made his way to Rosie, sniffing her shoes and then leaning against her leg so she could fuss him.

'You're such a good boy, aren't you?'

'He knows how lucky he is,' Max added. Then staring at the sky, examining the colours of the night, he said, 'Maybe I should remember that more too.' Their eyes met as they had earlier when she'd been so sure that they'd been flirting, his dark and intense. How did this man trigger so many emotions in her? If only she could forget what she'd overheard and rid herself of his words repeating in the back of her brain.

'Goodnight, Rosie,' he said, drinking the last of his beer and placing the bottle on the table.

Looking into his face, which for once didn't seem so heavy with worry or frustration, she didn't have the heart to ask about Johanna – something that might bring the storm clouds back again. It was clear he was dealing with more than just a break-up. His career seemed to be poised on a knife edge. She'd never found her passion before, passing from job to job, but now she had, she didn't want to lose it. They were alike in that way: her doing everything she could to keep her tiny pitch at the flower market and build it into something else, him trying to regain his. She had to find a way to get him painting again.

Watching him leave, Zoon following along behind him, she felt the urge to speak – to see his face one last time. 'Maybe see you tomorrow?'

He turned and smiled, but she had a feeling they'd delved too deeply tonight, and he'd given far more away than he'd intended. When he spoke, the single-word reply told her she was right.

'Maybe,' he said, slipping his hands into his pockets, but she knew he'd withdraw again, hiding in his boat until the rawness of the evening's exchange had passed.

As the first raindrops began to fall, they fled in opposite directions, away from each other.

Chapter 15

When Rosie left for the flower market the next morning, there was no sign of life from Max's boat. During the night, she'd listened to the gentle tapping of the rain on the water and fallen asleep thinking of the day they'd spent together. She'd never imagined he would dance so freely or speak so openly. A smile grew on her face as she glanced back over her shoulder, but he must still have been asleep or taken Zoon for an early-morning walk.

It was still raining, and she enjoyed the cooler weather after the weeks of heat. The air smelled fresh and earthy, and though the sky was grey, the clouds amassed in heavy, navy-blue banks, she enjoyed it. The wind was picking up too and Rosie quickened her pace.

By the time she arrived at the flower market, the rain was pelting down, puckering the surface of the canal. All the vendors were watching the sky, chatting about the storm everyone knew was to come. Bas had just arrived with her flowers when there was an almighty flash of lightning. A huge rumble of thunder seemed to shake the ground beneath their feet, and the rain increased in intensity, hitting the canal with such force that the water jumped back up.

Bas took shelter with them. There was no point trying to deliver flowers in this weather. The incessant rain would damage the delicate petals and ruin them before they made it inside. Unsurprisingly, the tourists had stayed away, and the market was as quiet as the grave. This was not what Rosie was hoping for today. Inspired by the sights she'd seen with Max, from the canal house garden to the Milkshake Festival, and the beauty of the Amsterdam skyline, she wanted to make bouquets and arrangements. She'd have to reduce the price of her stock, too, which meant less profit, something she couldn't really afford. But some of the flowers were going past their best and needed a home as soon as possible. She began marking them up, ready for opening.

Emma came over, offering Bas a cup of tea. He said thank you and followed it with something else in Dutch Rosie couldn't make out.

'What did he say?' she asked Emma.

'He said, he needs to get on with his deliveries here at the market. He can't stand here all day, or he'll end up late for everyone, but he's worried about the flowers. We need to protect them.'

'Will this do?' She picked up the umbrella she'd used

that morning. It was one of her dad's golfing umbrellas – ridiculously wide, enough to protect three people. Bas grinned widely at Rosie and nodded. 'Come on, then.'

They made their way to the van and before long, everyone was helping. Everyone except Finn. He stood by his pitch, watching them work with his arms folded over his chest. With a wave of his hand and a harsh word he sent a few of his staff to retrieve his flowers, which was something, Rosie supposed, but not quite the coming together everyone else was doing. Rosie felt sorry for his employees. She might not be the most successful florist in the world but at least she was her own boss. She'd worked for people like Finn before; bullies who loved having power over others. No wonder no one in the market liked him.

As the last of the flowers were unloaded, Bas hugged Rosie. '*Bedankt*, Rosie! *Bedankt*.'

'You're welcome, Bas. Have a good day!'

'Have a good day,' he repeated in staccato English.

'Thanks for helping,' she said to Emma. 'And you too, Noah.'

Despite Emma's dismal attempts at flirting at the Milkshake Festival, Noah was still clearly keen and was lingering around after everyone had gone. Emma turned to him.

'We needed your big strong muscles, didn't we?' She grabbed his bicep, squeezing it.

'Ow!'

Emma immediately let go as Noah, eyes wide in surprise,

rubbed his bicep. 'I'll see you later, Emma. I – I better go. Bye, Rosie.'

She waved as Emma turned her back on him and buried her head in her hands.

'Really?' Rosie asked as Emma peeked at her through her fingers, a grin pulling at her mouth.

'Don't! I just keep opening my mouth and this – this rubbish comes out. I don't know what's happening to me. I've never been like this with a guy before. No wonder he hasn't asked me out again.'

'You only saw him yesterday; give him a chance. And you didn't see the way he glanced over his shoulder at you.'

'He did?' Emma asked, her voice rising with hope.

'He did. And he had a cheeky grin on his face. He might not have liked the terrifying death grip on his bicep—' Emma groaned. 'But he likes you. Definitely.'

'He won't if I keep going on like that.'

'You just need to flirt more subtly.'

'I don't know how to do that.'

'Well, I'd suggest drawing attention to you rather than grabbing at him. Touch your lips and see if his eyes follow. Flick your hair back and tilt your head.'

Emma shook her head in wonder. 'How much experience have you had at this?'

'Too much,' Rosie replied. 'No matter how many frogs I kiss, I haven't found my prince yet.'

'What about Max? If all frogs looked like him, I'd be happy to kiss them.'

Rosie sighed, thinking of her offer for him to come with her today and his refusal. 'I just don't know where I stand with him. One minute he's flirty and fun, the next he's pulling back.' She told her about Johanna and the conversation she'd overheard, but didn't mention about his creative block. For some reason, she just knew he'd want to keep that private, and as much as she loved Emma and their new friendship, it didn't feel right to share something so personal yet. 'It's . . . confusing,' Rosie finished with a dramatic shrug.

'Men are very confusing,' Emma agreed. 'And I might be bad at reading them, but I know that that—' she pointed, and Rosie gasped as she followed Emma's finger '—is a good sign and not at all confusing.'

Rosie couldn't believe what she was seeing. Max, looking gorgeously rumpled, his hair slicked down from the rain like some kind of 1950s Hollywood star, was striding towards her. Zoon, in a cute rain jacket, trotted along at his heels.

'Oh. My. God,' Rosie whispered.

Was Johanna's hold over him as strong as she'd thought? Or was he here for something else? Was he here for her but as a cheap replacement, just a rebound? Someone to pass the time with while his heart healed? Was she really just his too cheerful English neighbour? Whatever she was, she couldn't resist the way her heart pounded faster, matching his stride.

Emma grinned. 'Hi, Max.'

He smiled widely as he approached. 'Emma, wasn't it?

How are you? Did you have fun at the festival? I'm sorry I didn't get the chance to say goodbye.'

'That's okay. It was our fault for running off.'

'I've just seen Noah, actually. I think I'm going to have to stop by his stall on the way home and grab some of his delicious cheese.'

'Don't forget I have a gorgeous selection of breads and meats that'll go perfectly.'

Max chuckled. 'I won't.'

Emma left, winking at Rosie as she went.

'Hi,' Max said, sounding almost shy.

'Hi.' After a second, she gathered herself. 'You came.'

'It was an offer I couldn't refuse.'

Zoon barked.

'And you brought this little guy too!' She reached down and scratched him behind his ears. His tail began wagging so furiously his whole body shimmied from side to side.

'So,' said Max. 'What're you doing today?'

'Well, it kind of depends on the weather. Do you think this rain will last all day?'

'There's no sign of it stopping anytime soon. I guess we'll just have to wait and see.'

'In that case.' Rosie turned and stared at her flowers, her hands on her hips. 'I'll have to mark down some of these flowers to try and shift them or they won't be worth buying.'

'These are beautiful,' he said, picking up a particularly lovely rose.

'They're one of my favourite flowers.'

'Do you mind if I sketch it, and maybe these too—' He dropped Zoon's lead and moved to a large tub of anemones.

'Of course not.' She was thrilled to see him pull out a small sketchbook and stubby pencil, making marks on the paper. She took Zoon's lead and placed the handle under the leg of her stool so he could move around but not run off. He sniffed the different tubs, enjoying the unfamiliar smells.

Rosie began to sort her delivery, marking down her flowers and putting them in a bucket out front with a 'sale' sign stuck on. Now the market was open, a few customers who'd taken shelter from the rain perused the shops, admiring the myriad bright blooms before stopping at her stall. Gratefully, she handed over a large bunch of lilies she'd just reduced to a customer and thanked them for giving them a good home when Finn marched over.

He spoke – well, shouted – in Dutch.

Rosie felt heat climb up her spine, tingling the back of her neck. He was so angry she felt almost intimidated. Max stepped forwards, into her peripheral vision, and she was glad to know he was there. The other shopkeepers were watching and, she hoped, would intervene if Finn continued but first, she'd do her best to defuse the situation. 'I'm sorry,' she said calmly, holding up her hands for him to stop. 'I don't—'

'What do you think you're doing?' He pointed at the flower tub she'd placed out front.

Had she put them in the walkway or something? Was

she breaking some kind of health and safety code she hadn't been aware of?

She stared at them, then him, wondering what he could be talking about. 'I'm just reducing the price on them.'

'You're trying to undercut me.'

'I am not!' she exclaimed.

Max stepped forwards, his frown firmly back in place as he scowled at Finn. His hand gently touched her lower back protectively. 'What's going on?'

'Nothing to do with you,' Finn replied, lifting his chin as though his whole assault on her was justified. Max took another step towards him, opening his mouth to speak, but Rosie had never needed a man to speak for her and wasn't about to start now.

'It's all right, Max,' she replied, doing her best to control the quivering in her voice. 'I can handle this.'

He glanced at her, and then nodded before stepping back, trusting her, but remaining near enough that he could intercede if she needed him to.

Finn, his complexion turning ruddy, planted his feet and crossed his arms over his chest. It seemed to be his favourite pose. '*You* are trying to steal my business.'

The heat that had been rising in her spine now spread through her whole body. She could feel anger and frustration rising but having dealt with rude customers before, she knew just what to do. She kept her voice calm, her tone soft. 'I just need to get rid of these flowers before they're past their best or they won't be worth a customer buying them. You do the same sometimes – I've seen you.' His eyes widened at her response. He obviously hadn't thought she'd answer him back. Well, he might intimidate other people here, but she wasn't going to be one of them. From the corner of her eye, she saw Max smile.

'That is not— You can't—'

Zoon growled, edging closer to Rosie's feet, protecting her.

'And you've brought a disgusting dog into the market.'

'It's my disgusting dog, actually,' said Max, reminding Finn he was there.

The older man's gaze sprung once more onto Rosie. 'Who do you think you are?!'

'Who do you think *you* are?' she echoed back to him, her voice rising. Shouting at her over a perceived slight was one thing, but insulting Zoon, who was the sweetest, most well-behaved dog she'd ever known, was another. 'And I'll tell you another thing,' she continued, resisting the urge to point her finger at him. She'd stood up to her bullying bosses before (not always a good idea, she had to admit, but she wasn't going to stop now). 'I'm just starting out and everyone here has been so helpful and supportive except you. I have no idea what your problem is, but I suggest you get over it sooner rather than later. I'm entitled to reduce the price of my flowers if I want to. I've got a business to run. And unlike you, this is my only spot. I don't have extra shops, so I'm allowed to do what I need to do to make a living.'

'How dare you—'

'How dare you! You've marched up to me and instead of talking to me about your concerns, you've had a go at me in front of everyone. Not very grown up, is it? Now if you'll excuse me, I've got work to do.'

And with that she turned away and continued sorting her flowers from the morning delivery. Finn stood for a second in the silence that had fallen. Behind her, it was like someone had pressed pause on the world, the only noise the rain pummelling the awnings and the water of the canal. People stood still, muttering to each other; the stallholders, too, had stopped what they were doing. She was vaguely aware of Finn working his jaw as though preparing for a second round, then he thought better of it and marched off back to his own pitch.

The *Bloemenmarkt* filled with noise again and a second later Max was at her side. 'Are you all right?' The weight of his hand on her shoulder was reassuring, calming her racing heart.

'I'm fine. I won't be bullied like that.'

'You were . . .' She looked at him, willing him to finish the sentence. The smile he gave sent her heart beating against her ribs, and it had only just calmed down. 'Marvellous.'

She opened her mouth to speak but couldn't get the words out. Max went back to the seat he'd made for himself from an upturned bucket and continued sketching. In a daze, she returned to work, catching the smiles and thumbs-up gestures from the other vendors. A wonderful sense of belonging calmed her; she just wished she hadn't had to have an argument with Finn to feel it.

The rain continued unceasingly. Customers were few and far between, so Rosie and Max took a break, drinking a coffee from one of the other vendors. Max had refused to show her his sketches, but she'd loved seeing him at work. There was a light in his eyes as he turned the paper this way and that, his arm moving swiftly. Every part of him was absorbed in his work – a sign of true passion, she believed. She just hoped this would lead on to more – that the feeling would snowball and soon he'd be painting again, teaching and making the most of his talent. As they sat, chatting about the different flowers and if this storm would ever end, Rosie's attention was drawn to Finn's stall.

He was nowhere to be seen, but the awning seemed to be sagging with the weight of water sitting on it. In fact, it wasn't just sagging, it was positively bowing.

'What is it?' asked Max. 'You're scowling.'

Rosie pointed to Finn's stall. 'Is it just me, or does that look like an accident waiting to happen?'

'It doesn't look good, does it? But it'll serve him right for treating you the way he did this morning.'

'But if that falls, the water's got to go somewhere. It'll drown all his flowers.'

'I thought flowers liked water.'

'They do, but not that much and look—' She picked up a flower that had been caught in the rain during the delivery that morning. She gently lifted a petal, showing him where the delicate flower had torn from the force of the raindrops. 'This is water damage. And even if some survive now, the amount of water could make them die quicker.'

'I doubt he'd care about that. He'd probably still sell them and take his customers for a ride.'

'I hope not.' Rosie sipped her coffee as the raindrops beat a rhythm on the ceiling. She couldn't stop glancing at Finn's stall. 'I'm going to have to say something.'

Max looked up. 'To Finn?' His tone was incredulous. 'Why would you bother?'

Rosie stood up. 'Because he might not be a nice person, but I am. It's what my mum would do. Here, can you hold this?' She handed him her cup and walked over.

Finn saw her coming and met her just outside his stall. He really did have beautiful flowers, and so, so many. Though a pang of jealousy hit her, Rosie reminded herself she could get to this stage one day if she kept going.

'What do you want?' Finn asked.

She almost turned and walked away at that moment, leaving him to his fate. But she couldn't do it. If it was the other way around, she'd want someone – even her worst enemy – to tell her. She'd take the moral high ground. After all, they were going to be working together till at least the end of the summer. And the end of the summer was looking more and more likely with her small flower stall barely breaking even and repairs needed on the boat. She shoved that thought to the back of her mind.

'It's your awning,' Rosie began. 'Have you seen the amount of water on it? I was worried that—'

'My flower stall is none of your business.'

Her anger flared. 'You know—'

But she couldn't get another word out as a deafening crack of thunder smothered all sound. Several flashes of lightning followed in quick succession and the rain grew even heavier. It was as though some being above the clouds had turned on a tap or hosepipe and was spraying it down on the flower market. The loudest rumble of thunder echoed around them, and water began to rush in from the sides of the awning as it started to collapse.

'Quick!' Rosie shouted, gathering Finn's plants and moving them out of the way as the awning crumpled in the middle under the weight of water. A waterfall rushed forward, splashing over some of his plants and knocking others on their sides. The stall keepers opposite tried protecting their own goods.

Finn was pinned to the spot, but Rosie couldn't move quick enough. Max rushed to help, moving Finn's stock before it was washed away on a tide of rain and stagnant water. A moment later, the left side of the awning completely collapsed, taking a few tubs of flowers they'd been unable to clear with it. Just as her boat had been not long ago, his shop flooded, water seeping into her trainers, soaking her feet.

The water reached into the neighbouring pitches and Finn turned to them, his face ashen. Rosie surveyed the scene, her eyes falling on the devastation the water had brought for Finn and the others closest to him. As she brought her eyes up to his face, expecting to see him angry and ready to blame someone else, her heart lurched, and she felt sorry for him.

'I – I—' He looked like he might cry. All the pomposity leached from his face, making him look like a frightened, vulnerable man. 'I'm so sorry,' he said, turning around to face every one of the vendors who had been affected. 'I'm so very sorry.'

They stared at him in silence, some of them concerned, others scowling with anger. She felt a lump of emotion in her throat as her heart went out to him. For a moment, no one moved, but Rosie knew they couldn't just stand here. They needed to act.

'Has anyone got mops and buckets?' she asked loudly, jolting them all into action.

'I do,' Emma replied, running to Rosie's side, joining her in the battle to help.

'Me too,' said Noah, jogging back to his shop to fetch them.

The remaining stallholders bustled into life as Rosie took the mop and bucket from Emma. Emma handed them over and their eyes met for a moment, emotion written all over their faces, confusion and sadness overriding any negative feelings they'd had towards Finn. Emma grabbed a flower tub and was attempting to haul up as much water as she could, emptying it back into the canal.

'Finn,' Max said, placing a hand on his shoulder to bring

him round. He hadn't moved and stood gazing, his mouth hanging slightly open. 'Finn?' he repeated gently. 'Let's try and fix the awning, shall we? Stop any more water coming in.'

'I— You—' He peered around wildly, but the extent of the devastation still hadn't sunk in yet. 'You'll help me?'

'Of course. Now, we need to get this out of the way.' Max lifted the heavy, pale cream awning. Where the water had been sitting on it, algae had turned it green, and the smell of stagnant water filled the air. 'You'll need to get a professional in to fix it properly. It needs tilting more, so the rain falls back into the canal. But we can at least do something for now.'

'Th–thank you,' he stuttered, following Max's instructions.

It took a while but eventually they made some progress. Even some of the customers helped, sensing how devastating this could have been not just for Finn, but for everyone around him. Almost three hours later, the awning was fixed back up, the rain had eased somewhat, and Finn's stall was mostly back together. His staff thanked Rosie for jumping into action, especially given how rude Finn had been to her earlier, but Finn had remained silent. After working with Max, he'd continued alone, salvaging as much as he could. Rosie didn't know if he was embarrassed, angry or just trying to get a handle on the situation.

'Aren't you angry?' Max asked her.

'About what?'

'About Finn. You save his shop, and he doesn't even say thank you.'

She watched him move tubs around, shifting the same one from one place to another, glancing at the awning every time as if checking it was safe. Finn paused and looked down at his trousers. The bottoms were soaked, the pale beige fabric turning darker from the water.

'To be honest, I think he's in shock. You saw how out of it he was when it happened. Maybe he'll say thank you tomorrow when he's calmed down. It must have been horrible for him.'

'I still don't really know why you helped him when he was so rude to you.'

'Why did you?' she countered. 'You helped him as much as I did. What made you do it?'

He thought for a moment, and a wry smile tugged at the corner of his mouth. She'd trapped him. 'Because it was the right thing to do. And perhaps because I had a good morning sketching. I haven't had that in a while, and I felt . . .'

'Yes?'

'Happy.' She couldn't stop the inane grin pulling her cheeks tight. 'You are . . .'

'Amazing? Beautiful? Clever?'

'All of those things.' His cheeks reddened as if he'd said it by accident while her eyes pulled wide. 'And also, annoying and way too cheerful.'

'It's been said before.'

'I'd like to say thank you.' He picked up Zoon's lead.

'Let me take you out tonight. I have something I'd like to show you. Another thing in Amsterdam you must do.'

'As a tourist or a local?'

'Both.'

'Do I get to know what it is?'

'Of course not.' He laughed and stroked Zoon's head. 'Come on, Zoon, let's leave Rosie to her day. And after all that dirty water, you need a bath.'

'Are you talking to me or the dog?' she teased.

His eyes raked over her as if imagining her naked, and heat burned through every nerve ending in her body. 'Zoon, of course,' he replied, but his voice was hushed, like it was taking an effort to control it.

Rosie watched him go, her mind so focused on Max and the way he'd looked at her, not to mention what he might have planned, she didn't hear the person clearing their throat next to her.

'Rosie?' She turned to see Finn, still pale and shaking a little in front of her.

'Finn! Sit down, you look like you're going to pass out.' She ushered him to the stool and waited while he sat. He gripped the sides of it, as if nervous he might fall off, obviously unable to trust his legs. Rosie wished she had a biscuit or something sugary to give him. He really didn't look at all well.

'I – I wanted to say thank you,' he began. 'Thank you for helping me today. I didn't deserve it. I'm sure if you hadn't urged everyone, they'd have stood by smiling, enjoying my shop getting destroyed.'

She thought that more than a little uncharitable but didn't say so. She was sure everyone would have helped no matter who needed it. Some might have been reticent, but most had been more than friendly to her. Some people just weren't good in emergencies, that was all.

'Nobody wants to see someone else's livelihood destroyed,' she said gently. 'What will you do?'

'I'll get someone in to fix the awning tomorrow. I haven't lost much stock, thanks to you.' He lifted his head to look at her, colour returning a little to his cheeks. 'I'm sorry for the way I've behaved towards you.'

Rosie's mouth hung open. She hadn't been expecting him to say anything like that. To be honest, she'd thought after he'd calmed down that he'd go back to his usual selfish ways, giving only a cursory thanks to those who helped him. He still might, she supposed, but this version of Finn sitting in front of her was so different to the one she was used to, she didn't know what to do.

'Oh,' was all she managed to say.

'You weren't expecting me to say that, were you?'

'No. Not really.'

'I'm not normally . . . how I've been lately. It was wrong of me to speak to you the way I did earlier. You're right, it's your pitch and you're allowed to do what you want.'

'And the talks?' she asked, wondering just how far this change of heart went. They'd played such an important role in increasing her takings she didn't want to lose them, and she wasn't interested if this was just a surface-level apology, if tomorrow, he'd be back to his old ways. She kept her voice soft and un-accusing, not wanting to seem mean after the day he'd had.

Finn blushed, colour flooding his cheeks under the dark tan of his face. He seemed a little more alive than he had before.

'I'm ashamed of that.' Rosie noticed him toying with his fingers, pushing the thumb of one hand into the palm of another. 'It was a good idea, and I shouldn't have stolen it.'

'You could have just spoken to me, and we could have sorted out a schedule.' This thought clearly hadn't occurred to him. She turned over an empty metal bucket and sat in front of him. Again, keeping her voice soft, as she had done with unruly customers in her waitressing jobs, she asked, 'Why did you feel the need to steal my idea?'

'I don't know. I always worry when someone new starts that they'll be a threat and take my business. I'm always waiting for the day to come when it all goes wrong.'

That was clearly a trauma response if ever she'd heard one, but she wasn't going to ask anything more about the cause right now.

'You think this tiny pitch is going to make a dent in your profits? I don't think so. You've got that enormous spot and two shops, so I hear. I don't think you need to worry about me. Not yet anyway,' she added with a grin.

Finn smiled and a softness infused his face. 'This is how I started.' He motioned to Rosie's tiny pitch. 'I'm sure that in a while you'll definitely be competition I should worry about.'

'You started with a tiny pitch like this?' She couldn't keep the shock from her voice. For some reason, she'd always supposed he'd started with the enormous bit he had, or a shop first. She'd also assumed he'd had money to start up his business, that it had all come easily to him. A judgement, she realised, she had absolutely no evidence for.

'Actually, I started with this tiny pitch and a bike.'

'A bike?' She couldn't stop the laugh from escaping her mouth as she imagined this refined, well-tailored man pedalling around Amsterdam.

'I was younger then,' he added with a hint of amusement. 'As soon as I could afford even a little help, they'd work here, and I'd ride a bike around Amsterdam selling flowers from the basket. It was hard on the legs.' He rubbed his thighs to prove his point and Rosie laughed again. 'Everything grew from there. I saved up enough for a deposit on a shop and then did the same for a bigger one.'

'Well, that fills me with hope. I've got to admit I'm not finding any of this easy.' The end of the summer felt like a million miles away, but it was only a month or so. 'I've moved all this way, and I can't afford for this not to work.'

She realised with an ache in her heart that as much as she loved her family, she didn't want to return home. She loved the city and the flower market, and the thought of making her life and career here filled her with a sense of purpose she'd never really had before. She'd worked in jobs and as part of a team, but nothing gave her the sense of friendship this place – this city – did.

'You've been very brave moving countries. That's quite a commitment. I didn't know you'd done that. Listen—' He stood up, far more stable on his legs. 'I'll stop giving the talks and if I can help with anything, don't be afraid to ask.'

'Why don't we try and work together?' Rosie said. 'Fenna loves to stock bulbs; you stock, well, everything, but lots of tulips, which is the national flower—'

'Well done.' That teasing tone was back again, and Rosie had the strange feeling she might actually get to like Finn if he carried on being like this.

'And I love herbs. Why don't we work out a schedule? See if Fenna wants to be involved too?'

'That's a—Wow! That's a good idea.'

'Here—' She took her phone from her back pocket. 'What's your number? I can set up a WhatsApp group for us.'

A hint of the Finn she'd known before resurfaced as he hesitated. Then he said, 'Are you sure she'll want to talk to me?' and her heart melted.

'Of course. We're all in this together, after all.'

He gave her his details and went back to tidying up his stall. Rosie did the same, running over the conversation again in her head. She couldn't believe the man who'd just sat and talked with her was the same one who'd been eyeing her so suspiciously since she'd started working there. Knowing he'd begun in a similar way, with a small pitch and the basket of a bike, filled her with hope. The rain eased to a gentle tapping and the clouds began to clear. Rosie headed home with a spring in her step and a smile on her face, and that was before she even knew what Max had in store for her.

Chapter 16

'There you are,' Max said as she approached her boat. 'You need to get changed.'

'Okay. Into what?' He looked at her like she was an alien and had started speaking some strange language he had no hope of understanding. Typical man, Rosie thought. 'Like, casual clothes, party outfit . . . what?'

He frowned. 'Something you can eat dinner in.'

'Yeah, but dinner where?'

'Do you always have to ask so many questions?' He checked his watch.

'When you're a woman deciding what to wear to a—' She almost said 'date' but stopped herself just in time. Was that what this was? Or we he just being her tour guide still? 'To an event, then yes, we need to ask questions. For example, is it a jeans evening or a dress evening?'

Max shrugged. 'Dress, I suppose.'

'But you don't know?'

'You'll look nice in anything,' he said quickly, then scurried back to his boat, calling over his shoulder, 'I'll be back in half an hour.'

'You said three-quarters of an hour a minute ago.'

'Then you asked questions for fifteen minutes!'

Rosie giggled as he headed back inside his galley, and she did the same. She'd grown used to the gentle rocking of the water and found it comforting whenever she stepped inside the *Forget-Me-Knot*. For a second, Rosie took in her new home. The events of the day had made her realise just how much she wanted the summer to last forever. The colourful rugs and cushions gave the place a sense of warmth, and alongside it, Rosie felt a freedom and happiness that almost overwhelmed her. Max might have been shocked at how chaotic her bright, colourful décor was, but she loved it.

After grabbing a glass of water, she jumped in the shower and quickly washed away the dirty rainwater from the day. Though her bedroom wasn't private, she'd drawn all the curtains and had a towel wrapped around her. As she emerged, her phone rang.

'Hey, sis,' she said. 'You okay?'

'I'm fine. Why won't you accept a video call?'

'Because I'm naked,' Rosie replied matter-of-factly.

Her sister giggled. 'Oh. Fair enough.'

'I just got in.' As she dressed and began to towel-dry her

hair, Rosie told her about the events of the day and that Max was taking her out for dinner.

'So you've got a hot date! Good for you, Rosie.'

Rosie threw her dressing gown on over the towel and quickly began her make-up. 'I don't know about that. To be honest, I don't know what's happening.'

'But you fancy him? Even though he's grumpy and rude and shouts at you from his boat like a crazy old neighbour?'

'Yeah. It doesn't sound great when you say it like that, but he's not that bad really. Not once you get to know him.'

'And does he fancy you? He must do if he's taking you out on a date.'

'I don't know! Sometimes I think he might but then he's all grumpy and quiet and I have no idea. And I overheard him talking to someone – a friend – and he said I was just some crazy English tourist neighbour and that there was definitely nothing between us. He's also getting over a break-up, I found out. A bad one, I think.'

'Wow, that's a lot, Rosie. Why didn't you tell me?'

'I don't know. I've just been really busy, and I guess I needed to figure some things out in my head.'

'Normally in this situation you'd just come right out and ask him. You've done that before.'

Once when a guy Rosie was working with was sending her mixed signals, she'd simply asked him outright and as a result he'd asked her for coffee and they'd gone out for a total of six dates and a few hot and steamy nights too.

'Maybe I will, but I don't know. I just think that approach won't work with Max. He's too reserved. Did you ask the doctor out yet?' she asked, trying to change the subject.

'Urgh, no.'

'You've missed your deadline twice now,' Rosie reminded her, teasingly.

'I just can't get the courage up to do it.'

'Let's make a deal,' Rosie said. 'If I ask Max about his ex, you have to ask the doc out. Fair?'

'No! No deal! I can't cope with this sort of pressure. It's all right for you, you're an extrovert. You don't mind talking to people. You're like mum in that way. But me – I just can't. Let me do it in my own time.'

'Oh, all right. If you're going to be such a baby about it.'

'Hey!'

Rosie giggled, then seeing the time on her phone, turned to her wardrobe. She chatted with her sister about the day at the flower market, how things were going, and her sister's plans to come out and see her one weekend. Excitement at the thought filled her stomach. 'I'd love that. Do you think Dad'll come too?'

'Definitely. He can't wait. He's never stayed on a houseboat before.'

She looked around the room. 'I'm not sure I've got enough room for you both.'

'Don't worry, we can always rent one or get a hotel. We just want to see you and the flower market and your little pitch. Have you thought of a name for it yet?'

'No!' Rosie took out a black dress, form-fitting with three-quarter-length sleeves. It had served her on many occasions when she hadn't known exactly what to wear. It hadn't let her down yet. 'I was toying with The Canal Stop Shop.'

'Eww.'

'What's wrong with that?'

'It sounds like a garage or an all-night minimart.'

'Yeah, I suppose it does. Hey, Mels, what do you wear to dinner when you have no idea where you're going? I don't want to be overdressed—'

'Or underdressed.'

'Definitely not.'

'A little black dress is always the answer. Classy and elegant and you don't have to wear skyscraper heels; you can keep it casual with accessories.'

'You are wasted in nursing, you know that?' She took the black dress from her wardrobe and sniffed it, checking it didn't smell of any of the lingering damp that she sometimes caught a whiff of after the flood.

'Have you thought about naming the shop something to do with Mum? Like Botanist's something . . . I don't know.'

Rosie paused from struggling with the zip at the back of the dress. 'I love that idea, Mels. Mum would love it too.'

'And Dad,' Melody added.

It would honour her mum's memory and make her a part of her future too, even though she wasn't there to see it.

A second later, after getting her dress done up as far as her waist, she let out a grunt.

'Umm, Rosie . . .' Melody said. 'What are you doing?'

At that moment, with both hands struggling behind her back, Rosie's balance failed. 'Argh!' She fell to the side, missing the built-in dining table by millimetres.

'Rosie? Rosie, are you all right?'

'I'm okay,' she replied, pushing herself upright and back up to standing. 'The bloody zip's stuck and I just fell over trying to fix it. I'm going to have to go and see if I can get it sorted.'

'Okay. But don't kill yourself over a dress. Speak soon, sis. Love you.'

'Love you too!'

Rosie spent another five minutes struggling with the zip and gave up. She was getting far too hot and sweaty. She took a break, leaving it undone, and spritzed on some perfume. The good thing about having short hair was she didn't have to do anything to it, which gave her more time to think about what Melody had said. Naming the shop something to do with her mum would be perfect. But what? She tried one more time and couldn't get the zip to move, which meant she had no other option. She'd have to ask Max to help.

Rosie slipped on her shoes to see Max step onto the deck and knock at the open galley door.

'Ready to go?'

She couldn't help but take him in. Instead of his usual

paint-splattered jeans and T-shirt or oversized plaid shirt, he wore clean fitted jeans that wrapped around his thighs like a second skin. His other ones were so baggy she hadn't noticed before how muscly his legs were. Drawing her eyes up, she saw his smart shirt and blazer gripping his broad shoulders and chest. His hair was a little wild, but she liked it that way. Her pulse began to race as he studied her too and the way his eyes roved over her curves said he liked what he saw.

She forced her gaze back to the mirror, checking her reflection one last time. 'Ready, but can you just do my dress up for me, please?'

'Your . . . why?'

She spun, so he could easily access the zip. 'It's stuck.'

She heard his sharp intake of breath and felt a prickling of enjoyment as he cleared his throat. 'Umm . . . yeah – sure – okay.'

Max stepped into the galley, pausing behind her. The zip was stuck at her mid-back, just below her bra line. She could feel his shaky breath brush her bare skin. He fiddled with the zip and it began to move. As it neared the top, his fingers swept the skin on her back, sending a shockwave through her. The touch had been soft and she couldn't help but imagine him gently placing his hands either side of her face as he guided her towards him for a kiss, or his fingers sweeping down her waist as he explored the curves of her body, or—

'There,' he said gruffly. 'Done.'

She forced away those thoughts as an internal fire burned inside her. 'Is this outfit okay?' she asked, turning to look at him, hoping to see mirrored on his face the longing she felt inside. It was there momentarily as his eyes scanned the length of her body once more.

'You look lovely.'

Her breath hitched and time seemed to pause as they stood only inches apart, watching each other. The pressure built, but with neither of them speaking, Rosie panicked and asked, 'So where are we going?'

'For dinner.'

'Yes, but where?'

He moved outside and she locked the door of the *Forget-Me-Knot* behind her.

'You'll see. Stop asking so many questions.'

She giggled as he offered his arm and they walked side by side.

***

Rosie looked at the boat they were about to have dinner on. She'd imagined a fancy restaurant where she might have felt uncomfortable or out of place. She should have known Max would take her somewhere special. Somewhere out of the ordinary.

The boat looked like one of the high-end ships Rosie had seen on some of the prestigious canals. It was at least twice the size of the *Forget-Me-Knot* and felt more like a giant yacht that footballers owned. The captain's bit (she hadn't learned the proper name for that yet) was shiny and black but without a giant wheel, like sailing ships had. Instead, it had a small control deck and behind it, a small but elegant restaurant had been laid out.

'Are we going on a dinner cruise?' Rosie asked excitedly. Not only was she hungry but since she'd arrived, she'd longed to jump on one of the canal tours of the city, seeing her new home from its most famous landmarks. Max grinned, showing she was right. 'But I thought you hated touristy things?'

'I do, and if anyone appears with a backpack, I'll throw it overboard. But I have to admit, it's a brilliant way to see the city and this place serves some of the nicest food in Amsterdam.'

'Have you been before then?'

'Yes, once.'

He didn't add any more, and Rosie wondered if it had been with Johanna. The depth of her jealousy surprised her and threatened to dislodge her smile and her enjoyment of the evening. She told herself not to be so petty. First of all, this wasn't a date and secondly, she'd taken dates to the same pub often enough. They were both adults and they both had baggage.

A man in a black uniform with shining brass buttons, who definitely wasn't the captain, assisted her onto the deck and a waitress took over, showing them to their table. The inside was all shining varnished wood and linen tablecloths. Rosie felt like she'd walked onto the canal version of the

Orient Express. There was such an old-world feel to the place, helped by the piano jazz playing quietly through the speakers. Other diners were already seated, perusing the menu.

'Not a backpack in sight,' she whispered to Max.

'Thank God.'

The waitress explained she'd be back to take their order shortly and everyone would be served at the same time to enable them to then depart for the cruise as scheduled. They ordered their drinks, which were delivered within minutes, given it was such a small space.

'This is incredible,' Rosie said as the waitress poured them wine from the bottle of red they'd decided to share. 'Where do they cook the food?'

Max pointed to a building opposite them. 'The kitchen is there. They cook everything fresh.'

'Amazing. So—' She turned to Max and for a second considered asking him if he'd brought Johanna here, then decided better of it. 'What were you sketching today and has it restarted your creativity?'

He laughed, pushing his hair back from his face. 'It doesn't quite work like that. At least it hasn't for me. I haven't suddenly started painting again, but I did enjoy sketching. It was nice to feel it come naturally again, even just for a little while.'

'So what do we do to get you painting properly again? Is it like, repeat what we did today but times a million? Really ramp it up?'

'Rosie,' he said with a laugh. 'You can't fix everything straight away. I think I just need to keep doing this sort of thing and I'm sure it'll help.' He didn't sound entirely convinced, but he was right that she couldn't solve it immediately.

If she'd learned anything from her years of working jobs she didn't care about and then suddenly seeing the video of the *Bloemenmarkt*, it was that everything happened when it was supposed to.

'Have you thought more about going back to teaching? Maybe it'll help spark your creativity again?'

'Maybe,' he said. 'I have got an appointment to show some pieces to a new gallery. The work isn't new – they're older pieces that've been in storage, but it might work out. Anyway, enough about that. Let's talk about something else.'

'Okay,' she agreed cheerfully. She didn't want to ruin the evening by pushing. 'What shall we talk about?'

They started with the places she still wanted to visit, and she said that her dad and sister might come and stay, and Max shared information about his family. By the time they'd finished eating, she knew he had a sister who lived in a small town outside of Amsterdam and that he'd studied art at university. 'I haven't really travelled, but that doesn't bother me. I love it here. Amsterdam has everything I need.'

The first course was served and Rosie felt like she was in an exclusive Michelin-starred restaurant. She'd ordered super savoury black-truffle-flavoured potato rosti in a truffle cappuccino – a frothy sauce that was utterly delicious. Her taste buds reacted to the first excellent bite and she ate the small starter quicker than she should have, finishing before Max had barely touched his caviar. Unlike some dates she'd been on – even though this wasn't a date – the conversation flowed easily. Max's dry, ironic humour made her laugh out loud several times and she even made him chuckle. A warmth shone from him this evening, one Rosie had known was there – that she'd seen glimmers of, but never this freely. There was way more to Max than met the eye and she felt as if a layer had been stripped from him, revealing the real man underneath.

As the main courses were delivered, she made a mental note to eat slower. She didn't want him to think she couldn't be taken out in public. Her cod in a Pernod-infused hollandaise sauce elicited several sounds from her that made him look up, her cheeks colouring as she dipped her eyes back to the meal. When it came to dessert, it was her turn to look at him as he enjoyed his bergamot and limoncello coconut cream. She stuck with the *stroopwafel*, which was like the ones she'd eaten already, but with the decadence turned up by a thousand. There were fancy restaurants in London and even some on the banks of the Thames, but they were nothing like this.

After the meal, as the boat began to move away from the dock, they stepped out onto the deck. The boat cruised through the canals. One side of the sky held the setting sun, a deep yellow glow, and from it grew shades of orange and apricot. On the other, where the storm clouds were clearing, cobalt and navy were underlined by mauve and pink. It was breathtakingly gorgeous. They passed the picturesque houses, the beautiful buildings reflected in the water.

'It's a beautiful city, isn't it?' Max said.

Next to him, Rosie felt the heat of his body. 'It is.'

'Not everyone thinks so. Some people who were born and raised here can't wait to get away.'

Was this her chance to ask about Johanna? She longed to know more about what had happened, still sure that she had something to do with Max's inability to paint. A part of her knew it could ruin the lovely evening they'd had and was warning her she should shy away, but another was desperate to see him back to himself – the man she knew was in there under the doom and gloom, the man she was seeing more and more of – and she couldn't help herself.

'Max,' she began tentatively. 'When we had dinner on your boat the other night, you said being a painter doesn't pay very well, and that some people find that hard to deal with. Who were you talking about?'

'You are very nosy,' he replied, and though his brow had pulled together, the tone of his voice was light. He turned to look at the sky once more, watching the distinctive canal houses pass by. Where it was getting darker, some of the lights were on and a warm glow shone from the windows. He glanced at Rosie. 'My girlfriend – well, ex-girlfriend now – she . . .' She held her breath as he paused, considering his words. 'I think she wanted more from me than I could give on an artist's salary. She had enough of being penniless and saving for everything we wanted, so she left.' His matter-of-fact tone didn't hide the hurt written across his features.

'I'm so sorry. How long ago was that?'

'A year – maybe a year and a half now. But we all have someone who's broken our hearts, don't we?'

'I'm not sure I do actually. The only person who's broken my heart is my mum and she didn't do that on purpose. She died.' She gave a small, sardonic chuckle. 'I've never had my heart broken because of romantic love before.'

'Never?' As he twisted his body to look at her, he drew closer. Her eyes followed the line of his jaw beneath his trimmed beard, ending on his mouth.

She'd never had her heart broken by a man because she'd always kept a piece of herself back. A piece shrouded in grief, a piece where the pain and loss over her mum acted like a shield against the possibility of love. Her parents had loved each other so deeply, and though her dad tried to get on with his life, she knew he still mourned her mum. In the months after her mum's death, she'd thought that the loss was even greater for him. They'd had so many years together – had lived a life together – and would have had so many more if given the chance. Because of that, she'd been too scared to open her heart fully to love. She'd always thought herself quite an open person and that a lasting relationship hadn't come her way because she'd never found the right man. But now she realised, as she stared at Max, and felt a depth of emotion she'd never had before, it was clear that she'd never really allowed anyone into her whole heart, and that maybe she'd been doing herself a disservice.

'You've gone every quiet,' Max said gently.

'Sorry, I—' She plastered on her normal smile. 'I don't know what came over me.'

'Yes, you do,' he said. 'You don't need to lie. What were you thinking?'

Under his kind, understanding gaze, with all traces of his grumpiness lost, she found herself telling him the truth, repeating the thoughts that had circled in her mind moments before.

'Perhaps you have kept a piece of yourself back. It's understandable. Though I don't know where that piece is, given you always say what's on your mind.' She smiled at his joke, grateful for his attempt to lighten the mood. His face grew grave as he looked at her, his eyes meeting hers and refusing to look away. 'I don't think I've ever met anyone who knows themselves as well as you do,' Max said. 'It's . . . reassuring. There are no games with you.'

Rosie was aware of his arm pressing against her own. She could feel the tension in his muscles through the fabric of his blazer. As the boat swayed on the water, her body leaned against his and she had no desire to move.

The sun had set, and the sky was lit with glistening stars. The moon, bold and bright – a silver disc in the sky – shone down on them and on the water, bringing strands of platinum light to its surface.

When Max spoke again, his voice was husky and taut

with control. 'You've made me think about things differently with your incessant cheerfulness and fix-everything attitude.'

'I have?'

He turned to her, and she copied him, their bodies now facing each other. They were barely inches apart. He studied the shape of her eyes, the curve of her lips. His fingertips rose to her cheek, gentle and soft as they brushed her cheekbone, just as she had imagined them. Her body came alive at his touch, flaming from his proximity. He leaned in, his mouth finding hers, kissing her gently. The warmth of his lips exploded her nerve endings. His tongue swiped at hers gently, and she opened her mouth to encourage him further. Soon he was kissing her passionately and she had never known a longing like it.

Men had tried to kiss her like that before, but it was nothing compared to this. She edged her body against his, and her fingers stroked the back of his neck. His hand shot into her hair, holding her close.

As they melted into each other, the world around them disintegrating to nothing, her heart opened and the shell of grief that had kept it protected – isolated – fell away. She was almost certain that if she looked down, she'd see it on the floor at her feet. Freedom lightened her body and, for the first time, she knew. She was in love.

Chapter 17

'Hey Dad!' Rosie trilled as she quickly made tea the next morning.

After the kiss (or should that be kisses) she and Max had shared the night before, which had swept her off her feet, she was still walking on air. Following the moonlit boat ride, she and Max had cuddled and canoodled, walking back to their boats hand in hand. She'd wanted him to invite her in, and had toyed with the idea of asking herself when the words she'd longed for hadn't been forthcoming. But something inside her had held back. Max was only just opening up, laughing and relaxing, enjoying himself again, and somehow, she just knew that she was better off taking things slow, going at his pace, giving him space. The realisation of how she'd been holding a piece of herself back for years had rocked her too and she needed time to get her head around that before she threw herself headlong into something else. Even though the ache in her heart, and in other places, pleaded otherwise, she ignored it. Whatever jealousy she'd felt over his ex, Johanna, had left and Max had clearly felt it was time to move on too.

'You sound very chipper this morning,' her dad said, and she did her best to control the smile on her face reflecting too much in her voice.

'I am. I'm in Amsterdam, things are going well at work and I'm happy. That's good, isn't it?'

'Amazing. I'm very proud of you.'

'Thanks, Dad. So what's the call for? Just checking in or is something going on?'

In the background she heard her dad's old kettle click to a stop. 'Just a check-in. I wanted to make sure you were all right. Melody told me about the guy at work who was being horrible.'

'Yeah, but I think that might be sorted now too.' At least she hoped so. They'd ended on such a positive note the day before, she couldn't imagine him going back to being moody and stand-offish, though nothing was impossible. She'd find out today.

'Well, I guess I'll leave you to it.' There was a note of sadness in her dad's voice and she realised that with everything that had been going on, she'd been neglecting to call as regularly as she should.

'Why don't I call you again tonight, Dad? We can have a video chat over dinner, and it'll be just like old times.'

He immediately brightened. 'Yes, let's do that. We should cook the same thing too.'

That was a lovely idea. 'Okay, what do you fancy?'

'How about your mum's salmon and new potatoes? That was always your favourite growing up.'

It had been and she still cooked it for herself when she was feeling low. It was her go-to comfort meal. 'Brilliant. I'll make sure to get some on the way home.'

Rosie bid her dad goodbye and finished getting ready. As she stepped outside, she was glad to see Max already up and about. He came to her as she stepped off the dock, placing a gentle kiss on her cheek.

'Hi,' he said sweetly. 'Off to the market?'

'Yeah. You? You're up and about early.'

'I've got a meeting at a gallery at nine. It's a new place opening up in De Pijp.'

'Is that why you were there the other day?'

He nodded. 'I don't know if they'll want my work but—'

'Of course they will. They'd be stupid not to.'

'Thank you.' He bent his head and gave her a gentle kiss on the lips. As warmth flooded through her, along with need and longing, she threw her arms around his neck. Eventually, they pulled away from each other and she stepped back, feeling light-headed.

'Did you want to have dinner tonight?' Max asked.

'Yes! No! I'd love to, but – I'm sorry, I can't. I'm having dinner with my dad, over video chat. I think he's missing me.'

Guilt suddenly washed through her. With their mum gone and Melody working long shifts at the hospital, they'd often seen each other more than most fathers and daughters. She should have been making more time for him rather than just using him as a sounding board when she needed a pick-me-up. She swallowed, summoning up some positivity. She couldn't change the past, but she could definitely change the future. From now on, she'd make more time for her dad. Maybe schedule in a weekly meal like they were having tonight? That was a good idea, and she'd suggest it this evening.

Any disappointment Max had felt vanished in an instant, to be replaced by something like pride. 'You should definitely see him. You can always pop over for a drink when you've finished.'

'I might just do that. Okay. I'll see you later.' She extracted herself from Max's arms, which had stayed around her waist, and reluctantly started her walk to the flower market. 'Good luck with the gallery!'

Her day at the flower market was one of the busiest she'd ever had. She hardly saw Emma, who was also rushed off her feet, and Rosie was sure that part of her unusual number of customers came from Finn, who she caught once or twice pointing people in her direction, urging them to listen to her talks on bergamot and sage. She gave him a grateful smile at the end of the day as she left for home, ready to pick up her ingredients.

As Rosie wrapped the salmon in paper and popped it into

the oven, before adding new potatoes to a pan of boiling water, she could have been back at home in the family kitchen. She sliced sweet cherry tomatoes onto a plate, and her thoughts ran to her mum and how proud she would be of her. It was something her dad had said often, but as she'd drifted from job to job, never really sticking at anything, the words had felt hollow. Not because of anything her dad had done, but because they simply hadn't rung true to Rosie herself. Now she was earning them.

When her dad's cheerful face popped up on the screen, Rosie could feel the love across the miles between them. 'Look!' he said, turning the camera to show he'd set the small family table, complete with a napkin and glass of wine. Rosie burst out laughing, turning her own phone around.

'Great minds think alike!' She'd set her own place, laid a tablecloth over the tiny table and added a bright blue placemat. There was also a glass of crisp white wine waiting. Seeing the smile on her dad's face sent a lump into her throat and threatened another wave of guilt to ready itself, but she pushed the negative feelings away. 'I just need to get mine out of the oven.'

'Me too.'

When her dad's face next appeared as they set their plates on the table three hundred and fifty miles apart, his glasses were steamed up from the oven and he had to tip his head to see her.

'You look like you're about to tell me off,' she teased.

'You always used to tip your head like that when I'd done something wrong and you wanted to scare me.'

'It worked, though, didn't it?'

'Sometimes.' She cut into the salmon, the smells triggering memories of home and noisy dinners together. 'So tell me about your day.'

Her dad went through the trials and tribulations of his work, and they chatted about his colleagues and hers. She mentioned Finn's changed attitude and that the atmosphere at the flower market was now much more relaxed. The boost to her daily profits was, she hoped, a sign of things to come. Her dad updated her on Melody's long, tiring hours at the hospital, the stresses and strains she was under working for the NHS, and how he wanted her to get a bit more of a life, so she wasn't working all the time. Rosie didn't ask if her sister had asked the doctor out yet. That was a purely sisterly conversation, and Melody would not be impressed if she let it slip to their dad.

By the time they'd finished eating and talked through the washing-up over another glass of wine, it felt like they'd spent the evening together in the same room, within touching distance. She longed to give her dad a hug and told him so.

'Me too, sweetheart, but this has been fun.'

'It has. We should do this once a week.'

'It's a date.'

'I'll text you tomorrow, okay?' Though she normally texted good morning and goodnight, it was another thing she'd let slip recently and she resolved to start again.

They said their goodbyes and she headed outside into the cool evening air. Now the storm had passed, the weather was heating up again and though the sun was setting slowly in the sky, the air remained warm. Max was out on his deck, working on his sketch while Zoon barked at the passing ducks. He looked up as she stepped out.

'How did it go at the gallery?' she asked.

'Good, I think. They like what I do, and I think I've scored you a job too.'

'Me? How?'

He gestured to the empty seat beside him before pulling it closer. Wine glass in hand, she sat down, and his arm snaked around her shoulder. 'They're looking for some floral displays for the gallery opening and I recommended you.'

'Me? Why?'

'Don't sound so surprised.' He chuckled. 'Why wouldn't I recommend you? I wasn't about to suggest Finn.'

'But . . . what do they want? I mean, what type of thing are they looking for? Big? Small? Ab—'

'If you say "abstracty" I'm taking that wine away.' She pulled her glass close to her body and protected it with her other hand. 'You'll have to go and see them to find out. Here's the guy's card. He said he'd be around till mid-morning.'

'Okay, I'll nip by first thing. Thank you. That was kind of you.' Max's soft gaze made her tip her head up and plant a kiss on his lips.

'He'll be blown away, I'm sure.'

'And I'm sure he'll want your work too.'

'Let's hope.' He raised his glass in a toast.

In the short-term relationships she'd had, nothing had felt so natural as being with Max. Some of the guys she'd seen hadn't shown this level of affection even after four or five dates, except in the bedroom. Yet Max was happy to hold her hand, kiss her forehead and put his arm around her. It had only been a day, she reminded herself, but what she was experiencing now fitted so well with the flashes of the real Max she'd seen since she'd arrived, and she wondered how Johanna had ever let him go. Money wasn't everything. There had been times when her parents hadn't had any money, but they'd had each other, and that had been all that mattered. Once you found someone you loved, you couldn't let them go. She knew only too well how life could be cut short.

'You're being quiet again,' Max said, breaking into her thoughts. 'I don't like it.'

A cover of coots passed by, their little black heads peering at everything around them. Zoon had gone to his bed but lifted his head before deciding to ignore them.

'I was just thinking about my parents and how much they loved each other. When you find the right person, you can't afford to let them go.'

Realising this may have been too much too soon, Rosie froze, expecting a heavy, difficult silence to follow, but Max's body language remained the same.

'I agree,' he said softly, pressing a gentle kiss to the top of her head.

As she snuggled into his shoulder, they watched the sun go down. When the velvety night encircled them, bright stars began to shine overhead, and a slight breeze picked up. It wasn't cold, but she could feel a slight chill on her skin.

'I'd better go to bed,' she said, standing.

Still holding her hand, Max followed. He pulled her close and kissed her passionately, his fingers threading into her short hair and cupping the back of her head. She savoured the feel of his lips on hers, and the soft brush of his beard. He tasted of the wine they'd been drinking. When his right hand fell to the curve of her waist, drawing her even nearer to him so their bodies were pressed together, every nerve ignited.

'You could go to bed here,' he said gruffly, and Rosie didn't need words to respond. The passion of her kiss was enough. He led her inside and as the night unfolded, their bodies intertwining, it was clear Max was falling in love with her as much as she was falling for him. Whoever Johanna had been, she was well and truly forgotten. It was now just them and the future that lay at their feet.

Chapter 18

De Pijp was rapidly turning into one of Rosie's favourite areas of Amsterdam. Café tables were already full of early-morning tourists, vans unloaded trays of goods to restaurants and those on their way to work called in at the gorgeous bakeries to grab an early-morning treat. There were so many art galleries and artisan shops she could have stayed there all day, but instead she made her way to *the* gallery. Max explained it was named *Opstand*, which meant revolt, after the Eighty Years' War that had resulted in the forming of the Dutch Republic.

She'd called ahead and the owner was happy to meet her there at nine o'clock. It meant opening a little later at the flower market, but she'd texted Bas and told him to leave her flower delivery, which she could only do now she was confident Finn wouldn't sabotage them. Rosie approached the modern-looking building. It had a wide glass window at the front through which she could see canvases of modern art, some similar to Max's – all slashes of paint – others clearly inspired by Andy Warhol or Lichtenstein. She knocked on the glass door and a young man in a blazer and drainpipe trousers that stopped at his ankles, with an enormous quiff and black eyeliner, let her in.

'You must be Rosie,' he said, as he beckoned her up the steps into the gallery. 'I'm Jeroen.'

'It's lovely to meet you. Max said you wanted some floral displays for the gallery opening.'

'That's right. He said you were bold and bright and that's just what we're looking for.'

Good job she'd worn a bright pink T-shirt and had a yellow headscarf tied over her head. As she looked around the space she could see that was definitely a theme. Though the walls were white, all the pieces were colourful and bold. Even if they were painted in paler colours, something about their execution was vibrant and new.

'What sort of thing did you have in mind?' Rosie asked, taking out her phone to make some notes.

He led her through the gallery, motioning to the spaces she was to fill and describing what he'd like. 'Max mentioned you doing something inspired by the different places in Amsterdam. I have to say, I love that idea.'

'They're not replicas,' she said quickly. 'I feel I should make that clear. They're more . . . abstract.' She went on to describe the arrangements she'd made so far based on the places Max had taken her.

'That sounds perfect. As you can see, we're a modern gallery. We love our classical artists, but there's also a vibrant new art scene and I plan to be the go-to gallery for work of that kind.'

'You're ambitious, like me. Do you want to see some samples and I'll send you a quote?'

'No, it's fine.' He waved a hand dismissively. 'I know most of the florists here in Amsterdam and they're all very traditional. I don't want tulips. They're a definite no. I want exactly what you're describing. The opening is in two weeks. Is that all right?'

'Yes, of course.' She was buzzing at the opportunity. It would mean an initial outlay from her, which would make her finances even tighter, but she just had to hang in there until the gallery paid up and then she'd have a small profit to put towards boat repairs or expanding her business. 'Thank you so much. I'm so excited to get to work.'

'When are you seeing Max next?'

She felt her cheeks colour. 'Probably tonight – we're neighbours,' she added, unsure as to why. It wasn't really a secret that they were sort of together. At least, she didn't think it was. 'He'll be so pleased. He—'

'Can you tell him that I'm sorry but we won't be stocking his paintings? Not this time anyway.'

'W – what?' Her stomach hardened as a heavy feeling of

dread suddenly formed, reaching up into her throat so she couldn't swallow.

'I love them,' Jeroen said, holding his hands up in defence. 'But unfortunately, the rest of the team weren't convinced they'd sell and as you can see, we already have someone similar.' He gestured to a piece she'd spotted through the window.

'But shouldn't you tell him? It's not really my place to—'

'I won't be able to call him till tomorrow. I'm busy all day and he needs to know soon. I had hoped to have better news for him, especially after all he's been through.'

'What do you mean?' Her throat tightened and she forced herself to take slow, even breaths.

'Did he not say? Typical Max.' Jeroen tutted. 'I probably shouldn't say. If he hasn't told you, he—'

'I'm sorry,' she said, shaking her head. 'You can't expect me to deliver bad news to him without knowing more.'

'Actually, I can.' He crossed his arms over his chest. 'I am employing you, after all.'

'To make flower displays. I'm not your PA.' She raised her chin. No matter how much she wanted and needed the opportunity, she wasn't about to let this guy off the hook. 'And you can keep your job, thanks. I'll be just fine without it.'

A smile raised the corner of Jeroen's mouth. 'He told me you were feisty. All right then, I'll tell you. After Johanna – you know about her?' Rosie nodded. 'After she left him he went to pieces, couldn't paint, couldn't teach. She destroyed him. All because she wanted him to have more money so they could go out to restaurants and take expensive vacations. She liked the idea of an artist and an artist's soul but she didn't like the reality of that life, which is that it's hard. He didn't take it well and in response, she made it personal, told him he wasn't good enough. That he wasn't getting exhibitions because he wasn't as good as the newer upcoming artists. She destroyed his confidence. He's only just getting back on his feet, been in touch with the art school again.'

'How do you know all this?'

'The art world is a small place, especially in a city like Amsterdam. Everyone knows everyone else.'

Perhaps that explained some of his reserve too. If all his friends and acquaintances knew his business, she could easily see him withdrawing from the world. Relying only on himself.'

Jeroen continued. 'All of that after his mother was so controlling . . . I hate to do this to him, but it isn't my choice.'

'So why should I tell him all that? I'm sorry, but this feels like your job, not mine.'

'I know this isn't regular,' Jeroen said, smoothing the hair on the back of his head.

'No, it's not.'

'But you care about him, don't you?' She felt herself blush again. 'I can tell he cares about you from the way he spoke. I hadn't seen him like that in a long time. Trust me, he'll take it better if you explain all this. If I tell him, he'll see it as the end of his career again.'

'Can't you convince them to stock his work?'

Jeroen shook his head. 'I would if I could, but if Max found out he wasn't selected on his own merits, he'd be livid. The way he spoke about you, about how you just get on with things, he'll take it better and it won't damage him as much.'

Though she didn't like this one bit, a part of her agreed. Jeroen might deliver the news in a businesslike fashion but she could imagine the fallout. It had taken a lot for Max to break out of his creative slump and this could send him straight back down that dark hole he'd described if it wasn't handled well.

'I don't like this at all,' she said, making deliberate eye contact with Jeroen. 'It still doesn't feel right, but I'll do it.'

'Thank you.' Jeroen visibly relaxed. 'But do let him know we want him to try again. We'll have a number of exhibitions coming up and just because it wasn't right this time, doesn't mean it won't be next time. Now, I have to go. You've got my number if you need me for anything.'

He showed her to the door, closed it behind him and disappeared into the depths of the gallery. Rosie was left standing on the steps, dumbstruck. Whilst she was pleased she'd got the job, how the hell was she going to tell Max he hadn't?

Chapter 19

Though she wished she could go straight home and see him, she couldn't. She had a job to do and flowers to sell. Rosie had hoped it would be a welcome distraction, but she could already picture the look on Max's face and the thought that his confidence would again be knocked back made her feel sick. No matter how hard she tried, it was going to be difficult to put a positive spin on this, and Max would quickly see through any attempts to do so. He'd see them as meaningless platitudes even if what she said was true: that there'd be other chances, other opportunities.

The day passed excruciatingly slowly and as closing time neared, Rosie found herself lingering. She wasn't ready to go home and hurt Max's feelings. She wanted them to stay in the perfect bubble they'd created.

'That was a crazy day,' Emma said, nibbling on a bar of

chocolate as she approached. She'd gone for another pair of harem pants today, this time in a sage green with a pale vine print on them. She'd let her red hair down and Rosie could make out dark brown roots creeping in, which somehow only added to her individual look. 'Same for you?'

'You have no idea.' Rosie tossed a damaged flower into a tub and flopped down onto her stool, ripping off her headband, the yellow now seeming annoyingly bright.

Emma frowned. 'What's happened? Don't tell me Finn's up to his old tricks again?'

'Finn? No, he's being lovely, even sending customers my way.'

'What is it then?'

Rosie explained everything, including the night she and Max had spent together.

Emma squealed at that point. 'I knew there was something between you.' But as Rosie carried on, her face darkened. 'Oh no. Why did you agree?'

'I just thought I might be able to tell him better than Jeroen. Jeroen would call, say it bluntly and then hang up, leaving Max to dwell. I thought if I was there – if I told him face to face – I might be able to minimise the damage.'

'Rosie, I really think you should call Jeroen and tell him you've changed your mind—'

'No.' She shook her head. 'It's better if it comes from me, but I hate what it's going to do to him.'

Emma reached out for her friend's hand. 'All you can do is be there for him. He'll be disappointed at first, but I'm sure with you there he'll be better in no time. Shall I walk out with you?'

'Thanks. Maybe a quick drink for some Dutch courage?'

'You do know that's insulting to Dutch people, don't you?' Emma tilted her head. She wasn't cross or annoyed, just speaking matter-of-factly.

'Is it?' Rosie was mortified. 'I had no idea. Doesn't it just mean you guys like a drinky or two?'

'No, it's saying we're not brave unless we have a drink.'

'I suppose it is. I'm so sorry, Emma, I didn't mean to insult you.'

'That's okay.' She giggled. 'You haven't said it to anyone else, though, have you?'

'Thankfully not.'

'Good. But no, I can't join you for a drink. Sorry.'

'Seeing Noah?' Rosie raised an eyebrow, glad at least her friend was having a better time of things than she was. But Emma's face paled.

'No, he hasn't spoken to me since the bicep incident and I'm sure he hides whenever I go near his shop.'

'I'm so sorry. Are you sure it's not just a coincidence? Maybe he has something else going on?'

'I'm sure.' Emma gave a resigned shrug. 'I think I've ruined that chance by being so – so – stupid.'

'Hey, you're not stupid.' Rosie put both hands on her friend's shoulders, catching her eye. 'And if he can't see how amazing you are, he doesn't deserve to have you.'

'See, you'll have Max smiling again in no time.'

Oh how Rosie wished to believe it but somehow, she doubted it. She doubted it very much.

She approached the *Forget-Me-Knot* with a heavy, aching heart, wishing – for the first time since arriving – that Max wouldn't be there. But what she saw as she approached was worse: he was painting.

A huge canvas stood on the easel and Max, in paint-splattered overalls and a tight T-shirt that hugged his chest, swiped paint to and fro. He paused, stopping to study the canvas, tilting his head this way and that, then closed his eyes as if manifesting or visualising something. The paint splatters on his clothes, she noticed, were brighter. Colours that matched her chaotic, overly bright living room. After taking a deep breath, he opened them again and began to paint once more. It was the first time she'd seen him in action and she hated the fear bubbling inside her. She loathed the idea that she was going to wipe the smile and look of contentment from his face. A look that had only recently appeared there. She swallowed down the acidic bile stinging her throat.

Max grinned at her in such a carefree way she nearly turned tail and jumped on the first Eurostar back to England. She couldn't do this. She couldn't hurt his feelings and she hated Jeroen for asking but herself even more for agreeing.

'Hey! How'd it go with Jeroen?'

'Yeah, umm . . .' She stood awkwardly nearby, taking a step towards his boat and then changing her mind and shuffling back. 'Okay.'

'What's wrong?' Max placed the palette and brushes down, moving to the edge of the deck. 'Was he rude? Jeroen can be like that. He's quite blunt – says what he thinks – but he's a nice guy underneath it all. I hope he didn't upset you.'

'No, no.'

'So what is it? Come in and sit down.' He ushered her to the small table on the deck. Zoon came over as soon as she sat and pushed his nose into her hands, determined to get a fuss, but even his cute face couldn't make her smile. 'Didn't he like your ideas? I mentioned about you making something inspired by Amsterdam and its history, its places. He seemed excited when I told him.'

She felt a stab of pain in her heart. He'd fought her corner, been so nice promoting her that she couldn't get the words out. Pushing them past the lump in her throat, she knew it was better to get it out there.

'He liked the ideas,' Rosie began, thinking how clumsy she was being. She should play it down, ignore her success. 'It was just that, umm . . .'

'If he was rude to you I'll call him now.' Max grabbed his mobile from his back pocket.

Oh God.

'No, Max, he—' She took his hand and he lowered himself into the chair. 'He said I had the job but . . . Oh God, I'm so sorry, Max. He said he was sorry but they couldn't display any of your paintings.' The colour drained from his face, now pale and ashen against the strawberry blond of his hair. She wanted to stop and hold him, pulling him close and wrapping her arms around him. She continued, wanting to explain – to make it better. 'Jeroen said that he wanted to, but some of the team weren't convinced because they already had someone producing similar work.'

'Why . . .' His voice was thick and he wouldn't look at her. 'Why didn't he tell me himself?'

Rosie sighed, knowing she should have stuck with her instincts and said no, forcing Jeroen to do his job. 'He wanted me to tell you because he was worried you'd be upset.'

'Like a child who needs his mother to comfort him?' His tone was sharp with hurt and anger and Rosie didn't blame him. She'd made a terrible mistake by agreeing and instead of the news being delivered professionally, she'd merged those lines and embarrassed him.

Max tried to withdraw his hand but she wouldn't let him and held it firm. 'I don't think he wanted to treat you like a child. He said he was really sorry. He just didn't want you to stop painting when you'd only just started again. He said you're a great artist and—'

'Stop it, Rosie.' His voice was stone cold and harsh as he dragged his hand out from under hers and stood up. Her fingers hit the table with a slap. 'You don't need to sugar-coat this for me. Despite what Jeroen thinks, I'm not a baby. It's fine. I get it. They didn't want my work.'

'It wasn't that they didn't want it. It was that they already had someone similar. It was just bad timing.'

'Rosie—'

'It's not a reflection on you and your art, it was just one of those unfortunate things—'

'Rosie, please,' he said again, his voice still cold but with a hint of desperation threading through it.

She knew she should listen to him but she couldn't. She just wanted to see the smile back on his face, to see him shrug it off and return to the easel, picking up the palette and brushes and beginning to paint once more. If she kept talking she might hit on one thing that made him feel better. 'Maybe if you try another gallery, or wait a bit longer, they'll change their—'

'I'm not waiting for anyone to change their minds anymore.' In the quiet of the late evening, the words rang around them. Zoon pricked up his ears, turning to his owner. 'I think you should go, Rosie. I don't think I'll be very good company tonight.'

'That's okay. We can just sit and watch the stars or we could go and watch a movie. I can cook dinner—'

'No.' He picked up the dustsheet and threw it back over the easel. She wondered what damage it had done to the wet paint underneath it. Had it smudged it? Ruined the painting? She sat very still, her heart beating hard against her ribs. Max was hurting and though she hadn't been the direct cause of it, she was partly responsible. She chided herself for not saying no to Jeroen. 'Go home, Rosie, please. I'd like to be alone.'

Without saying another word, he headed inside. Sensing something was wrong, Zoon followed, casting a glance over his shoulder at Rosie. Max closed the galley door and pulled the blind down on the small window, obscuring her from view. A second later, the remaining curtains closed, Max shutting out the world. Shutting out her.

Tears pricked her eyes as she made her way back to the *Forget-Me-Knot*. If only Max knew her heart was breaking as much as his, and that she'd give anything to give him the job she'd won.

Chapter 20

Rosie ate her breakfast whilst staring out of the window at Max's boat. There was no sign of life and though she knew he needed space, she wanted to see him – she needed to see him. She needed to know he was all right, or that, even if he didn't feel it right now, he would be in time. This was just a blip. A hiccup. If he kept trying, one of the chances would work out, she just knew it.

Fed up of this limbo and gathering her courage, she threw the remains of her toast down, unable to stomach another bite, and grabbed her keys. With a firm knock on Max's door, she waited for him to answer. Zoon barked and she heard rustling within. He was definitely in there. The blind that covered the galley door was pulled to one side and Max's scowling face with hair ruffled from sleep, grimaced at her. Reluctantly, he opened the door.

'What is it, Rosie?'

'I wanted to see if you were okay?'

'I'm fine.' He went to close the door again, but she put her hand on it, pushing it back.

'You're not fine.'

'Then why did you ask?'

She could smell the faint tang of alcohol on his breath. He must have continued drinking after they'd parted. Drowning his sorrows. She didn't blame him, but he couldn't go on like this. 'Max,' she said gently, 'please.'

He threw a hand through his hair. 'Please what?'

'Let me in.'

Though she only wanted entry to his houseboat, it was clear she meant more. He was shutting her out. They both knew it and their eyes locked. His were bloodshot, marked underneath with the same bruised blue he'd painted on the canvas. He wavered as if he wanted to, but something held him back. 'I need to go back to sleep.'

'You need to talk about this.'

'There's nothing to say.'

'Max, I know you—'

'You don't know me at all!' His words felt like a physical blow and she rocked backwards onto her heels. 'We met a month ago. That's all.'

He swallowed and looked at the floor. She knew the pain his words had caused had flashed across her face – that the pain was still there. She certainly felt it stabbing at her heart and winced. Her heart was bruised and for once she was lost for words.

'I'm sorry, Rosie. I—' His voice softened. 'Have a good day, Rosie.'

The door closed before she could stop it and she stumbled back in frustration and sadness. She knew Max was hurting but that was no reason to treat her this way. Yes, they had only met a month ago, but that didn't mean anything. She *did* know him, just as he knew her. With the door shut, he'd made his intentions clear. Perhaps he just needed a little more time.

There was nothing more she could do. She needed to get to work. Stopping on the way for coffee, Rosie headed straight to Emma's deli.

'It didn't go well, then?' Emma asked, after gratefully accepting the cup.

'You could say that.' After explaining how the evening had panned out and their interaction that morning, Emma clicked her tongue. 'I know he's upset but he shouldn't take it out on you.'

'I know. I don't think he means to and at some point I'll tell him so. He's just hurting. It took a lot for him to put himself out there like that and despite his demeanour, his confidence was pretty low to start with.' She took a sip, enjoying the hit of caffeine, the bittersweet liquid coating her tongue. 'What do I do?'

'You're asking me?' Emma let out a sarcastic laugh. 'I can't even flirt with a guy who likes me. I'm not the best person to give advice.'

'Noah still staying away?'

She nodded. 'I've definitely frightened him off for good.'

'We know he's super shy. Maybe he just needs to gather his courage. Or maybe he's just been busy.'

Emma cocked her head. 'Let me believe that. It might make me less embarrassed.'

'You know once,' Rosie began, 'I was trying to flirt with this guy and I thought I was on fire, making him laugh and stuff, and I noticed he kept only catching my eye briefly. I thought he was being coy so I ramped up the flirting only to catch my reflection in a mirror and see my skirt was tucked in my tights – at the front! Everyone could see my knickers!'

Emma burst out laughing.

'So we've all got embarrassing flirting stories,' Rosie told her.

'That's actually made me feel better,' Emma said, cupping her drink.

'Good.' Rosie checked her watch. 'I better go. Bas has just gone by with my delivery and I need to get started on arrangements for the gallery opening.'

'I know it's hard, but try and look at the positives,' Emma said. 'This could be a great way to build a name for yourself.'

She was right. Rosie's natural positivity was struggling to shine through at the moment, but there were some things to be grateful for. One day she hoped to have a shop in Amsterdam, just as Finn had, and this event would take her one tiny step closer to that dream. Her mum would be proud of her. At the reminder that she'd only just let those final walls down to let Max in, her bruised heart ached even more. Maybe she should have kept those walls firmly in place. As he'd said that morning, they hadn't known each other very long. Maybe she'd been too hasty in letting him under her skin. But her feelings had been stronger for him than for anyone she'd ever met. With a sigh, she banished thoughts of Max from her brain and began work.

In between a steady flow of customers, Rosie researched places in Amsterdam that might serve as her inspiration and made some preliminary sketches. Her profits were growing at the small flower stall and with the event money too, she could actually begin to think of herself as a businesswoman and not just an ex-waitress-cum-barista-cum-office-temp who was playing at being a florist. That legitimacy gave her a sense of pride that not even Max's comments could dent. As her equilibrium returned to something nearer normal, she determined to call in on Max again before the end of the day and see if having had some time to get over his initial disappointment had helped him gain some perspective. He might not welcome her arrival, but she wasn't about to give up on the relationship they were beginning to explore, or his career as an artist. She believed in him; he just needed to as well.

But as Rosie approached the *Forget-Me-Knot*, her plans were scuppered when she found Piet waiting on the pavement next to the houseboat. He was pacing backwards and forwards in agitation, a piece of paper in his hand. Rosie wondered what could be wrong. She'd paid her rent on time and hadn't been making too much noise. Max seemed to be her only neighbour as she'd never seen hide nor hair of the people on the other side of her, and surely he hadn't complained. Anytime he had, he'd done so directly to her. Her brain tried to replay memories of their first few meetings, just to make her feel even sadder, but she refused to pay attention to them.

'Hi, Piet, everything okay?'

'No. No, it's not okay.' The last time she'd spoken to him he'd gotten away from her as quickly as he could, so to see him lingering, shuffling his feet and avoiding eye contact made her more than a little wary.

'Okay, well . . . do you want to come and have a cup of tea and tell me all about it.'

'Yes. Yes, I think I better.' He pushed a hand through his hair, sweat pricking his hairline, and followed her onto the deck of the *Forget-Me-Knot*. Piet crumpled into one of the small metal seats she'd put outside.

As she made tea, Rosie couldn't stop her eyes drifting towards Max's boat, but there was no one around and no sounds from inside. She wondered where he was and what he was doing, hoping that his mood had lifted even a little. She brought out the mugs of tea and placed them on the table. 'Do you want sugar?'

'No, thank you. Just milk.'

She sat opposite him. 'So what's wrong, Piet?'

He placed the piece of paper between them but it was all in Dutch. She studied it, trying to understand some of the words but despite carrying on with her pitiful attempts at Duolingo, she couldn't get to grips with any of it. She pushed it back towards him. 'I can't read this, Piet. What does it say?'

'It's from the city council stating that the houseboat doesn't meet residential codes. Renovations must be made or I have to evict you.'

'What?' Her hands were shaking so much she almost spilt tea all over her lap. 'How – how do they know this? When did they come and inspect it?'

Piet dropped his eyes, looking suddenly sheepish. 'I have to fill in some information each year and they might have come while you were at work. They don't always need to look inside; they can tell a lot from the outside.'

The cheek of the man! He hadn't bothered to let her know any of this was happening and then had allowed them to come and prowl around her home without letting her know. 'So what are you going to do?' she asked sternly.

'Me?' He seemed shocked by the question and anger began to rise in Rosie's chest.

'Yes, you. This is *your* boat. You rent it to me. As the landlord, you need to make the repairs.'

'I can't! I – I can't afford to.'

Rosie couldn't believe what she was hearing. She stood up, aware of Zoon barking somewhere inside Max's boat. 'But you have to, Piet. I can't afford to. I'm only just making enough to live on. I haven't got the money for expensive boat repairs. And I wouldn't even know where to start.'

He didn't answer and Rosie knew that getting irate and

shouting at him wasn't going to help. She sat down again, taking a deep, calming breath. Perhaps the repairs wouldn't be that bad. If it was cosmetic stuff, she might be able to do much of it herself. 'What exactly needs doing?' she asked calmly.

He placed the piece of paper between them, pointing to a list of bullet points at the bottom and explaining the first one. 'All the wood needs repainting with a protective waterproof film, epoxy, or marine spar varnish.'

'Okay.' She could do that, couldn't she? How hard could it be to paint the deck and the outside of the galley? Max had even mentioned that needing doing before winter, so that wasn't a big deal. 'I can do that,' she told Piet.

He scowled. 'Even the bits that are underwater?'

'They need doing too?'

He nodded. 'Of course.'

Her heart sank. 'What else?'

'The engine needs servicing and the bilge pump needs replacing.'

She had no idea where the bilge pump even was, so that was definitely a job for an expert and probably a costly one.

'The electrical and plumbing systems need checking and there should be safety equipment here.' His cheeks coloured and again he avoided her eye.

'Well you can pay for that,' Rosie said coldly. 'If I'm supposed to have safety equipment and I haven't, that's your job as landlord.'

'Yes,' he replied, in apologetic tones. 'Yes, I will sort that out. You're right. I'm sorry. It's just – I've been so busy with my family and the other units I run. I didn't think this was going to happen until after you'd gone back.'

'But I told you I wasn't planning on going back.' She sat back, her shoulders tense. 'You didn't believe me, did you?'

'It seemed such an odd thing to do,' he admitted.

Great. Brilliant. This was exactly what she needed right now.

'I really am sorry, Rosie. I can help with some of the costs, but I can't cover everything. I understand if you need to move.'

Move? Up until that moment the idea hadn't occurred to her. Her eyes moved to Max's boat. Was that her only option? The gallery opening was one small piece of business but she wasn't making enough day to day to cover repairs and her living costs. She couldn't afford a higher rent. The *Forget-Me-Knot* had been blessedly cheap and now she knew why.

As she looked into the galley, she saw her bright-coloured cushions, the rug, the plants, the pictures on the shelves, and it was like something punched her hard and fast in the stomach. She'd made it a home. Her home. The new-found connection to her mum, to the feelings of fulfilment she'd never had before, to the life she was making for herself were as tied to this slightly scruffy houseboat as they were to the city. And now she was going to have to give it all up.

Having barely drunk his tea, Piet stood up. 'I really am sorry. I know this is a shock.' He left the piece of paper on the table and edged away, looking resolutely forwards as he continued down the street.

So that was it.

In the space of twenty-four hours her life had been completely upended. She searched again for signs of life on Max's boat. She wanted him to hold her, to tell her it was going to be okay. To turn up with his box of tools and help her fix this like he had her leaky tap.

She wanted her family. Her dad's kind words and her sister's gentle encouragement. She moved inside and began running sections of the paper through a translation app, hoping Piet had read it wrong. But she knew he hadn't, and when the app confirmed it, she couldn't stop the tears misting her vision and rolling down her face. What choice did she have but to move back home?

Her dream was over and it hadn't even really begun.

Chapter 21

'What are you going to do?' asked Melody, her voice ringing with concern in Rosie's ear as she walked the streets of Amsterdam.

After seeing Piet, she couldn't sit still. Every time she tried, the unreadable instruction from the city council stared at her and Rosie spun between anger and tears. She'd needed to move, and as the summer evening was bright and the sky still clear and blue, she'd decided to go for a walk.

'You mean once I've called Piet and kicked him squarely in the nuts for doing this to me?'

Melody giggled. 'Yeah, after that.'

'Come home, I guess.'

'What? You're giving up?'

'It's not really giving up, is it? I've been backed into a corner.'

A bike bell tinkled behind her and she moved out of the way. The streets were still busy, bars and restaurants full of people. She saw the roof of the Rijksmuseum in the distance, the abundant blossoming trees dotting her line of vision.

'There must be a solution, surely?'

Rosie headed away from the busier road and darted down several quieter streets until she found herself on one that was virtually deserted. The houses were laid out before her like a painting. With their flat fronts and windows all lining up with each other, it was as though someone had drawn them. Old Victorian-style lights stuck out of each one, just above the doors, and the numerous windows reflected the golden evening sun. On another night like this she might have sat with Max on his boat. They might have gone on another canal cruise or ridden their bikes around the city, finding hidden spots together. But that was another reason that made it impossible to stay. Something special had been taken away from her. Max was throwing their chance at happiness away.

'Rosie,' her sister said. 'There must be something you can do.'

'Like what? I just don't have the money to make all the repairs the boat needs and the landlord can only help a bit.'

'So what's he going to do?'

'I don't know. Evict me and get rid of the boat, I suppose. Or maybe it'll sit there unable to be used until he can get someone to get rid of it. I didn't ask.'

After a few more minutes, Rosie found herself on a picturesque bridge over one of the canals. Flower baskets overflowed with tiny purple, blue and pink blooms. A bike leaned against the red brick and she watched the water flow beneath her.

'Can you find somewhere else to live?'

'Not with the money I'm making.' She'd done some mental maths before her sister had called and she simply didn't have enough to pay another deposit, let alone a higher rent. Most of all, she didn't want to.

'When I realised the boat was called the *Forget-Me-Knot*, it felt like a sign from Mum. Like I was right where I was supposed to be. Plus, now I've made the place my own and it feels like a home. I don't want to give that up.'

Not to mention she didn't want to stop living next to Max, even though he seemed to have given up on them.

'Rosie,' Melody said firmly. 'This isn't like you at all. How many times have you urged me to find solutions rather than dwelling on problems?'

'This isn't just a problem, Mels. This is a *big* problem. Like, a huge problem. This is the problemest problem of them all. I don't think there is a solution to this – not one that I can afford. I can't afford to move – nowhere's within my price range and the thought of it makes me feel sick – and I can't afford the repairs either.'

'It seems to me you're not thinking straight at the moment, Rosie-Roo.'

'You're usually the one telling me to have my feet on the ground.'

'I know, but . . . when you get a problem, you don't think

in straight lines, like the rest of us do. You think in waves and circles, finding solutions that no one else would think of. It's your creative brain, I guess.'

'Maybe it is, but there's no beating reality. I just don't want to leave,' Rosie admitted, feeling tears sting the back of her nose once more. 'This is the only place I've felt like I belong. Where I've felt like I have a purpose. Where I might be able to build a future and actually make something of myself. I can't go back to doing temp jobs or taking whatever work I can get that pays the rent. When I go to work every day here, I love it. I can't wait to see what the day brings. Even if I'm missing you and Dad, I know this is where I'm meant to be. The flower market, the houseboat, they just make me feel like I'm finally . . . me.'

'Oh, Rosie,' Mels said. 'Have you spoken to the city people? Is there a way to work out a schedule of repairs that gets them off your back?'

Rosie paused, the water flowing under the bridge in ripples and waves. She hadn't thought of that. She'd been too caught up in her anger and annoyance over Piet's terrible landlording and Max's withdrawal that she'd closed her mind off.

Her sister's voice pierced the silence. 'You've gone quiet.'

Rosie realised she'd been standing there thinking, leaving her sister hanging on the other end of the line.

'You might be on to something there.'

'Are you telling me that I might have come up with a solution?'

'I don't know if it'll be a solution exactly, but it might buy me some more time at least. Maybe I'll go and see the city council tomorrow and try and figure this out.'

'Ha! See! I told you there'd be a solution – or at least, part of one. Glad I could be of service. You're welcome.'

Rosie giggled and the tension eased slightly from her neck and shoulders. The canal waters flowed, as they always did and always would. It wasn't a whole plan for dealing with this mess, but it was part of one and who knew, maybe tomorrow would bring another solution.

'Have you asked the handsome doctor out yet?'

'Are you changing the subject?'

'Yes, but I want to know as well. You might have hit on something but I need time to think it through.' She might also need Max or Emma to act as translator. 'So?'

Melody groaned and Rosie could picture her head falling into her hands. 'Not yet.'

'Why not? You promised you would and you're already well over deadline.'

'Because I just can't. We work together.'

'Only a bit. You don't see him every day, do you?'

'No, not every day.'

'So work isn't the problem. You just need to be brave.'

'I know, I know.'

In the background, Rosie could hear her sister making a cup of tea. The kettle hissed and she wished she was there in her flat, about to curl on the sofa next to her.

'Well, I'm going to keep bugging you until you do. Do

you want me to text you at lunchtime every day to see how you're doing? Give you a little reminder?' Teasing her sister was bringing the first smile to her face she'd had all day.

'No thank you. I can do this. And so can you.' Melody's voice turned stern. 'If this really is where you've felt the most like you, the most happy and the most at peace, you can't give it up. You can't just give in because you've faced an obstacle. It's a big one,' she added quickly as Rosie inhaled to make a case for her self-pity. 'But you've overcome much worse. You've done so amazingly well to get where you are; you can't let this beat you. You know I was nervous about you moving there, but I've seen how good for you it's been. You've always thought outside the box. Do it now and I know you can fix this.'

'Thank you,' Rosie whispered, a small, hard lump forming in her throat. She was so lucky to have the family she had. A family that loved and supported her and always had. 'Love you.'

'Love you too. Me and Dad – we're both really proud of you, and I know Mum would be too, no matter what. But she'd be especially proud you're working to make yourself happy. I have to go. I've got to get to work. I'm on nights.'

Rosie said goodbye and stared at the canal. The sun was dipping in the sky and a slight breeze ruffled the bushy leaves of the trees. She wanted to be here to see the trees turn red and russet, and their leaves fall to litter the streets.

She wanted to see the city at Christmas, to experience the Amsterdam Light Festival and watch the bright displays highlight the city. No, she wasn't prepared to give up. She didn't have the answer yet, but there must be a solution somewhere. She just had to find it.

Chapter 22

Rosie returned home, walking the red-brick streets, watching the birds and ducks bob on the waters of the canals. Bikes whizzed past, the smell of traditional Dutch apple cake wafted strongly from one particular bakery and Rosie took a deep breath, the scent of cinnamon calming her nerves. She wasn't even hungry, which showed how stressed she was, but she did quite fancy another of those *tompouce* she'd had on her first day. It seemed a long time ago now. How could it only have been a month? So much had happened in that time, it made her head spin.

As she came back to the *Forget-Me-Knot*, seeing for the first time all the things that needed fixing on the cute little houseboat, a flash of her normal optimism came back. If she had enough time, she could turn the *Forget-Me-Knot* into the most beautiful houseboat on the canal. She could even sell flowers from it. That would be her first shop. Her flower pots were beginning to bloom, and once the deck and galley were varnished, it would look magnificent. Maybe one day she'd even have a gorgeous mural painted on the side of a giant forget-me-not, the pretty, delicate blue flower with a bright yellow centre shining out at the world. But her positivity soon vanished. After today, she'd be lucky if she was still here at the end of the summer.

Max was approaching his boat, having just taken Zoon out for a walk, and Rosie felt her breath hitch as she spotted him. She turned away, unsure what to do. Should she smile? Be angry with him for pushing her away? No matter how much she wanted to be, he was hurting and if their roles had been reversed she may have felt the same. She'd probably lash out too and the sign of a good friend was one who stuck around, even in those difficult moments.

Max too seemed unsure what to do and glanced at her before unclipping Zoon's lead and shooing him onto his boat. The tiny dog refused to do as he was told and instead headed straight for Rosie, jumping up at her, his tail wagging enthusiastically. She ruffled the hair behind his ears and then bent down and pushed her fingers into his wiry hair.

'Hey,' Max said, coming closer. 'How're— You've been crying.' Shock registered in his voice and guilt flashed across his features. 'Rosie, I . . .'

She waited, hoping to hear an apology for why he'd pushed her away when he could have leaned on her for support. But his words floundered and silence filled the air. Her pride drew her up. She didn't want him to think she'd been crying over him, even though she had.

'It's the boat,' she said firmly, making her point. 'It needs a ton of repairs and I can't afford them. I don't know what I'm going to do.'

Tears threatened again and she forced her gaze back to Zoon, who still stood on his hind legs, his front paws pressed into her thighs, waiting for a fuss.

'I'm sorry to hear it. What did Piet say?'

She went over her conversation with him and added, 'I'm going to go and see the city council tomorrow. Try and work out a schedule of works that might buy me some more time.' She wanted his help and to have him by her side when she pleaded her case. 'Do you think you could come with me? To help me translate?'

'Rosie, I—' He took a step backwards. 'I'm sorry, I already have plans. Can you ask—'

'It's fine,' she said quickly, heat racing up her neck into her cheeks. Gently, she pushed Zoon back down and away from her. 'No worries.'

'I'm sure—'

'Goodnight, Max.' She walked past him and onto the deck of the *Forget-Me-Knot*.

'Zoon, come,' Max commanded, his words underpinned by a note of sorrow. With a glance at Rosie, Zoon did as he was told.

If Max was planning to say anything else, Rosie didn't

give him the chance. She'd held out an olive branch and he'd batted it back to her with such force she was surprised it hadn't hit her in the face. Whatever had started between them was obviously over and she wasn't going to wait around for any more pitying remarks. Without looking back at him, she opened the galley door and disappeared inside, closing it firmly behind her.

***

Rosie was able to rope Emma in to coming with her to the council offices. Emma had organised her assistant to cover at the deli, but Rosie had no option but to open late. It wasn't ideal. She couldn't really afford to lose business, especially at the moment, but she didn't have any other option. As they began to leave the deli, Rosie was surprised to hear Finn calling her name.

'Is everything all right?' he asked as she and Emma passed him.

'Yes, of course. Actually not really, but that's a whole other story. What can I do for you?'

'I just noticed you were . . .' Finn glanced back at her small pitch all closed up.

'Yeah, I need to go somewhere.'

'But you'll lose money.' She was surprised at his genuine level of concern.

She shrugged. 'Can't be helped, I'm afraid. Something's come up and I need to deal with it now.'

'Would you . . .' He hesitated. 'Would you like me and

my guys to keep an eye on things? We can always serve people for you? I have enough staff on today. If that'd help?'

Rosie didn't know what to say and opened and closed her mouth without making any noise, which made the hesitant Finn positively alarmed. She told herself to get a grip. 'That's so kind of you, Finn. Are you sure?'

'Of course. It's the least I can do after you helped me the other day.'

Rosie fished in her bag and handed over her keys. 'Here.'

'You don't want to do that yourself?' Finn asked.

'No, it's fine. I trust you. And I really need to get going. I've got a meeting with the city council and I'm told they don't like to be kept waiting.'

Finn took the keys, wishing her well, and she and Emma made their escape. Rosie noticed Noah glancing at them as they left, his eyes lingering on Emma for as long as possible. There was still hope there for her friend, she was sure. Emma's disastrous flirting attempts might have stalled her progress but they hadn't stopped it altogether. Rosie just wished that hope still existed for her and Max. He would have to be pushed to the back of her mind while she dealt with the most pressing problem: the boat.

'What's the plan?' Emma asked as they approached the city council offices.

'Beg and plead without self-respect or dignity until they help me out?'

Emma giggled. 'Let's just see how it goes, shall we? I can be quite charming when I need to be.'

'Just don't try and flirt, okay?' Rosie asked with a gentle, teasing shove.

'Hey! I'm getting better at it, actually. I'll have you know I had a whole conversation with Noah yesterday and I didn't even try to flirt once.'

Maybe that explained why things seemed to have improved.

They entered the city council offices and anxiety settled in Rosie's limbs, weighing them down, slowing her movements. Her chest felt too heavy to breathe properly and her legs didn't want to climb the stairs to the correct department. Eventually, she was called forward to a man at a desk and Rosie began speaking. When it was clear he knew some English but was struggling to keep up with Rosie's rushed, worried speech, Emma took over.

Rosie watched as the conversation flowed back and forth, Emma pointing at various sections of the notice Piet had left with her, and the council man doing the same. Emma occasionally paused to ask Rosie a question, or translate and then provide her answer. As the meeting progressed, the council man seemed to get more and more frustrated with her as the conversation went on. The tension in Rosie's shoulders and neck was vice-like.

After half an hour of intense discussion between the three of them, some in English, some in Dutch, Emma turned to Rosie and Rosie's heart sank at her expression.

'I'm sorry, Rosie. It seems there isn't much room at all. According to Mr Classen they'd already given Piet several warnings before this. Which he ignored. They can't give any more time. I'm so sorry.'

Determined not to cry in front of this total stranger, Rosie nodded to Mr Classen and thanked him for his time.

'What will you do now?' Emma asked as they stepped back into the light of the warm, summery day.

'I don't know, but we better get back to the flower market or I won't have any money to do anything with.'

'It was nice of Finn to keep an eye on the place for you.'

'It was, wasn't it? Seems he's not that bad, after all.'

'I think it's you,' Emma replied, catching her off guard. 'I think you bring out the best in people and bring them together. The community at the flower market is much nicer now.'

An idea buzzed somewhere inside Rosie's head. Something about the word 'community' sparked the beginnings of a nebulous concept, but then it faded as she avoided a cyclist who, for once, wasn't very friendly at all.

He shouted something in Dutch, waving one fist so violently he wobbled and nearly fell from his bike.

'Sorry! Sorry!' Rosie shouted after him.

He said something else and Emma began laughing. 'He just called you a potato.'

'A potato! Why would he call me that? Is it some weird Dutch insult?'

'I've no idea.'

'Do you think I look like a potato?' Rosie asked worriedly. She had worn a cream top and a long cream skirt today.

'No! He was an idiot – just ignore him.'

'Maybe you should teach me some Dutch swear words so I can swear back.'

'I'd love to!' Emma squeezed her arm as they walked along.

As they continued towards the *Bloemenmarkt*, the niggling in Rosie's mind remained. Something about community and bringing out the best in people reminded her of the Milkshake Festival she'd been to. The memory of Max dancing and the time they'd enjoyed bit at her, but it was the feel of the place that was sparking something. If only she could identify what.

'Is that Max?' Emma asked, breaking into her thoughts.

Rosie followed the line of her finger and sure enough Max was walking into a café with a beautiful woman on his arm. Her long dark hair glimmered with shades of coffee and chestnut and her beautifully tailored clothes (which screamed designer label) hugged her body like they'd been made to measure.

Max had opened the door for her and as she walked through, he followed, placing his hand gently on the small of her back. He'd done that with Rosie and it sent shockwaves through her nerve endings. She could almost hear as well as feel the physical ripping of her heart as it tore into pieces. Max was smiling and something lit his eyes the same way it had when he'd been painting. Rosie bit the inside of her lip. She had no idea who the woman was, but it was clear they were enjoying each other's company.

'Maybe they're just friends,' Emma added. Rosie made no reply. Her throat had stuck together and her body had forgotten how to breathe. A sharp ringing pierced her ears. 'Come on. Let's get going.' Emma gently tugged on her arm, leading her away. 'Let's get back to the *Bloemenmarkt*.'

Though Rosie didn't want to, she couldn't help but glance over her shoulder to see them looking dreamily at each other over coffee cups, the woman reaching across the table towards Max and his hand reaching out for hers in return.

Chapter 23

Rosie finished her day at the flower market and trudged home. After cooking herself a delicious meal in an attempt to make herself feel better, she sat out on the deck. Voices sounded from Max's boat: his deep baritone and a higher, lighter one prone to giggling. She'd rapidly decided she hated that voice and knew it must be the woman she'd seen Max with earlier. The image of them together had stayed in her mind all afternoon, no matter how she tried to get rid of it.

Through the evening, Max had been laughing – actually laughing – and every time she'd caught the sound, her heart had shrivelled just a little bit more. She wasn't sure it actually existed anymore and there wasn't just an empty hole where her heart had previously been. Though Rosie was facing away from him, she heard the galley door open and Max and his guest step onto the deck. Unable to stop herself, she glanced over her shoulder and again saw the beautiful brunette who'd been with Max earlier that day.

They'd spent the whole day together? She swallowed her wine, willing it to soothe the burning in her throat. Catching Max's eye, she spun back to hear him say: 'Goodnight, Johanna. I'll see you tomorrow.'

Hearing his ex's name, she had to choke down a sob. He was back with the woman who'd broken his heart? The woman who hadn't wanted to be with an artist, on an artist's pay. How? How could this have happened? She hadn't thought they were in touch.

'Goodnight, Max,' Johanna replied. There was silence and the sound of her kissing his cheek. 'Sleep tight.'

Johanna walked down the road, her heels tapping a rhythm on the pavement. Fire began to burn in Rosie's belly, reaching up and igniting in her lungs so she felt as if she were actually breathing fire. She knew it was none of her business, that they'd barely been an item and she should keep her nose out and just move on. But she'd never been very good at doing that, and to think that only days ago he'd slept with her. Then, in the days between doing that and pushing her away, he'd started bedding his ex again? All of that was enough to force her from her seat. She turned and stared at Max.

'How did it go at the—'

'Don't bother acting is if you care, Max. We both know you don't.'

His features froze. 'What do you mean?'

'I mean that a few days ago we were making love and then as soon as you had some bad news you pushed me away and started shagging your ex.'

'Rosie, I—'

'It's fine,' she said, holding up her hands to stop him. His eyes widened as she hit the mark. 'As you said, we barely know each other. Maybe I was an idiot for falling for you so quickly.' She watched his mouth close, his jaw working hard.

'You were falling in love with me?'

She suddenly realised that in her anger she'd blurted out the true extent of her feelings. Her breath hitched, her lungs fluttering as if they had no idea what they should be doing. Rosie ignored his question. What was the point in admitting it again when he'd only say how sorry he was? Give her meaningless platitudes. 'You know the thing that makes me so mad I can hardly breathe?' She clenched her fists to her sides. 'What annoys me most is that you said that she didn't like the life you could give her. She never really believed in you, but I did from the moment I saw your paintings. From the moment I met you and you talked about what you did, I believed in you and I still do.'

'Rosie, I appreciate you saying—'

'But actually . . .' She gave a sad, angry laugh as the thought crystallised in her mind. 'The thing that actually annoys me beyond all of that. Beyond you pushing me away and racing back to your ex, is that even now, you don't believe in yourself. You're so busy caring what one gallery owner in too-short trousers says that you let that knock you.'

A slight hardness came to his features. 'You don't understand. When you put your work – your creation, a part of yourself – out there, and people reject it, it . . . it hurts. It's not always easy to pick yourself up and see everything in a positive light. Some of us aren't built for seeing the rainbows in the world.'

'Oh, because that's what I do, isn't it?' She felt like a firework about to catch light and explode into the air. Her anger was on the verge of boiling over, tumbling out of her and hitting everything around. 'I just tootle around looking at rainbows and baby birds and fluffy clouds, thinking how wonderful life is and how lucky I am to be alive. I might try and be positive, but I'm not a robot. It isn't always easy for me either, Max. Don't you think I get hurt sometimes too? Having to tell you about the gallery's decision hurt me as much as it did you. You hurt me the other day when you pushed me away. Losing my mum nearly destroyed me.' He had the good grace to drop his eyes, shame-faced, but she had to get these final words out. If she didn't, they'd sit inside her and fester. 'I was a child when she died and I miss her every damn day. Just because I try and keep my chin up doesn't mean I'm bulletproof and you know what else?'

'What?' he asked, his chin lifting but his voice trembling.

'These boat repairs might be the straw that breaks the camel's back. The council won't give me an extension on the deadline because they sent useless Piet so many letters before he deigned to deliver this one. So it looks like the only thing I can do is pack it all in and move back to England.'

Rosie gulped in a breath on this final word, it all hitting home one more time. Her emotions were spent, and she felt like her favourite old T-shirt. The one that had once been a bright vibrant red and was now faded and worn out. She'd lost her colour, her enthusiasm, and her hope.

'Isn't there something we can do?' His use of the word 'we' stung instead of giving her hope.

If there was, she had no idea what. She stood and picked up her glass. 'I don't think so. It's been nice knowing you, Max.'

She knew she sounded melodramatic given that she was going to work at the flower market until the very last moment – until she was forcibly evicted and had no other choice but to get on a plane home – so she'd be seeing him every day for the next few weeks at least. But hey, every girl was allowed a moment of drama now and again. After sweeping inside and closing the door on him, she pulled the curtains. The only thing she could do now was enjoy the days she had left until it was time to say goodbye.

Chapter 24

Rosie found it difficult to smile, even for the customers, though she did her best to act as cheerfully as possible. Her colleagues had noticed the change in her, as Finn was constantly glancing over and Fenna had also popped round a few times to talk about things that they wouldn't normally talk about. Emma had delivered her three coffees and Noah (along with Emma) had delivered her a lunch and forced her to eat it while they took it in turns to serve her customers. The support she was receiving was almost overwhelming and though she appreciated it, she couldn't wait to leave at the end of the day and be alone to cry.

As the work day drew to a close, she pulled down the shutter over her tiny pitch, and turned to see a small army led by Emma marching towards her.

'Emma told us what happened,' said Finn.

Rosie shot Emma a poisonous look. 'What? I asked you not to say anything about Max breaking my heart by sleeping with his ex who has the most annoying, stupid tinkly laugh I've ever heard.'

'Actually,' Finn said, his eyes darting between them, 'she didn't mention any of that. She just said about your houseboat.'

'Oh.' Rosie's face flooded with heat. It crept up from her neck, over her cheeks and across her scalp. 'Sorry, Emma.'

'I should think so. Of course I didn't spill our girl-chat secrets.'

Finn cleared his throat. 'We need to talk.'

Everyone else – which included Noah and Fenna – nodded.

'Okay,' Rosie said nervously, stretching out the word. 'But if this is some kind of intervention, can we at least do it in the pub?'

'Definitely,' Emma said and the group marched outside and along the canal to one of the restaurants in a small side street. A large umbrella shaded them from the evening sun, and the bright green climbing plants decorating the houses, their bushy leaves reaching out over the buildings, gave the small space a cosy, secluded feel.

Noah asked Rosie what she'd like to drink, and took everyone else's order. 'Emma, would you help me with the drinks, please?'

'Oh,' she replied, her eyes widening in surprise. 'Of course.'

Rosie bit back a smile – her first genuine one of the day – as the two still-completely-besotted-with-each-other idiots headed inside.

'Emma told us everything,' Finn said. 'Well, everything about the boat and the cost of repairs and you possibly heading back to England.'

'I get she didn't mention about Max and our brief, but amazingly intense relationship.' One that had held so much promise she felt the same stab of pain that had plagued her since their last argument.

'Umm, no she hadn't mentioned that.'

'But I'm sorry it didn't work out with him,' Fenna added. 'He was very handsome.'

'He was,' she said with a sigh.

Finn cleared his throat. 'The boat. It's just bad luck. Houseboats do take a lot of looking after and your landlord should have done a better job. Not all landlords in Amsterdam are like that.'

'I know,' Rosie replied with a laugh.

Fenna nodded. 'Do you have to return to England, though? Is there nowhere else you could live?'

Rosie shook her head. 'That boat was literally the only thing I could afford to rent and I know this sounds silly but . . . well . . . you know my mum was a botanist. She died when I was young and so, when I came across the *Forget-Me-Knot*, I thought it was a sign from her that this was where I was meant to be. Everything just seemed so right, but now I'm not so sure. Everything seems to be going wrong. I don't have enough to fix the damn boat and even if I did, what then? It's going to take me years to build up enough money to open a shop with the small pitch I've got. I just feel like I'm better off leaving at the end of the summer when my final penny runs out.' She shrugged, helplessly. 'Maybe packing up now and going home before I land myself in enough debt to make me bankrupt is the best thing to do. No one can say I didn't try, can they?' She gave a small, pathetic smile that she in no way felt.

At that moment, Emma and Noah returned with a bottle of wine in a cooler and five glasses. He poured the wine and silence fell for a second.

'I can understand why you feel how you do,' Finn said, surprising everyone with his empathy and kind tone. 'But you mustn't give up. You remember I said I started with a tiny pitch at the flower market and a bike. There must be something. Could you sell flowers from the houseboat too? If it's done up?'

'I – I don't know,' she confirmed, dropping her eyes to her glass, then taking a sip of the delicious liquid. She'd hoped that one day she might, but she hadn't explored that option; she'd considered it but hadn't thought through if she'd have employees. It all seemed too much to hope for.

'You can,' Fenna confirmed. 'I know lots of people who sell goods from their houseboats.'

'So you could also start selling from home, as well,' Finn said.

'But I need a home for that to happen,' Rosie replied. 'Look, I know I sound all doom and gloom and it's really kind of you all to try and help me, but I really don't think there's enough money to make this work.'

'Can you get the money somewhere else?' Noah asked. 'Your family or a bank loan?'

Having worked so many low-paid jobs and living perpetually off her overdraft for such a long time, any bank would laugh her out of the building if she asked about a loan. 'There isn't,' she replied, feeling guilty for being so grumpy. Was this how Max had often felt? It was a vicious cycle. She felt hopeless and because of that, her brain refused to look for positives. She'd believed before that there were always solutions out there if she just looked for them, but she couldn't lift this veil of defeat that obscured her vision. She had to fight this overwhelming urge to run and hide from the world.

As silence descended and Noah tutted. 'Look at that—' He pointed to where someone had purposefully dropped some rubbish. 'How can people do this to our beautiful city?'

'I agree,' Fenna said. 'The historic part of town – especially the flower market – needs protecting from things like that. The city does what it can but people don't realise the significance of it. It's our history, our heritage, and it's getting worse. So many areas are falling into disrepair.'

Rosie suddenly lifted her head. No one had noticed except for Emma, who was watching her quizzically.

Suddenly, the nebulous idea that had floated in her head after her visit to the council offices began to take shape. Fenna's words mixed with the thought that had struck her the day before but that she couldn't quite grasp. As soon as she'd heard the word 'community', she'd thought of the Milkshake Festival, of people coming together in love and support of one another, encouraging respect and understanding, acceptance and pride. The wheels in her brain were turning, the part of her that sought solutions firing back to life. After another gulp of wine, she finally had it: a solid idea.

'I've come to know that look,' Emma said. 'What are you thinking?'

Rosie had no idea if it would work, and they might all laugh at her for even suggesting it. But the word was circling, details starting to cling to it like iron filings drawn to a magnet. For all she knew, there was already something of that kind and the idea might go nowhere, but she was with exactly the right people to ask.

'A festival!' Rosie declared. 'I was thinking about organising a festival that celebrates the canal community, its heritage and those who look after it. Something like a floating canal festival.' Fenna and Finn looked at each other while Emma and Noah both dropped their eyes. 'What?'

Finn was the one to speak. 'There is already a canal festival. It's held in August each year, called *Grachtenfestival*. It's a music festival and people perform all around the canal areas.'

'Oh.' Rosie's shoulders slumped. But a spark had come back to life and she refused to let it peter out again. She'd had a taste of being a grump and she didn't like it one bit. Now she was beginning to think more clearly, she knew the idea had merit. 'So maybe a floating canal festival is too broad. Besides, it would take too much organising to get the word out everywhere around the city and to get people to attend. When I worked in a marketing team, I was told people had to identify their niche.'

'Well, our niche is the floating flower market,' Noah said, and everyone nodded.

'So could we organise a floating flower market festival?' Rosie asked. 'We could raise funds for people who need help keeping their heritage protected in the *Bloemenmarkt* and canal district?'

'It sounds like a great idea,' Finn said, smiling widely. His face looked completely different now he'd relaxed, and he seemed much happier. 'I more than anyone realise now how important community is. If you're organising this,' he said to Rosie, 'can I suggest we pay you a fee from the profits? The rest of the money can then be dealt out to those who need it. That way, no one can accuse you of anything underhand.'

'Will that be okay, do you think?'

Everyone nodded, though the worry remained as to what she'd do if it wasn't enough. But it was a start. She'd just have to work hard to make it successful.

'Does anyone know anything about organising festivals?'

Fenna asked. Her blonde-grey hair hung loosely around her shoulders, catching the soft evening light. More people were joining them in the small, secluded spot and the noise level rose.

Noah's cheeks coloured and he pushed his thick-rimmed glasses up the bridge of his nose. 'I used to work at an events company before I started the cheese shop. Maybe some of that knowledge might come in useful.'

'Actually,' Fenna began, 'my daughter works for a graphic design company. I'm sure she could help put together some flyers or something. Get a discount on getting them printed.'

'We definitely need a theme, though,' Rosie said, pushing her wine glass to the side and leaning forwards on the table. 'What exactly are we trying to achieve? Because raising money is the goal, but what else? We want to . . . ?'

'Raise money to preserve the cultural heritage of the canal community,' Finn said, making a note on his phone.

'And,' Emma added, 'showcase the talent of people in the *Bloemenmarkt* area.'

Noah smiled at her, nodding as he slipped his arm around her shoulders. Emma grinned widely. 'And wider if we can. If we get enough interest. We want to showcase everyone around the *Bloemenmarkt* and who lives and works on the Amsterdam canals. Though that might be a bit too big a goal.'

'I don't think so,' Rosie said. 'And we might as well aim as high as we can. If this doesn't work and I end up going home, it won't be for lack of trying. I'll go out with a bang!'

'You won't be going anywhere,' Emma assured her, taking her hand and squeezing it.

Rosie swallowed down the lump in her throat. 'So what do we do first?'

Finn looked up from his phone, where he'd been typing furiously. 'First, we need to inform everyone in the *Bloemenmarkt*. Let's call a meeting for tomorrow morning. I'll contact everyone I know who works there. If we all do the same, we shouldn't leave anyone out, and we can catch up with anyone who misses it during the day. Agreed?'

'Agreed.' Finn nodded.

Rosie could see why Finn was such a successful businessman. He might not be the most creative of thinkers, but he was focused and organised – exactly the skills they needed for this. She was grateful to have him and everyone else around her.

'Thank you, everyone. I don't know what to say.' She forced the tears back from her eyes.

Emma hugged her, as did Fenna as they were closest. Noah and Finn glanced at each other slightly awkwardly before Finn raised a glass. 'To the floating flower market festival!'

Rosie grabbed hers, eager for a top-up. 'It has a nice ring to it!'

Now she just had to make it a reality and in the smallest timescale imaginable. She took another glug of her wine, draining the last of it from the glass. Her natural good cheer, which had only just returned, was in danger of disappearing again, but she had no option but to grit her teeth and dive straight in. If nothing else, her mum would be proud of her for trying.

Chapter 25

Rosie sipped her takeaway coffee as Bas delivered her flowers. Everyone was gathering by Finn's large corner pitch for the meeting. The market had become her second home and an intense tugging at her heartstrings pulled her spirits down. She looked around at the different stalls, the displays of bright blooms, the buckets of bulbs, those silly tiny windmills. She loved this place and hoped – prayed – that this crazy, still as yet unorganised, idea would work.

As Rosie unpacked her flowers, slotting them into buckets to keep them watered, she peeked at Finn's pitch and see if anyone else had arrived. They hadn't. And she worried that with Finn's reputation, people had chosen to stay away. Perhaps they were nervous they were going to get a telling-off, or worse, from the previously arrogant stall holder. She had to hope that his natural authority would bring them to him.

'I heard about the meeting,' Bas said, in stuttered, broken English. 'I might come.'

'You should,' she replied, cheerfully. At first, she wasn't sure what he'd be able to do, but then it occurred to her that he delivered to so many places around the city, he'd be perfect for handing out leaflets and flyers. 'We'll be starting in a minute. Why not stay?'

He checked his watch, sucked air through his teeth, then nodded. Rosie smiled, glad that curiosity had won out over his demanding schedule.

As eight o'clock neared, more and more vendors began to gather at Finn's. She knew most of the faces, but there were definitely some people she hadn't met before – people who worked down the opposite end of the market, she presumed. Turnout was impressive. More than she could have wished for. She just hoped they could get everyone on board. With a deep breath, Rosie and Bas wandered over.

'Right, everyone,' said Finn to the assembled crowd. 'Thank you all for coming over for this meeting. I realise this is taking time out of your morning set-up, so thank you for being here. We've got a new, exciting proposal to share with you all. Ah, here's Rosie, the mastermind behind the idea, and as she's English, can we stick to that, please?'

Rosie gave an awkward wave as Finn stood aside for her to speak. A lump formed in her throat. So much was riding on this being a success and not just for her. She wanted it to work and to be of value to everyone. Nerves bit at her stomach so she almost placed her hand there. Instead, she clasped them together in front of her. 'Hi, everyone,' she began nervously. 'Umm . . . I have been practising my Dutch, I promise. But thank you for agreeing to discuss this in English. I don't know how much Finn has told you, but I'm hoping we can work together to do something incredible. Something that I don't think has been done before but will benefit us all.'

She saw Emma, Noah and Fenna at the back, all smiling and nodding. Finn stayed at the front with her, and she was grateful for his support. As she got into her stride, explaining about the festival and where the proceeds would go, her nerves faded. She was honest about her own story and most people smiled and nodded in response, keen to do everything they could to promote their businesses, but some were not convinced.

'Why should we bother?' one particularly grumpy old man asked. Rosie recognised him as another flower seller from further down the market. He then mumbled something in Dutch.

'English, please,' Finn reminded him.

He glowered, but switched back so Rosie could understand him. 'Sounds like it'll be a normal day for me, and if people can't afford to keep their homes or businesses in a good state of repair, that's on them.'

'I don't believe in charity,' another said. 'People should learn to help themselves. You can't rely on other people to fix your problems for you.'

'I understand your point of view,' Rosie said. Though she didn't really. People didn't take charity for the heck of it. They took it because they needed to, often with feelings of shame attached. And she believed in community – people coming together to make life just a little bit better. 'Really, I do. But, if we're honest, life isn't always that easy, is it? Lots of people struggle and it isn't because they're not putting in as many hours as they can. It could be because they're having family problems, marriage problems – maybe their kids are struggling at school? I'm happy to be honest about my case.' She glanced at Emma, who nodded encouragingly. 'I rented my houseboat when I came here from London, and the owner didn't keep it up to scratch. I didn't know this at the time, obviously, and now he can't afford all the repairs and if I don't find a way, I'm going to lose everything. I know I'm not as in need as a lot of people, so if this works, I'll only be taking a small fee for organising it – an amount I intend to put back into the fund as soon as I can. But it made me think how hard it is to keep such a beautiful space as this protected.'

She signalled to the *Bloemenmarkt* around her. 'This city is beautiful. The flower market is beautiful! It's the only floating one in the world! Isn't that worth protecting? Heritage is important. It's why I wanted to come here and I'm sure it's why you all feel so proud to work here too.'

Those who were already on board continued their nodding but the two naysayers weren't to be convinced.

'No,' one replied, shaking his head. 'I still don't agree.

Why should I give some of my profits to a fund for people I don't know?'

'I agree,' the other added. 'I'm not interested.'

Finn suddenly stepped forwards. 'That's absolutely fine.' He held up his hands in surrender. 'No one is going to be forced to be involved. You'll benefit from the crowd we'll draw in, but you don't have contribute if you don't want to. The only thing is, you won't be able to request any money from the funds we raise if that's the case. And if anyone else wants to opt out, that really is fine. Please don't feel obliged if it isn't something you want to do. But the more we come together, the more successful this will be in not only raising money, but also in raising the profile of the *Bloemenmarkt* and us as people who work here. For me, it's a way of thanking those of you who supported me when my awning collapsed. We've all relied on the friends we've made in the *Bloemenmarkt* community at one time or another, and this is a way of giving something back. All it is, is putting on something a little bit special during that working day when you'd be here anyway, encouraging donations and maybe helping with some tasks like putting up posters.'

'That's right,' Rosie said, speaking up once more. Finn had done a great job of quietening the miserable ones and moving the conversation on. 'What we really need is contacts. If you know people who can design the flyers or get the word out online about what we're doing, please let us know. We just need to let everyone in Amsterdam know what we're doing and encourage them to come along.'

'Sorry,' a younger woman said, raising her hand. 'I'm confused. What exactly will happen on the day itself?'

'Well, I'm planning to hold some special talks and Finn's planning on teaching people about arranging flowers.'

'I'm holding a cheese tasting,' Noah said. 'There'll be samples everywhere for people to try.'

'Same for me, but with meat and crackers,' Emma added, smiling at him. 'I'll be showing people how to pair meats and cheeses perfectly and what things they need to go with them.' Noah grinned back and Rosie felt her heart skip a beat for them, before this quickly reminded her that Max had broken her own heart and that her love life was an absolute disaster.

'You can do anything you like,' Rosie told the crowd, drawing her attention back to them. 'Just make it something a little different to usual. But we've only got three weeks, so we need to get started with spreading the word. That's our priority.'

'I can deliver . . . things,' Bas added, sticking his hand in the air, and Rosie had to resist the urge to hug him.

'Thank you, Bas,' she replied. 'That will be so helpful.'

'I suppose I could talk about the history of windmills to the tourists,' the young woman said, and Rosie immediately recognised her as the owner of the windmill stall.

'Yes! That would be amazing!'

'Or children can build their own. I've been designing a paper kit to sell. This could be a good way to see if it works.'

'That sounds wonderful,' Finn said, smiling at her and then Rosie.

The crowd nodded their assent and disappeared, chatting to one another as they went. Finn, Fenna, Noah and Emma all remained behind.

'That went well, I think,' Fenna said.

'Why do some people have to be negative, though?' Rosie asked, fully aware that she'd been exactly the same recently.

'That's people. You can't make everyone happy all the time, and it is their right not to take part. Some people just don't like change.'

'Or putting themselves out there,' added Noah. His glance at Emma seemed to speak volumes. Was he admitting he'd been holding himself back? Emma smiled shyly then dropped her eyes.

'There is one thing, though,' Rosie said, annoyed that the thought had only just occurred to her. 'How are we going to pay for flyers and posters?' She looked around the group, nerves tightening her stomach that this might prove the stumbling block that tore her plans down. 'I can't afford to pay for anything. We don't have any upfront money to cover those initial costs.'

Once again, she'd been impulsive and forged ahead with an idea before thinking all the details through. If she had to call everyone back and say the idea was already a no-go, she'd be a laughingstock.

'I'll do it,' Finn said and Rosie, along with the others, were surprised at his generosity. 'Don't all look like that.' A note of sternness crept into his voice. 'I know I haven't always acted as nicely as I could but I'm not a complete ogre.'

'We know that now,' Emma replied cheekily. 'But still. That's more than anyone expects, Finn. I'm happy to add some money in too.'

'Me too,' Noah agreed, with a firm shove of his glasses up his nose. 'I can afford some and, with any luck, we could make this an annual festival.'

'We could,' Finn agreed excitedly. 'This could be very good for business. I've never known this community come together as much as it is now. It's wonderful to see. I'll set an initial budget of five hundred euros—'

'Five hundred euros!' Rosie shouted, louder than intended, making everyone jump. 'That's – that's—'

'Enough to get us started. We don't want this to be a flop.' Finn straightened up as if he'd brook no argument, and any protest Rosie was about to make died on her lips. 'We need to sort out city permits and paperwork,' he added. 'But I can handle that. My assistant will take care of everything.'

Rosie managed to keep her voice at a reasonable level this time, even though she was more shocked than she had been at the five-hundred-euro starting budget. 'You have an assistant?'

'Hashtag life goals,' Emma added, and Finn chuckled.

Fenna, who had been quiet up to this point, turned to him. 'It's nice to see this side of you, Finn. I remember when you first joined the market, you used to be like this all the time. It's good to have you back.'

'Thank you,' he added, shuffling his feet as though

uncomfortable. 'I have to admit, things have been difficult for me lately.'

'Sorry, I wasn't fishing for information.'

'I know,' Finn said gently, placing a hand on her arm.

'You really don't have to tell us anything,' Rosie added. 'It's fine if you'd like to keep things private. I get not everyone's an over-sharer like I am.'

He smiled fondly at her. 'No, it's okay. I've been bottling things up for a while and taking my bad temper out on everyone else. My staff were too polite to point it out to me. I'm lucky I still have them. You talking about the problems people are having, Rosie, it was so true. That's why I forgot to get the awning fixed. I—' He took a deep breath in, avoiding their eyes. 'I used to be married but my husband and I separated.'

Fenna gasped. 'He used to meet you sometimes when we closed. Oh, Finn, I realise now he hasn't been around for a while. I'm so sorry – I should have asked.'

He shook his head. 'No, no! I don't know if I'd have been able to answer even if you had. And at the same time, my mother, she has Alzheimer's, and it's been getting worse. She's now in a home.'

Rosie couldn't help but reach out and rub his arm. 'That must have been so difficult for you.'

'It has been hard,' he admitted. 'But I know I made life harder for myself by staying away from everyone. I could have had a lot more support if I hadn't taken it out on everyone else. I was just so worried that I'd lose the business, and it felt like the only thing I had left. And I needed the money for my mother's fees. I was so concerned about not making money, not making profit, feeling like it was the only thing in my life I was good at.'

'Oh, Finn,' Rosie said, shoving her arms around him, taking him by surprise. 'I'm so sorry for everything you've been through.'

'If I can do anything,' Noah said as Rosie let Finn go, 'please just let me know.'

'And me,' Emma agreed.

'Maybe we should have lunch later?' Fenna suggested to him. 'It's time we got to know each other again.'

'I'd like that very much, thank you.' There was no hiding the tears in his eyes as he clapped his hands together. 'Now, we had all better get back to work!'

'Definitely,' Rosie agreed. 'I've got to get arrangements made for the gallery opening.'

If nothing else, Rosie reflected, she had at least done something to help relieve Finn's burden and for that, her mum would be proud, whether the floating flower festival was a success or not.

Chapter 26

By the time Rosie had finished the last arrangement, after a wonderfully busy day, her feet ached and she wanted nothing more than to get home and curl up on the sofa with a glass of wine and a good Netflix movie, but tonight was another dinner date with her dad. She was shattered, her back aching, but she was at least ready for the event the following evening and had already agreed with Jeroen that she would deliver the arrangements at 5 p.m., ready for the opening at 6 p.m.

As happy as she was to have the work, and of course the money, she couldn't help but wish Max would be there too. The gallery – and its rejection of Max's work – had been the beginning of the end of their short but wonderful relationship. How different things might have been if they were both going to be there tomorrow night, enjoying their relative successes together.

Thoughts of Max and the night they'd shared, the romantic canal boat ride and the first time he'd kissed her, played in her head as she made her way home, so that when she saw him on the deck of *The Rembrandt*, sitting out in the evening sun, she should have been prepared for the surge of emotion that hit her. She longed to feel his lips on hers again and to shout and scream at him some more for throwing away their chance of happiness. Because that was exactly what he'd done. By pushing her away he'd given up any possibility they had of making it together. And now he was back with Johanna. Their love hadn't even been worth fighting for.

She pressed down her need to tell him again what a fool he'd been and instead, made her way towards her boat. He was reading something on his phone and looked up, a nervous smile flitting across his features. He raised a hand in greeting, which she pointedly ignored and continued onto the deck of the *Forget-Me-Knot*. Zoon, however, had other plans and bounded away from Max, onto the street and around to her boat.

'Zoon, come back here!'

Rosie tried to walk past, but he danced in between her legs. 'Zoon, go home,' she said gently, giving him just the lightest of fusses because she couldn't resist his cute face and silly sad eyes.

'Zoon! Come!' Max bellowed, but he was completely ignored. With a sigh, he placed his phone down and came to retrieve him. 'I'm sorry.'

'Don't be, I've missed him.'

'You have?'

The air stilled around them as she stood and met his gaze. She wanted to open her mouth and say how much she'd missed Max too, but she couldn't force the words past the giant football-sized lump of hurt that still remained lodged in her throat.

'You look tired,' he said gently and though she knew he didn't mean it as a criticism, but she still felt rankled.

Who was he to say such things to her? They weren't friends anymore. And they wouldn't be neighbours for much longer. Her anger burned like a flare lit into the night sky, sparking in her body.

'Do I? Maybe that's because I'm working all the hours I can to try and save my boat.'

Max visibly paled, rocking backwards. 'Rosie, I—'

'You know, you can't just go around telling women they look tired. That's like, bloke advice 101. No woman wants to be told that. Ever.'

'I know, it was a stupid thing to say. I just . . . just wanted to make sure you were okay.'

'I don't know if I'm okay, Max. Ask me in three weeks when I know if I've saved my boat or not.'

As she hadn't been given an extension on the repairs deadline, she'd be cutting it fine. But she did have a month, so if the event went well and she got started on the repairs straight after it, she'd hopefully get most of it done before the deadline. And they wouldn't force her out when she'd nearly finished, would they? She shook the thought away. There was too much to worry about already without thinking of things that hadn't happened yet and that she had no hope of controlling.

'Three weeks?' he echoed, slightly puzzled. 'Why? What's happening?'

With everything that had happened, he hadn't earned the right to that information as far as Rosie was concerned. She stepped away from him, hyper aware of his strong arms, of his woody aftershave and the distracting bulge in his biceps. 'It doesn't matter.'

'Rosie, I wanted to tell you that—'

She couldn't bear any more of his platitudes or apologies. 'Goodnight, Max. Night, Zoon.'

'Rosie—'

She gave the dog a final scratch behind his ears and moved inside as quickly as possible. 'I have to go. I have a date with my dad.'

***

When her phone rang and she saw her dad's face on the screen, she almost cried. She wanted to tell him everything that had happened and though she'd given him some highlights over text, he had no idea of how wrong everything was going. Keeping up a cheerful exterior for the next hour was going to take all of her non-existent acting skills and a whole lot of grim determination.

'Hey, Dad,' she sang. 'How was your day?'

'Good, good. Oh, I've missed your face. But this is nice, isn't it? Are you ready?'

She turned her camera around to show the table laid up again, just as she had before, and her salmon was plated and keeping warm in the oven. 'All ready,' she confirmed. 'So, tell me all about what you've been up to.'

Her dad ran through all the gossip from his work, the day-to-day things he'd been up to, and started on the subject of someone he knew who was getting divorced after thirty-five years of marriage.

Rosie's mind ran to Finn and all that he'd been dealing with until her dad said: 'You know, I don't think Linny would have let me get away even if I'd wanted to. Not unless she'd got to keep the house and garden. Sometimes I think she loved that garden more than me.'

Rosie couldn't speak. She actually had it: the name for her shop. Not that that was looking likely anytime soon, but she finally knew what its name would be: Linny's Garden. As she ran it around in her mind, she knew it was right. The sound it made was perfect: soft and gentle as she was, welcoming and friendly. Exactly the type of person her mum was, and it would be a place where people felt better just for being there. The way she'd always felt around her mum.

How ironic that she'd found the name just as the chances of her making a success of life in Amsterdam were disappearing, the odds stacked against her.

No, she thought, straightening her spine. *No!* She was

done thinking negatively. She was done feeling sorry for herself, especially with the new-found friends she had around her, all of whom were working as hard as they could to make the festival idea a success. She wouldn't be the one to fail. Not when Linny's Garden needed opening.

'What are you smiling at?' her dad asked. 'That joke wasn't that funny.'

'Your jokes are always hilarious, Dad. But thanks to you, I think you've just nailed what my shop'll be called when I finally open it.'

'Oh yeah? What's that? Not "Steve and Isla's Divorce", hopefully.'

She giggled. 'No, Dad. Linny's Garden. It's perfect, isn't it?'

Tears made his eyes glassy and bright. 'Oh, sweetheart. That's wonderful. She'd have loved that.'

He was right. She would have, and it was up to Rosie to make that happen. Yes, her heart was bruised and sore from Max's behaviour but she'd never once let a man affect her decision-making and she wasn't about to start now. If Max didn't see how perfect they were together, then that was his problem. She had her mum's memory to uphold, her own future to carve out and a life to live here. And she'd do everything she could to make that happen.

Chapter 27

Rosie knocked on the gallery door, trying her best not to drop the arrangements she'd made and brought with her in a taxi. The tallest one had sat next to her on the seat, her hand held over it like a seatbelt. The taxi driver had found it very amusing and Rosie laughed along with him at the absurdity of it all. She was excited to see her work in situ amongst the amazing pieces of art and a thrill rocked through her at the prospect of doing more of this type of thing, if the festival idea worked.

Jeroen had invited her to stay for the opening so she'd worn her favourite little black dress and a pair of kitten heels – not so high she couldn't be on her feet all evening, but stylish enough to make her legs look good. Despite her promise to herself not to think about him anymore, she realised that had things been different, she and Max could have been arriving together.

The taxi pulled up and Jeroen spotted her through the window, coming to the gallery door and letting her in. The kind taxi driver unloaded the displays from the trunk onto the pavement in front of the gallery.

'Thank you for driving so carefully!' Rosie said as she paid him the fare.

'I could have arranged a van if you needed it,' Jeroen replied. He was looking particularly stylish in another tight-fitting blazer and his signature ankle-grazing trousers, this time in a deep burgundy. Polished brogues and a yellow bow tie finished the look. He adjusted his thick horn-rimmed glasses before picking up one of the displays and carrying it inside. 'I bet I can guess what this is inspired by.'

'Have you just read the card?' Rosie asked teasingly.

He smiled. 'No. I can tell from the colours. It's the Milkshake Festival, isn't it?'

'Correct,' she replied, happy that he'd recognised it. 'How did you know?'

'Well, it's bright and colourful, the flowers are bold and vibrant, and you've added tiny signs with the names of the different tents. It's genius! I love it.'

'Thanks. Be careful of the glitter, though. It gets everywhere.' She'd included a few large fake flowers in different glitter-covered shades. It was big and bold and one of her favourite displays. She'd also made one of the garden Max had taken her to at the Van Loon Museum. That one was softer and calmer, with its blue and white theme and small delicate flowers. The one she adored most, though, was inspired by the canal boat ride Max had taken her on when they'd stared at the stars, and kissed in the moonlight. The memory of his kiss made her lips tingle. The round display combined blue irises that sprung out in all directions like the canals of Amsterdam, set off by gentle green ferns, like the tree-lined streets.

Rosie placed it where they'd agreed it would go and went back outside, eager to get the remaining arrangements off the street and into the gallery.

'Wow, Rosie,' Jeroen said. 'They look wonderful. And you have cards to go with them?'

'Yes, I named them as you suggested, just as the artwork is named. I'm afraid they're not very imaginative.' The one inspired by the Milkshake Festival was simply called 'Milkshake'.

'That doesn't matter. They look stunning.'

Soon the waiting staff arrived and Jeroen left to brief them on their roles. He hadn't mentioned Max once and Rosie thought it pretty mean, actually. Surely, given that he'd made her deliver the news, he could have atleast asked how Max was. Standing awkwardly with a glass of champagne at the back of the gallery, Rosie gazed at the artwork until the other guests began to arrive. As soon as there was a decent-sized crowd, she edged forwards, introducing herself and joining in conversations about the art. She was pleased to hear comments on the flowers and the beautiful gallery space, and when one woman gushed about the inspired arrangements, Jeroen introduced them, winking at Rosie as he stepped away to circulate.

'They really are wonderful. So unique and exciting. Normally –' she leaned in, speaking nearer to Rosie '– flowers can be so dreary. I'm honestly so bored of tulips. But I've never seen a display like "Milkshake" before. You know, it's my daughter's twenty-first birthday in a few months and I'd love to hire you for the flowers. Do you have a card?'

Rosie's cheeks burned. Not only did she not have a card, but could she commit to something a few months away when she had no idea if she'd even be here? Unwilling to let the opportunity go, Rosie decided she would somehow have to make it work. Even if she had to come back over from England and ask Finn for a workstation at his stall to do it. 'My cards are still being printed, but let me take your email address.' She pulled out her phone. 'And I'll contact you next week, if that's all right?'

'Wonderful!' The woman gave her details and then began speaking to someone else about the art piece they were standing in front of.

Rosie turned away, a huge smile on her face, but that smile faded the moment she saw the latest couple to walk through the gallery door.

Max, looking more handsome than ever in a suit and tie, his beard trimmed, the angles of his face clear, and his hair swept back so his gorgeous eyes shone brightly, was standing with Johanna. She was wearing a cream form-fitting dress and carried a Chanel bag. As Max's eyes scanned the room, they met hers and he rocked back in surprise. Clearly he hadn't known she'd be here. This must be why Jeroen hadn't offered an apology over the situation with Max or asked after him. He'd invited him, but why would Max come when it was going to cause him so much pain? Rosie didn't know what to make of it.

Max's eyes were still locked on hers and flitted over her body, quickly up to her face. If he hadn't been standing with his ex, she'd have been sure that his eyes were hungry, his mouth tightening as he resisted the urge to come and talk to her. She turned away, swiping a glass of prosecco from one of the passing waiters and swapping it for her empty one.

'Max and Johanna!' she heard Jeroen say behind her and she studied the painting hung on the wall in front of her. 'It's so good to see you. Max, I'm so pleased we were able to squeeze in one of your pieces.'

What? Unable to stop herself, Rosie spun around, but when Johanna's eyes were the ones to meet hers, she spun straight back again. The people beside her began looking at her strangely, like she'd just randomly decided to pull out a dance move even though there was barely any music and definitely no one else was dancing.

One of his pieces was here? Why hadn't he said? Or maybe he would have last night but she was too busy ignoring him, not giving him the chance to speak. Had Jeroen taken pity on him? How had this happened?

'Come and see it hung,' Jeroen replied to Max.

Their voices dissipated as they moved away and, unable to stop herself, Rosie glanced over her shoulder to see Max looking back at her. Thankfully, his hands were by his sides rather than wrapped around Johanna's waist. If she'd been met with that scene she might have cried. For a moment, she considered leaving, but the woman she had been speaking to previously had introduced another lady who was after flowers for a retirement party. And there was no way Rosie could pass up these and whatever other opportunities might be coming her way through the evening. She'd have to grin and bear it.

Grin, Rosie did. So much so that by the time she felt she could leave, her cheeks hurt. She'd collected four emails to arrange quotes for, and had received so many compliments on her work she was in danger of growing arrogant. Her mum would also say how unfair it was that men could speak of their talents and achievements and it wasn't considered big-headed but for a woman to do it, those comments had to be prefaced with platitudes. It wasn't fair and Rosie refused to have her achievements that night dimmed. Not only had she done something for her career, she'd faced Max and his ex and she'd survived.

As Rosie walked out of the gallery and down the street, the night air brushed her cheeks. Cooler than it had been before, it whispered through the trees in the quiet of the city.

'Rosie!' She spun at the sound of her name, and the

familiar voice. Max jogged down the street towards her. He paused, not out of breath, but his chest rising and falling. 'I was hoping to speak to you.'

'You seemed a little busy with—' She wanted to say *your girlfriend*, but didn't want to appear petty.

'Yes, it's been mad.'

The chronic over-sharer in her demanded more information and she refused to hold her tongue. 'Your girlfriend must be very proud, though you did say she wasn't exactly up for the life of an artist's partner.'

'My . . . ?' He glanced back towards the gallery. 'Johanna? No, no. She's not – we're not – it's not what you think.'

'It's fine, Max, you don't have to try and protect my feelings. I saw her at your boat. I know you two are trying again. I'm happy for you.'

'No you're not,' he said with a sly grin.

'No! I'm not!'

'Rosie . . .' He shook his head vehemently, his hair falling about his face. 'We're really not . . . an item. I mean, she did come by, but she wanted to talk. She wanted to let me know that she's getting married. She didn't want me to hear it from someone else.'

Rosie felt her jaw drop and hang loose. 'Oh,' was all she managed to say. Then a moment later, 'I'm sorry. What?'

Max smiled and his eyes burned into hers. 'She's getting married. And not to me. She wanted me to know rather than hear it through friends.'

'So you're not . . . You never . . .'

'No.'

'Then why are you here together?' She pointed to the gallery.

'She wants to buy her fiancé a painting. She might not have liked being an artist's girlfriend, but she loves art and wanted to get him something special as an engagement gift. We were here choosing a piece.' So they weren't together? Why hadn't he just said so? Her heart still felt broken at his pushing her away but he could have just told her they weren't an item. 'Isn't that a bit . . . weird?' She couldn't help but curl her lip as she spoke and Max burst out laughing, the sound filling the cool, quiet night around them.

'It is a bit. But she wants to be friends and I'm not childish enough to say no.'

'I heard Jeroen say you had a piece here.'

Max's eyes immediately lit up. 'I did. Someone withdrew at the last minute. It's not quite as good as being accepted from the start, but it sold and I'm not going to refuse the money.'

'I'm glad. I'm – I'm happy for you. Are you sending work anywhere else? Or teaching?'

He shook his head. 'Not yet.'

Despite everything, she wished she could give him the confidence he so desperately needed, but as she knew herself, that was a journey only he could take.

'I haven't seen you painting,' she replied, a part of her not wanting the conversation to end. 'Not on the boat anyway.'

'No, I – I miss it.'

The growing breeze ruffled her hair and sent goose bumps over her skin. She drew her arms around herself, protectively. The sky was lit with stars just as it had been the night they'd first kissed. A silver moon, momentarily obscured by a passing cloud, shone out again in all its glory, casting shadows over the ground.

Rosie's mind whirled with everything she'd just heard. She needed time to process her thoughts. Questions and statements were whirling through her brain at a thousand miles an hour. If Max was feeling better about his work and wasn't with Johanna, then why was he still pushing her away? Was it because he'd come to realise they weren't a good match? The only way she'd know was to ask but she couldn't face the humiliation. Not when she'd had such a successful night otherwise. It could only be that he'd realised he didn't want to take their relationship any further than it had already gone. Sadness rose like bile, a bad taste tingeing her mouth.

Over Max's shoulder, Johanna appeared in the gallery doorway. By the confused look on her face it seemed Max hadn't told her anything about them, or if he had, it was probably PG-rated with no mention of the night they'd spent together. 'Max?' Johanna called, moving to one side to let another couple leave. 'Can you help me? I'm running out of time.'

Max turned and raised his hand in acknowledgement and with a final glance at Rosie, which she wasn't sure was friendly or not, Johanna went back inside.

'I'd better go,' he said quietly. He reached out for her a little and Rosie's breath stilled, unsure if he was going to touch her. Her brain told her to not make this easy for him, while her heart wanted to feel his skin against hers, the weight and heat of his body nearer to her own. 'Will you be all right, Rosie?'

Her eyes were still locked on his wavering hand and she suddenly looked up as he said her name. 'All right to what?'

'To get home.'

'Yes, yes, I'll be fine.' She took a step backwards and continued on her way.

'Goodnight, Rosie.'

But she didn't answer, unable to say the words as her brain hummed. Her synapses fired but nothing was connecting into a coherent thought and her emotions were spiralling so she couldn't tell one from another. He'd said so much, but there were a hundred and one things buzzing in her head that remained unsaid. The only thing she knew was that despite saying she would be all right, she absolutely wasn't. She wasn't all right at all.

Chapter 28

A few days later, Rosie placed a poster for the floating flower market festival in the window of the *Forget-Me-Knot*. They'd had a number printed up and everyone was placing them around the city. Fenna's daughter had come through in her graphic design job and had illustrated the most gorgeous advertisement; the line drawing of the canal and flower stalls was like a work of art on its own. With Finn's funds they'd been able to get both larger posters and smaller flyers printed. Bas was delivering a huge number for them on his daily rounds of the city and had even asked some of his colleagues who worked different routes to do the same. Excitement bubbled in Rosie's stomach like a bath bomb fizzing in a tub of hot water. They were certainly getting the word out and they couldn't do much more than that. All she could do was hope that people liked the idea enough to turn up.

As her attention had been so focused on making sure the poster was square, she hadn't noticed Max until he stopped opposite her, Zoon at his heels. He bent down, peering in through the window and smiling at her. Now they were on speaking terms again – albeit strange, uneasy ones because she still didn't know what to do with all the information he'd given her – she waved back.

She still wasn't sure how she felt about the news that Max and Johanna weren't in fact an item. Standing under the stars and a bright, glorious moon, the attraction between them had been as fierce as ever. His eyes had swept over her hungrily, she was sure, and he'd been honest with her about his work, no longer pushing her away. There'd been so much more to say, though, and neither of them had had the courage to voice it. Trepidation slowed her movements, but leaving the poster, she edged off the tiny sofa and made her way outside.

Her summer in Amsterdam had been amazing and the sun was once again shining brightly. She couldn't help but feel happy under the aquamarine sky, feeling the warmth on her face and the gentle rocking of her boat on the water. The ducks were floating past, quacking to one another, and the *Forget-Me-Knot* felt more like a home than anywhere she'd ever been as an adult. Rosie made yet another silent prayer the festival would be a success.

'What's this?' Max asked, pointing to the poster as Rosie

met him on the pavement. Zoon raced away, the lead tearing from Max's hand. 'Zoon! Come here!' But the dog had no intention of coming back. Instead he ran onto Rosie's boat and into the galley, jumping up onto the sofa and curling into a ball, eagerly preparing for a nap.

'Long walk, was it?' Rosie asked, grinning at the dog.

'Not really – he's just very, very lazy.'

A heavy silence descended as she smiled at the dog, aware of Max's eyes on her.

'So?' he asked, his voice gruff, the word loaded. 'The poster?'

'Oh, yes.' She snapped her head towards it as if she needed to jog her memory. She'd been too busy thinking about Max and his gorgeous eyes. Eyes that were watching her so intently she could feel them like pinpricks over her skin. She cleared her throat and told him everything about the plan.

'You came up with this idea?'

'Yeah, along with a few others. Finn's been really helpful.'

'Evil Finn?'

She laughed. 'He's not evil. He was just ... misunderstood.'

'Like Darth Vader?'

'I think he was *actually* evil. He killed a lot of people. Finn's just been a bit grumpy because of some personal problems.' She wasn't going to say any more; it wasn't her place to. 'And anyway, he's trying to make it up to everyone now.'

'It's a brilliant idea. I should have known you'd come up with something.'

'It wasn't easy,' she added, remembering his barbs about her finding it easy to be positive.

'I know,' he replied, dropping his eyes, and she softened towards him at the evident regret on his face.

'I think for a while, I felt how you did. I couldn't find the positives in anything and it didn't even feel worth trying. I haven't felt like that in a long time, not since Mum died. But I'm glad I managed to pick myself up. I was lucky to have people around me to help.' Max looked towards Zoon, avoiding her gaze, and she realised the impact of her words. Her friends had helped her, but at the time Max had pulled away. She hadn't meant to make him feel uncomfortable or to punish him. 'Max, I'm sorry. I didn't mean—'

'It's okay, Rosie. You're right. I should have been there to help you and I wasn't.'

Stunned into silence, she couldn't think of what to say. She'd assumed he'd excuse himself from the conversation and disappear – push her away as he had before.

'I'm sorry.' She didn't know what to say and when a response wasn't forthcoming, he said, 'I'd better let you get on. Shall I . . .' He pointed to Zoon, asleep on her sofa.

'Yeah, sorry, I need to go to work, otherwise you could leave him.'

'No problem. May I—'

'Of course.'

He stepped inside and the way he gently lifted the dog as if it were a precious newborn baby made her heart thump in her chest. Not only that, her eyes were drawn to the tension in his biceps, the way his T-shirt pressed against his skin and tightened over his chest. Rosie chewed the inside of her cheek. Whatever was happening with them, her attraction to him was as strong as ever.

'I'll see you later,' he said as he squeezed through the door and walked back to his boat.

'Yeah, see you later.' Thank goodness he was leaving. Any more of that and she'd need a cold shower before she left for work.

***

The flower market buzzed with its usual busyness, but Rosie was sure there was an extra excitement in the air. There were more people than usual dancing around the stalls, and everyone was talking about the festival and what they were planning to do. Word was spreading, and even customers were beginning to ask questions about it. That had to be a good sign.

Emma, who had offered to dive out and get them some lunch as her colleague was working that day, arrived at Rosie's stall. Most of the flowers she'd ordered had already gone and she was just making a couple of smaller bouquets, hoping to use up some of the slightly older ones that would be past their best if she didn't get rid of them soon. It still astounded her how difficult it was to predict which flowers would be popular and when. Though she hoped that if she could stay here long enough, she'd see a pattern emerge.

'So how's things with Noah?' Rosie asked. It was a standard question now.

'I think I'm moving in the right direction, but he still hasn't asked me out on an actual date and I'm too afraid to do it in case I scare him off again.'

'Well, I have no useful advice. My love life is pretty dire so I don't think I'm in a position to help.'

'What's happening with Max? Have you seen him since the gallery?'

Rosie had already told her about the evening he'd set the record straight: the way he'd chased after her after she'd left and the bombshell he'd delivered about his still-single status. 'He's not been around. I don't know if that's on purpose or by accident, but we just haven't run into each other. He's out most evenings when I've sat on the deck.' She unwrapped the paper from the soft bun and studied it. 'What's this?'

'It's *broodje haring*.'

'Right. And that is . . . ?'

'Raw herring, sliced gherkins and chopped onions in a soft bread bun.'

'Raw herring?' Rosie asked, her mouth turning down in distaste.

'Don't knock it till you try it. You like sushi, don't you?'

'Yes, but . . . I don't know. This just seems a bit . . . weirder.' Emma snorted a laugh. 'No offence.'

'None taken.' Emma took a massive bite of hers and through a half-chewed mouthful mumbled, 'It's actually yummy.'

'Okay.' Rosie squared her shoulders, sizing up her sandwich, and took a bite. The fish tasted surprisingly mild and paired nicely with the pickle flavour of the gherkins and the sweet tang of the onions. 'Hmm,' she said, as she chewed. 'That's actually all right.'

'It's delicious.'

'Not sure I'd go that far but . . .'

'See, you're a proper Amsterdammer now.'

'Am I? Do I get a badge?'

'No, but you get to stay.'

'I hope so,' Rosie replied, the comment grounding her back in reality.

'Me too,' Emma added, leaning into her shoulder.

As they munched through lunch, they spoke about the festival plans and agreed to have a drink after work. They'd toyed with the idea of inviting Noah and the gang, but both women wanted some time to chat, and agreed that for now, it would just be them. If anyone else spotted them and asked to come along, they'd make room.

Rosie was just wiping her mouth on a napkin, when Emma nudged her furiously.

'Look! Look!'

'Ow! That hurt! What is it?' Rosie, who'd had her back

to the market, spun around to see Max making his way through the crowd. 'Oh!'

'I'd better leave you two alone,' Emma said. She winked at Rosie as she greeted Max with a quick hello.

'What are you doing here?' Rosie asked, then corrected herself so she didn't sound rude. 'I mean, hi! I didn't expect to see you around here. Today.'

'Have you got a minute to talk?'

'Yeah, sure. It's not very busy right now.' As they stood together in her tiny pitch, it suddenly seemed smaller than ever. The energy that bounced between them was like a gravitational pull, and fighting it took all her energy. 'What's up?'

'It's this festival you're doing. I—' He pushed his hand into his hair and shifted his weight. 'I want to donate some paintings.'

'You . . . ?'

'Want to donate some paintings. You can sell them and put the profits towards the fund to help people. I want to help. I . . .' He hesitated, and the seconds Rosie had to wait felt like decades. 'I want to help you.'

'Max, that's – I don't know what to say. Thank you, that's . . . that's amazing. How much did the one in the gallery go for?'

'Three thousand euros.'

'Three thousand euros? Really?' Rosie's mouth fell open and Max grinned.

'I don't imagine the ones I donate here will go for that

much, but if they're sold for a hundred euros, that'll still be worthwhile.'

'Max, I don't know what to say. Thank you.' She leaned onto her tiptoes and kissed his cheek. His hand went to her waist and, feeling her lips press his skin, the tiny hairs of his beard brush against her cheek, her stomach roiled with longing. As she pulled away, his eyes roved down to her lips, and she resisted the urge to wrap her arms around his neck and pull him in for a kiss. She was sure he wanted it too, but then he stepped back and away from her, a slight flush to his cheeks appearing over his beard.

'Shall I bring them here tomorrow?'

'Yeah, yeah.' She adjusted the 1940s headscarf tied over her short hair. 'That'd be great.'

'And if there's anything else I can do, let me know, okay?'

'Sure.'

He walked away, but after a few steps, paused and looked back at her. 'I'm in awe of you, you know. The way you've handled everything, the way you keep pushing forwards. I wish I could be more like that.'

'You just have to keep trying,' she replied gently. 'It isn't always easy, I know. But . . .' Her heart seemed to swell to three times its normal size. She knew this version of Max was in there; she just wished he had trusted her enough from the start to show it. Could she ever forgive him for pushing her away so coldly? 'I think that might be one of the nicest things anyone's ever said to me.'

'Your mum would be very proud of you.'

A lump formed in her throat. 'Did you know I've finally thought of a name for my business? If I can keep it, that is.'

'Yeah, what's that?' His smile was wide, lighting his entire face.

'Linny's Garden. After her – my mum.'

'It's beautiful. Truly beautiful.' He stayed watching her for a moment and she fought the urge to reach out for him. To try and hold his hand. 'I'll see you later,' he replied, his voice unusually tight as though he were pushing down emotions. But which ones?

Rosie knew what she was feeling. The anger and frustration that had burned her before had faded, and now she just felt desperately sorry for him, wishing she could give him the confidence in his work he needed. But what was Max feeling? He still seemed to be attracted to her and as Johanna wasn't actually in the picture, they could restart their relationship. Was that what she wanted? The fizzing in her blood and the tightening of her ribs told her it was. And though she'd always been happy to ask guys out, she wasn't sure she could do that with Max. Not now. And what would be the point if she was going to leave soon anyway? If the festival wasn't a success, she had no choice but to leave, and restarting a relationship just to hurt each other a second time seemed pointless. Masochistic even. Yet her heart ached to be with Max for as long as possible up to that point.

A customer came forward, interrupting her thoughts, and she pasted on a smile, encouraging a discussion about irises just to take her mind off her brooding artist neighbour and the aching deep in her soul that kept pulling her back to him.

Chapter 29

For the next few days, apart from exchanging polite greetings and some run-of-the-mill enquiries from Max about the festival, he and Rosie barely spoke, even when they saw each other on their boats. Whereas before they would have sat together talking, her teasing him about being grumpy, the air felt too charged with things unsaid and chances never taken, and so each retreated to their respective galleys whenever they had the chance.

Then late one afternoon, just as she was packing up for the day, Max turned up at the flower market, a gleam in his eye and excitement in his voice.

'I've been speaking to Jeroen at the gallery, and we came up with a plan.'

'What sort of plan?' This level of excitement from Max

was unprecedented and infectious, and she found herself almost giggling as she spoke.

'I'm going to paint a special piece for the festival and Jeroen's going to sell it in the gallery.'

'But you've already donated two paintings! I can't ask you to give up any more of your time – and profits – to this.'

'I wasn't asking your permission, Rosie.' His voice was stern but not unkind, back to the grumpy Max she'd known before.

'All right, grouchy,' she replied with a laugh.

'I'd like to do this and so would Jeroen.'

'That would be amazing. I can't wait to tell the others.'

Max grinned as Noah and Emma arrived, carrying what looked like a huge sack. 'The banner's here,' he declared excitedly.

Max helped them to place it on the floor and together they unwrapped it from the carry case and unfurled it.

'I can't wait to see what it looks like,' Emma added.

It was enormous, long enough to go across an entire street and Fenna's daughter had outdone herself with the design once again. Beautifully illustrated flowers flanked the central text and seeing the words 'Floating Flower Festival' in the centre, the event she had created, made Rosie's heart jump.

'Oh, Fenna,' Rosie said as she stood by her side. 'It's beautiful. The flowers are so bright and pretty. The text is so friendly and welcoming. Please tell your daughter thank you from all of us.'

'I agree,' Finn added, joining them. 'She's done an amazing job.'

The whole market were gathering round to have a look and all were murmuring their agreement. Fenna puffed with pride and Rosie gave her a hug.

'Now we just need to get it up. Has anyone got any ladders?'

Somehow, a few people did and to Rosie's surprise, Max was one of the first to say, 'Let me help.'

'Are you sure you have time?' Rosie asked.

Max checked his watch. 'I have an appointment but not till later. Let me do this for you.'

Those final words sent a thrill down her spine, and she smiled. 'Come on then, let's get this beauty up and in place.'

They'd already decided it would be hung at the entrance to the *Bloemenmarkt* and Finn's assistant had sorted all the permissions they needed. Whoever this person was, Rosie had already decided to buy them a thank-you gift. They'd been invaluable.

Max and Noah wrestled with the banner, urged on by the crowd, following their instructions for moving it up and down, left and right, until it was in the perfect place. With the ends secured, they climbed down, and everyone stood back to admire it. A round of applause broke out and as it faded and everyone went back about their business, Max's arm circled around Rosie's shoulders. She wanted to reach out for him too and leaned into the strength and warmth of his body. She didn't dare look up, worried that if she did, she might fall even harder for him.

After a few moments of silent admiration, Max let her go.

'We should go out and celebrate,' he said. 'And there's so much of the city you still haven't seen. I know of at least four more places you should visit, and these aren't tourist spots, so we don't need to worry about bashing into backpacks and being hit by water bottles.'

'You know, tourists aren't the only ones who wear backpacks and carry water bottles.'

'Maybe not, but they do have massive ones that they swing around and knock into things. And when they all get together you can barely move down the street without being pushed about.'

'Sometimes you really do sound like you're a hundred years old.'

'Do you want to come or not?'

As things were back to how they'd been when she'd first arrived, she couldn't resist. She loved teasing. 'Okay, you can show me another of your secret Amsterdam hideouts. Do I get any clues as to where we're going this time?'

'No. That would defeat the object. Come on.' He stepped outside of her shop and waited for her to close up.

As the late afternoon merged into early evening, the sky ablaze with colour, the city hummed with an energy she'd grown to love. The sun was dipping as it began its lazy descent. The canal lapped gently at the bridges and the air tasted of cinnamon and Dutch apple cake. Max led them to a nearby bike shop and rented two bikes. Rosie mounted and followed him through the city, far more confident and proficient than she had been the first time. They cycled for about fifteen minutes before Max pulled off the road and came to a stop.

Rosie followed, her eyes immediately finding what they were here to see.

'It's a windmill!' she exclaimed, a giant smile reaching over her face. 'Wow! I've never seen one in real life before.'

'Most tourists—'

'Ignorant tourists,' she added with a teasing smile as she removed her cycle helmet and clipped it to her bike.

He grinned. 'Indeed. Most tourists think there aren't any windmills in Amsterdam. This is the only one and it is the tallest in the Netherlands. What do you think?'

Rosie's eyes flew over the structure. It was made of a stone body and dark, almost black wood forming an octagonal shape leading up to enormous blades. Rosie let out a little squeal. Max's eyes caught hers, full of affection, and she revelled in his gaze before forcing herself to speak. 'It's very impressive.'

'And next to it is a microbrewery.'

'Ah! Is that why you brought me here?'

'No. Well, not entirely. Come on.'

She followed him towards the small brewery. 'Is it illegal to drink and ride a bike?'

'Yes, but we're only having one drink, and we can always walk our bikes back,' he replied with an impish grin.

'It's a shame we can't go inside,' Rosie said, pointing at the windmill.

'I know. But at least we can sit in front of it and enjoy the view. I'll get some drinks. You find a seat.'

Rosie rushed to grab a seat with a good view. She wanted to study the amazing building before she had to go home. And by home, she didn't mean the houseboat, she meant England. Though the houseboat and this city felt more like home than London. She'd miss that sense of belonging if the flower festival didn't work out. She took some photos for her dad. He'd love to see this. With the banner hung and posters around the city, surely some people would turn up? And with Max's work to sell too, that had to raise some funds. She'd have to call in at the gallery and thank Jeroen, as a piece sold in a stately gallery was bound to attract more attention than one sold at the flower market.

'So,' she said when Max joined her. 'How long do we have?'

He looked confused.

'Till your appointment?'

'Oh, that.' He checked his watch. 'Another couple of hours.'

'That's late,' she replied, sipping the hoppy liquid and enjoying the slightly bitter taste.

'It is. I've – I've got a new teaching job.'

'You have?' She couldn't believe he hadn't said anything

before. Then again, they hadn't exactly been speaking up until recently. 'That's wonderful! When did this happen?'

'Not long ago. I meant what I said before, Rosie. You are an exceptional person. You make things happen. You take chances. You're far braver than you give yourself credit for. You made me think I might be able to take some chances too.'

'Oh.'

It was quite a set of compliments.

Their eyes met and Rosie's stomach somersaulted. She was already glowing from his kind words but longed to hear him say more. To refer to the relationship they had begun and then abruptly halted. With her future uncertain it was unlikely anything more would happen between them, but she needed to know how he felt. She thought of all the times she'd just come out and asked a man how he felt, but now, sitting with Max in front of her, with the thought of his rejection forcing her chest to tighten and her heart to squeeze, she couldn't. She studied the amber liquid in her glass.

'I spoke to the college I used to teach at,' he continued. 'And I've started teaching a night class to adults who want to explore painting. It's only for beginners.'

'But you're enjoying it?'

'I am. I love their enthusiasm and helping them on their journey to making it a true passion. As it should be.'

'That's brilliant. I'm really proud of you. Actually, I meant to say that I got some extra work from the gallery opening. Two people have already hired me to make some arrangements for parties they're holding.'

'That's great, Rosie! That'll help pay for the boat repairs.'

She shook her head. 'Their events are after my deadline. If only they were before, it wouldn't all be riding on the flower festival.'

'Speaking of that . . . I was thinking . . . you're going to be busy that day—'

'Well, I hope I am.'

'Why don't I come and help? I can manage the stall if you need to go off and do anything and, hopefully, you'll be so busy you need two people.'

She didn't know what to say. She wanted him by her side while she faced the hardest day of her new career. So much was resting on its success and being near Max always felt . . . right.

'Are you sure you don't mind?'

'Of course not. I wouldn't have offered if I did.'

'Then thank you. That'd be great.'

They fell into an uneasy silence, words that she longed to say sitting heavily between them. Max began to talk of the windmill, giving facts about its history, and Rosie listened as best she could, but all she could see was the man she loved sitting in front of her. The man she was going to have to give up if this bonkers idea of organising a festival in three weeks didn't come off.

That she'd used the word 'love' didn't scare her because she did love him. She knew that now. Even if he was grumpy and difficult, prone to looking on the dark side of things, she loved the man underneath that armour. His kindness, his generosity, his passion and the intelligent, gentle soul underneath.

With their drinks finished, Max said, 'We should probably head back.'

'Yes,' she agreed, stretching out the kinks in her back. 'I'm quite tired.'

But she was pretty sure she wouldn't sleep at all as her life seemed to hang in the balance, and there was nothing she could do about it except wait.

Chapter 30

The morning of the festival finally dawned, and Rosie couldn't sit still. This was it. The day that would make or break her future and decide where she'd be calling home after the summer ended.

Nervous excitement buzzed through her system, and on another beautiful summer's day, she arrived at the flower market before anyone else. Her priority was sorting out her shop so she was on hand to help with any last-minute setting up, and she'd invested some additional money in even more flowers, hoping she would sell them all before the day was out. It really was make or break with only another week or so to get the bulk of her repairs done on the boat. She was cutting it fine. As she was unable to face doing anything until her future was secure, the list was getting longer and longer. If this whole thing was successful, in many ways her work was only just getting started.

'Are you ready?' asked Max, who had dived out to get coffee for them both. She was going to need all the caffeine she could get today. As always, Zoon was with him and settled on a blanket she'd placed at the back of her stall, next to a water bowl.

'Just waiting for Bas,' she replied, gratefully accepting the coffee. 'He said he'd be here early as everyone's ordered more flowers. It's been good for his business too.'

Before long, the rest of the team arrived: Finn and Fenna chatting as they came in, Emma and Noah shoulder to shoulder, both smiling with excitement and, Rosie thought, maybe a touch of love too. The atmosphere became more and more charged as everyone, (even the grumpy old doubters had finally come around) was as excited as she was, proud to be putting their area of Amsterdam on the map and to be saving the heritage of their city.

Once Noah, Finn, Emma and Fenna had set up their stalls, they congregated at Rosie's.

'Everyone ready?' she asked. 'Everyone excited?'

'Very much,' Emma replied. 'Noah and I decided to team up a bit today too. We've both got helpers in so we can show people how to pair meats and cheeses for the perfect dinner party.'

'What a wonderful idea!' Rosie clapped her hands together.

'There are people already waiting outside,' said Bas as he unloaded the last of his deliveries to another stallholder. His English really was improving.

Finn stood and stretched his arms over his head. 'I haven't felt this energised in years. I can't wait to open and get started.'

'Let's hope this works.'

'Judging by that crowd,' said Max, peering towards the street, 'it will.'

'Shall we, then?' asked Rosie and they all went to their pitches, ready to meet the customers who had turned out for the first, and hopefully not last, floating flower festival.

The day couldn't have gone better. Rosie didn't stop working and was glad to have Max at her side, though they barely spoke, except for serving customers. Zoon was proving quite a draw and adored the attention, getting cooed over and fussed all day long. She thought she might have to borrow him more often – if this all worked out. By midafternoon, she'd sold nearly all her flowers. Unfortunately, that was when the local media decided to turn up, including a photographer.

'Oh no!' Rosie panicked. 'What am I going to do? If they start snapping pictures, my place looks awful. I don't think even Zoon can save this one.'

Glancing around she saw that, while busy, the other vendors still had plenty of flowers to fill their tubs. They just looked busy while she'd be the laughingstock of the

Bloemenmarkt. That was the problem with such a tiny pitch!

'What can we do?' asked Max.

'I don't know. Tidy? Spread things out a bit?'

'There isn't much to spread out.'

She began rearranging things so she looked as successful as the other vendors whose crowds were still gathering, customers fighting for space in their shops.

'Here,' said Finn, as he and a member of his staff came over with three overflowing tubs of tulips.

'What's this?' she asked, her eyes widening at the quality of the blooms.

'A gift. And not just for the cameras.' He motioned to where they were coming closer, making their way around the market, photographing vendors and customers. 'You've done so much for this market – for the festival – and I have too much stock. I overbought and I won't sell them all. You sell these and keep the profits to help with your boat repairs.'

'Finn, I couldn't! That feels—'

'Right,' he said sternly, but not unkindly, cutting her off before she could protest too much. 'It feels right. For me. Please, do me this favour.'

'That's very kind,' said Max, stepping forwards and taking the buckets. 'Thank you.'

The two pieces of art he'd donated, which had been placed near her stall, had sold almost as soon as they'd opened but in the blur of activity, they hadn't had the chance to really celebrate. They'd shared a quick hug and she'd inhaled his strong scent and felt the warmth of his arms around her. Now, this offer from Finn threatened to send her emotions over the edge.

'Thank you,' she muttered, wiping away a tear and trying her best to hold back more. 'I don't know what to say.'

'Just keep going. Today is proving a huge success.'

'Quickly,' said Max. 'We better get these arranged.'

Rosie set to work and thanks to Finn, her stall didn't look like someone had looted it and run off with everything she had. As she was putting the finishing touches to it, Max's phone rang, his eyes widening as he read the screen.

'Sorry, Rosie. I have to take this. I'll be back in a minute, okay?'

She nodded, her concentration returning to the task ahead of her. The photographer was drawing closer. Thankfully, she just finished as he arrived with a reporter in tow.

'So you're Rosie Harper who's organised all of this,' the reporter said, gesturing around her.

'I can't take all the credit, I'm afraid. There's been a team of us working here to get it ready and lots of volunteers have given hours of their time to help design the flyers and hand them out. We couldn't have done it without everyone's help.'

'It's certainly an interesting new festival. What are your plans for next year?'

'Well, that really depends.'

She looked over to see Max had returned from taking

his call, his phone still in his hand. He was looking at her expectantly, hopefully, and her breath caught in her throat. She wanted more than anything to stay, but until the money was counted and she knew where she stood, she couldn't make a commitment to him or anyone.

'On what?' the reporter asked. 'This seems to have been a huge success.'

'I hope it has been, but we'll have to wait and see how much we've raised for those who need it.'

She was taking a fee from the profits but if there weren't any profits, there wouldn't be a fee. Which meant no money to fix her boat.

'Well, from what I've seen, everyone's keen for something like this next year. It's nice to meet you, Rosie. Keep us informed. We'd love to cover it again next year, maybe even be involved somehow.'

The photographer snatched a few more photos, including one of Zoon, who was worn out from all the attention and had fallen asleep on the blanket. Max edged towards her.

'Is everything all right?' Rosie asked.

'Yes, I— Everything's fine. Rosie, I—'

Before he could finish his sentence, Emma rushed towards her, grabbing Rosie by the shoulders and shaking her as she spoke. 'He asked me out, Rosie! Noah! He asked me out. We're going on a date tomorrow night. Can you believe it!'

'Of course I can,' she replied, giggling at Emma's unadulterated happiness. 'You're amazing and he'd be a fool not to see it. I'm just sorry none of my advice worked.'

'Are you kidding? Of course it did! I wouldn't have gone near him if it wasn't for you. Speaking of advice, perhaps you should take some of your own?' Emma nodded towards Max.

'There's nothing to say,' she said quietly, her body throbbing as she battled against her need for him. 'Not till I know if I'm staying or not.'

'Then as soon as we close, we better find out.'

The afternoon carried on as successfully as the morning and Rosie relaxed, finally beginning to smile. Thanks to Finn she'd made an extra few hundred euros and by the time the shutters came down on hers and everyone else's pitches, everyone was exhausted, but happy. There hadn't been time to ask Max what it was he was going to tell her, and nerves had tightened her stomach every time she looked at him.

'I might have to stay closed tomorrow,' Emma said, a thin sheen of sweat on her hairline as she came to join them. 'I don't think I've got any stock left!'

'Me neither,' said Noah, placing an arm around her shoulders. 'We could spend the day together, maybe?' His cheeks flushed with a subtle pink and Emma nodded emphatically.

'I'd love that.'

Finn and Fenna stepped forwards too. 'We should have a celebratory dinner tonight. Everyone is going to donate something from their profits, but from what I've seen and heard through the afternoon, we should have made at least a few thousand euros for the fund, and we agreed you'd take a cut, Rosie, didn't we? Will a thousand euros be enough to repair your boat?'

'A thousand?!' Rosie spluttered. She shook her head. Zoon woke up and made his way towards them, stopping at her feet. 'No, no!' She waved her hands wildly in front of her. 'It's too much!'

'Nonsense,' added Fenna. 'You deserve it for all the coordinating you've done.'

'You should take it,' Emma said gently, resting her hand on her shoulder.

This was exactly what she'd wanted and hoped for, but she couldn't help but feel guilty. 'I don't like having to do it, but I will, in the short term. I'm determined to pay it back.'

Finn stepped forward, handing her a piece of paper. 'That won't be a problem. Not with this.'

'What is it?' she asked, turning it over. Her eyes widened as she read the words printed on the front. 'A business plan? For – for—'

'For Linny's Garden,' Max said, appearing at her side, finishing the sentence she couldn't quite manage.

'For the next stage of your growth,' Finn added.

'I don't – I don't know what to say.' Unable to stop the tears spilling down her cheeks, Rosie swiped them away and half laughed, half sobbed. 'Finn . . . Max—'

Max's hand gripped her shoulder. 'Open it.'

She turned the first page to see a beautiful illustration of what her logo might look like.

The words 'Linny's Garden' were written in a beautiful cursive font of a bright golden yellow. Seeing her mum's name written down, tied on paper to her dreams, sent a swell of such strong emotion through her she almost stepped back, like a wave was hitting her legs and driving her backwards. Tears once more pooled in her eyes as she could almost hear her mum's voice telling her how proud she was of her. Rosie let it fill her consciousness, and she could almost sense her mum's touch. She'd worked hard to overcome so many obstacles and she was still standing. Rosie had never felt a pride like it.

The name was surrounded by thick line drawings of leaves and flowers, gently coloured in differing shades of green and pink. To the right-hand side was an enormous forget-me-not curling around the letters. Rosie gasped and placed a hand over her mouth. Her mum would have approved of this, and so would her dad and sister. It was a wonderful tribute to a woman whom they had all loved and missed every day.

'Max, it's beautiful.' His eyes met hers, and he raised his hand, gently brushing the moisture from her cheeks. Her skin almost burned with longing where he'd touched her. All she wanted was for him to cup her face and draw her in for a kiss. She wanted to feel his mouth on hers and push her hands into his hair. But he didn't move, and his hand slowly dropped away, back down to his side.

'There's something else too. Turn to page five.'

Her fingers were numb and undexterous, but eventually, she found the page. There was a sketch of the *Forget-Me-Knot*. Flowers flowed from pots and buckets, making it look more like a garden than a houseboat. She saw the outline of the houses on the opposite bank of the canal and ducks on the water. On the side of the galley was the logo Max had designed, but the forget-me-not was painted much bigger, and on the bow, the boat's name was painted in wide, high letters. It was exactly what she'd envisioned. It was exactly what she'd dreamed of.

'I don't know what to say.' She choked down a sob, determined to get the words out. 'It's perfect. It's everything I ever wanted.'

'We can make your dream a reality,' Finn said, kindly.

She turned her attention back to the document, aware of everyone's eyes on her, flipping the pages and scanning the words. Though she couldn't understand the details in such an emotional state, she could read the heading and subheadings. He'd outlined a step-by-step business plan working out possible profits, reinvestments and other income streams she might consider while she was setting up. He'd basically encapsulated her dream of running a shop from the flower market and from the *Forget-Me-Knot*.

'You've done so much, Finn! How can I ever thank you?'

'We'll need to go through it together and add in lots of details and actual figures, but this worked for me to get me started and that was before social media, so there's a lot we can add in that will help build your brand, but we might need someone else who knows—'

'I can help with that,' Noah suddenly piped up. 'I have a huge following on TikTok.'

'You do?' Emma blurted, covering her mouth as she realised how rude that sounded.

Noah laughed and adjusted his glasses. 'I might be shy around you, but that doesn't mean I'm shy around everyone.'

Emma immediately grabbed her phone and found him. 'You've got three million followers.'

He shrugged. 'People like cheese.'

Everyone laughed but Rosie's eyes searched out Max. He met her gaze and edged towards her.

'I hope you don't mind, but I spoke to Piet too. He's willing to sell you the boat. In fact, he's promised to sell it to you. As soon as you're in a position to buy it.'

'He better not try and add anything on after all the work I'm going to do on it.'

Everyone laughed and Rosie felt relieved that her equilibrium was returning. But he'd done that for her. And the question that floated in her mind was why?

'Jeroen called earlier,' he continued. 'The painting sold. That's some more for the pot too.'

'I can't believe it worked. You've all been so brilliant.' Rosie looked at the assembled group – her friends, her Amsterdam family – who'd stuck with this ridiculous idea and helped to make it a reality. 'And thank you, Max. And you, Finn, for this.' She held up the business plan. 'I can't believe I have a future again.'

'So . . .' Max said tentatively, stepping forwards. 'You're staying?'

'I am.' She glanced at the people around her, grateful for their love and friendship. Emma was winking and tilting her head towards Max. Was it time to take her own dating advice?

If she told Max how she felt and he was still against them having a relationship, for whatever reason, she'd be left embarrassed in front of everyone, and life would be unbearable as his neighbour. But if she didn't, what would happen? Would they continue as they were? Clearly attracted to each other but each waiting for the other to make the first move. If she'd learned anything from being in Amsterdam it was that it was time she went for what she wanted. She'd done it so far and had made something special of her life. Something that was only going to get better and better the harder she worked at it. And weren't relationships a lot like that?

Not only had she learned to fully open her heart instead of keeping a part of her back, protected for fear of losing the one she loved, but she'd learned that sometimes, working hard towards something was the best part. The journey was just as much fun as the destination. Turning to Max, she took a breath, her chest filling with air.

'Max,' she said, 'I know you think we should just be friends, but you're wrong.' His eyes flicked over the assembled crowd, silently questioning if she really wanted to do this now, in front of everyone, but as his gaze fell on her, their eyes met, and there was nothing but them. 'I don't know why we make such a good team, but we do.'

'Thanks. I think.' His brows knitted together, and he ran a hand through his hair.

There was a small titter from the rest of the group but, undeterred, Rosie carried on regardless.

'You're grumpy and stubborn, and like an old man sometimes, but you're also kind and funny and caring and gentle.'

'And hot,' Emma added, making everyone laugh again, including Max and Rosie.

'Yeah, that too.' Rosie met his eye defiantly, feeling confident, unbreakable. 'I've had the most amazing time here in Amsterdam. It feels like home. It feels like this was always where I was supposed to be and what I was supposed to be doing. And . . . you do too. You feel like home. When I'm with you, I feel like I'm with exactly who I'm supposed to be with for the rest of my life. So, you see, we can't just be friends. It's a stupid idea. We should be together . . . always.'

Max, whose eyes had been pinned to hers throughout her speech, took a breath and stepped forwards. He took the business plan from her and passed it to Finn, who smiled on affectionately. Suddenly, both Rosie's hands were in Max's, his thumbs running over her skin, but he wouldn't meet her gaze and Rosie's stomach dropped. A lump, large and heavy, formed in her throat. Her chest tightened, her body struggling to resist the urge to run away from his rejection and the subsequent humiliation that was to follow.

'Rosie . . . you are the most annoyingly cheerful person I've ever met in my life. You sing and dance at all hours of the day and you talk to yourself constantly. Loudly. You refuse to let people have their privacy and you have an opinion on everything.'

Everyone around them had fallen silent. Rosie could hear the blood pumping around her body, sending her into fight-or-flight mode. Her heart slammed rapidly against her chest as if trying its best to put itself out of its misery. This wasn't how she'd expected the conversation to go. It certainly didn't in the romcoms she loved so much.

'But you're also the best thing that's ever happened to me. I fell in love with you the moment you stepped onto my boat and bewitched my dog.' As he looked down at Zoon nestled between them, the dog gave a small bark. Rosie thought she might burst as love filled every cell in her body. 'You love me for who I am and I – I don't think that's ever happened to me before. After Johanna left, I didn't think I could follow my passion and make someone happy. But you made me see that I just needed to find the right person to share my life with. Those weeks when I stayed away from you were the worst of my life. I missed you every day. I missed seeing your smile and hearing you sing about chopping potatoes or being Queen of the Idiots.'

'Queen of the what?' Emma choked.

'Don't ask,' Rosie replied, not taking her eyes from Max's for a second.

'I – I felt like the luckiest person because you wanted to be with me and I'm sorry I threw all that away.'

'I love you, Max,' she replied, unable to keep the words inside any longer.

He stared into her eyes. 'You make me brave, Rosie. And I love you too.'

She pulled her hands from his, wrapping them around his neck instead. His arms engulfed her, tugging her close. Max's lips met hers with a gentleness that made her feel loved but left her desperately wanting more. As if he sensed her feelings, their kiss became more passionate, his hold tighter.

They forgot anyone was there until Zoon barked. When they broke apart, a sea of amused faces surrounded them.

'Sorry,' Rosie replied, unable to stop herself from smiling. Max loosened his grip enough for her to turn and face them.

'I guess,' said Emma, 'that a celebratory dinner with you two is out?'

'Rosie deserves to celebrate the hard work she's put into this. And we've got the rest of our lives to spend together,' said Max.

'But we might head off a bit early,' Rosie added, catching Max's eye. He raised a teasing eyebrow. All she wanted was to get him back to the *Forget-Me-Knot* and rip his clothes off. 'You know, I've got a lot of repairs to do on my boat and I need to get started.'

'We'll see you at the restaurant,' Finn said. 'Give you a few minutes to umm . . . pack up.' He handed back the business plan. 'Don't forget this.'

She took it and a second later, removed her arms from Max and instead put them around Finn, pulling him in for a hug.

'Thank you so much, Finn. You're amazing.'

He chuckled. 'We'll start working on this as soon as the boat's repaired. I've got some great ideas.'

'And of course,' added Fenna, 'we need to start planning next year's festival. If we can do this in three weeks, just imagine what we can do with a year!'

Where would she be a year from now? Rosie wondered as she moved back into Max's arms, his lips meeting hers once more. She couldn't be sure, but she had the feeling that the future held more than her fair share of success, and, more importantly, love.

With a wave, the others walked ahead of them.

'So, Rosie Harper, there's something else I need to tell you.'

'Oh?'

'Thanks to you, I was brave enough to send some images of my work off to a gallery in Berlin.'

'Berlin? And?'

'They want me to exhibit next year.'

She inhaled sharply and squealed, causing Zoon to drop his ears. 'Max, that's amazing!'

'It's because of you, Rosie. All because of you. I love you more than I ever thought I could love someone.'

'Even Zoon?' she teased.

'Even Zoon.'

And before they left to celebrate the festival's success and the new future ahead of them, he swept her into his arms and kissed her fiercely to prove it.

Epilogue

ONE YEAR LATER

The second annual floating flower festival was a huge success, with more businesses involved and more people helped by the fund Rosie had set up. Houseboats had been repaired, and shops in the flower market and local businesses on the Singel canal had been saved. The area was looking better than ever and, even better than that, there was a real community feel. The flower market vendors often helped each other out and it made working there the best job Rosie had ever had.

Her life in London – the grey, wet weather, the crowded morning commute, the carbon-copy office blocks – were a distant memory.

Thanks to Finn's business plan, Rosie's floristry business was growing. She'd been able to pay back the money she'd used from the fund and had even added a little extra as her own personal thank you. Finn was acting as something of a mentor to her and with his business acumen and Noah's social media know-how, she was now the proud owner of a slightly bigger stall at the *Bloemenmarkt* and Linny's Garden had officially opened on her houseboat. She even had a part-time assistant she was teaching the basics to, making sure to show them all the things her mum had taught her.

The repairs to the *Forget-Me-Knot* had taken almost three months to complete, but once work was underway, the council had been willing to let her continue. Max had helped where he could, which had kept costs down, and where he couldn't, the community around her had offered suggestions as to people she could use. Now, the hull had been repaired and cleaned, the deck had been repainted, the pipes checked and all leaks stopped, and the wiring was now up to code and good for at least another ten years. The safety equipment had been replaced by Piet so that she was now less likely to drown if anything went wrong.

The sale with Piet had just been completed and she couldn't believe she could finally call the place hers. There was still some decorating to do inside, but nothing gave her more pleasure than coming home from days at the *Bloemenmarkt* to her tiny houseboat with its mass of plants, flowers, colourful ornaments and soft furnishings, or to spend the day there working from it, chatting to her regular customers.

As she stood on the pavement opposite the *Forget-Me-Knot* after the final day of the flower festival, her feet ached, and her body throbbed. She hadn't stopped since six-thirty that morning and she was ready for a relaxing evening with her feet up. Max wrapped his arm around her shoulder and together they admired the large mural he'd painted on the side of the boat. The business name was exactly as he'd sketched, and the giant forget-me-not made her smile every time she saw it. She'd never forget her mum, and here she was with her as not just her business but her whole life flourished. She'd never felt more content or more fulfilled.

'Looks good!' her dad said and Melody agreed.

'It looks amazing. I'm so proud of you, sis.'

They were visiting more and more frequently, often staying on Max's houseboat as he slept in hers.

'What do you think?' Max asked Rosie.

'It's perfect.' She placed her hands either side of his face, the soft hairs of his beard tickling her skin, and kissed him, lingering in the kiss for as long as possible until they were interrupted by a screech.

'Max?' The voice came from an older lady standing on the deck of his boat, in front of an easel. 'Max! Help me! It's all going wrong!'

'It's all right, Anna. I'm coming.'

He pecked Rosie's lips and moved to the small class he was teaching to paint. Rosie had never seen him so happy. Between his tutoring commitments and the work he was now regularly exhibiting at galleries all over Europe, he was making a decent living. Not that Rosie wanted him for his money; she was making more than enough of her own. But she loved seeing him so fulfilled and knew that being financially stable made him feel better about himself. He loved sharing his gifts with other people and Rosie knew for a fact that Anna, in his seniors class, was one of his favourite pupils. He also spent time creating new work and as a fellow creative, that spoke to a part of her too.

Rosie's business had extended beyond the flower market to creating pieces for galleries and events, thanks to Jeroen and the two ladies who'd hired her that night at the gallery opening, giving her good reviews and spreading the word. She also still held talks and workshops, which people loved to attend.

Just as Max walked away, Rosie's phone pinged to let her know she had an email. She pulled it from her back pocket and read it through, her hand shooting to her mouth. 'Max! Max, come here.'

'What is it?' her dad asked, eating yet another *stroopwafel*.

'Dad, you can't have too many of those!'

'But they're delicious.'

After setting Anna back on the right path with her brush, Max came back to her. 'What is it? Is everything all right?'

'Yes. No. I mean – look!' She held her phone out to them all and Max's eyes grew wider.

'Rosie, this is amazing! I'm so proud of you.'

He took her in a hug and the painting class ambled over, Anna speaking first. 'What's happening? Tell us! You can't do this and keep it a secret.'

Rosie spoke while staring at her phone, reading again and checking everything was real. 'Linny's Garden has been selected for a feature in a travel magazine—'

'A prestigious travel magazine,' Max added.

'It's apparently a unique spot in Amsterdam – a secret delight, it says here. I can't believe it. Mum's name will be in a magazine.'

Her dad's eyes filled with tears. 'I'm so proud of you, Rosie!'

He hugged her and Rosie buried her face in his shoulder. 'I'm proud of you too!'

Max smiled. 'People will come from all over to visit once they read this.' Rosie wiped a tear from her eye and Max pulled her in for a hug, kissing the top of her head.

Melody slipped her hand into Ed the consultant's (former work crush and now boyfriend). 'Well done, sis. Good job.'

She'd finally had the courage to ask him out and things were going very well indeed.

With her family's constant messaging and video chats it didn't ever feel like she was that far away from them. Her dad visited when he could, though now he was in a cover band his evenings were a little busier than before. They'd also stayed at Christmas and Max had enjoyed taking them all on a canal cruise of the city during the winter Light Festival. The city had looked so different, the trees lit with magical fairy lights, the bridges decorated with spectacular displays and the water of the canals brightened by special installations. Amsterdam in the summer was pretty special but Amsterdam in the winter, the streets dusted with snow, was even more so. The more time she spent in this special city with its sense of love and respect and its buzzing, exciting energy, the more she felt at home.

'The boat looks wonderful,' Rosie said, slipping her hand into Max's. 'I can't believe this is my life. This place – this city – has been life-changing.'

'Obviously, because of me,' Max said.

Rosie batted his arm. 'Because of me. I've done all this. You're just better with a brush than me, that's all.'

'You have,' he said proudly. 'But I did help a little.'

'Yeah, I suppose you did. You fixed a few leaks and showed me a few unknown tourist spots.'

'Is that a euphemism?'

'Not this time. Oh, Max, I can't wait to tell Emma and Noah. And Finn. He'll be so happy for me.'

'And proud.'

Finn had become more than just a business mentor and was acting more like a second father to her. She and Max often had dinner with him and his new partner, and it was wonderful to see him so happy. Noah and Emma's relationship was going from strength to strength too, and Rosie was sure it wouldn't be long until they moved in together. She and Max both had their own boats still, though Max spent most of his nights at the *Forget-Me-Knot* and he'd grown used to her colour and chaos. Actually, she was pretty sure he secretly enjoyed it.

'This calls for a celebration,' Max declared. 'And I know just the thing.'

'Do I get to know what it is?'

'Of course not. Just be ready in an hour.'

Rosie rolled her eyes, but she loved the little surprises Max planned for her. He still took her to secret spots in the city and further afield in the Netherlands, and would sometimes surprise her with little things, like a sketch or a cream-filled treat from a new bakery he'd discovered.

Still buzzing from her email, Rosie returned to work and a short while later, Max's painting class finished, and the old ladies and gents left, patting Rosie on the cheek and congratulating her once more. Rosie changed out of her work clothes and into something 'nice' as instructed by Max.

'So where are we going? It must be fancy if Zoon and Dad and Mels can't come.'

The dog had been walked and fed, and was now curled up in Rosie's boat, on her bed, in his favourite spot to sleep.

'It is. But not too fancy. You'll like it.'

She followed him through the now familiar streets and down to a place she recognised. Her heart began to thump in her chest as they approached the canal restaurant they'd had dinner at on the night of their first kiss.

'Here!' Rosie exclaimed, smiling widely as she stepped down into the boat.

'I thought it was fitting after your good news today.'

As it was late in the evening, the sun was setting. A few velvety clouds gathered in the sky, obscuring the generous swipes of colour. Everything was infused with a golden glow from the still-warm sun, and she stood on the deck of the boat enjoying the fresh air, and the swaying of the ship on the water. Her mind flew back to over a year ago when she'd stood here with Max, the first time they'd kissed, and the first time she'd felt her heart fully open to love. Now all aspects of her life were full. She had friends, family, love and a profession that made her happy.

Max brought her a glass of champagne. 'I thought as it's a special occasion . . .'

'Thank you.' She took a sip, the bubbles floating on her tongue and popping against her cheeks.

'I'm so proud of you, you know.' Warmth flooded through Rosie at the compliment. He could still be grumpy, and always would be, but he was also kind and generous with his heart and his words. 'It hasn't always been easy . . .'

It certainly hadn't. Even after the flower festival, there'd been more than a few disasters. She'd varnished half her body while varnishing the boat and it hadn't been easy to scrub off. For a week she'd looked like she'd had a bad, patchy fake tan. She'd had days when none of her flowers had sold and more than once a private hire had asked her to change her displays, which had meant more expense and less profit. Not to mention the time she'd tried to surprise Max with a sexy night in and he'd arrived back at the boat with Anna in tow, promising to show her how to angle her brush correctly to ensure a particular finish. Thankfully Anna was open-minded and, Rosie suspected, had been a bit of a show-stopping tearaway in her youth, so she had simply laughed and asked for a glass of wine to settle her nerves. Rosie's cheeks still burned at the memory.

'But no matter what,' Max continued, 'you've never run away. You've always stayed and found a way through. You're unique, Rosie Harper. And that's why I want to give you this.'

For a second, Rosie's heart leapt into her mouth as Max reached into his jacket pocket. But instead of a small box, he brought out a sketch pad. Disappointment rushed through her, even though she hadn't realised until now how much she wanted Max to propose and for them to take their relationship to the next level.

'What's this?' she asked, the same disappointment fading as she flipped open the sketchbook. 'It's – it's me.'

Page after page was filled with sketches of Rosie, or Rosie and Max together. There were places they'd been and things they'd done, starting with the first day they'd met, when she'd walked onto his boat by accident. There was their visit to the Milkshake Festival, evening drinks on his boat, the day the pipe had burst and flooded the galley, and finally a gorgeous sketch, painted in delicate watercolours, of Linny's Garden. Her houseboat was colourful and bright with the large forget-me-not painted on the side and the buckets of flowers, their colourful blooms brightening the world around them.

'There's one more,' Max said, turning a few blank pages to come to a final sketch.

Rosie clutched her champagne flute tighter, emotion rolling up through her body like a wave on the sea. For a moment, in the fading sunlight she couldn't understand what she was looking at. The sketch showed her and Max, standing in front of their respective boats hand in hand. Zoon was at their feet with a big bow tie on his collar, but that wasn't what took her breath away. It was the fact that she was wearing a wedding dress – something large and poofy she'd never actually choose herself, but she could raise that point later – and Max was in a suit. A ring sparkled on her ring finger, and there was one on Max's hand too.

'Is this – are you . . . proposing?'

'I am,' he said quietly, his voice wavering. 'I left some pages blank to be filled with the memories we'll make between now and then. I don't ever want to let you go, Rosie. You're the best thing that's ever happened to me. The best person I've ever known. You have no idea how you make life better for everyone around you. You told me once that's what your mum was like – how everyone thought of her – and it's the same for you. But you make me a better person – a better human being – and it's those things I love most about you. I want to spend the rest of my life with you. Will you—' He swallowed hard, his eyes tearing, his words full of emotion as he dropped to one knee. 'Will you marry me?'

'Yes! Yes of course I will!' With her hands still full of a champagne flute and the sketchbook, she did her best to wrap her arms around him and pull him close.

He kissed her just as he had that first time over a year ago, only this time the love between them was even more intense, more assured. Their future lay together. She was sure of it and so was he.

'People say that their partner is their better half,' he said as they parted. 'But in this case, it's true.'

'Oh, you're not so bad,' she teased in reply, dropping the sketchbook and champagne flute onto a nearby table and returning for another kiss.

As their lips met, they heard someone nearby say, 'Awww,' and saw the flash of a camera. Both turned to see a couple watching them and smiling.

'Congratulations!' they trilled together, their backpacks knocking into the waiting staff behind them.

'Thank you,' Rosie replied cheerily, while Max mumbled: 'Tourists! I hate tourists,' before Rosie giggled and silenced him with another kiss.

She still had a little bit of work to do to make Max as cheerful as she was, but that was okay, they had plenty of time. They had forever.

THE END

Acknowledgements

This book was an absolute joy to write and that doesn't always happen! I really loved Rosie's positive attitude and making her and Max spark off each other was endless fun. First off, I'd like to thank all those who've picked this book and stuck around for the journey. Your time is precious and I really appreciate you spending it with me and my characters.

I always have to thank my agent, Kate Nash, for her unwavering support and, of course, the Avon team. Special mentions to Elisha Lundin who has now moved to Sphere but will always be a friend, and to Maddie Wilson who has stepped in as my new editor. As soon as we met, I knew we'd get on well and I can't wait to work on more books with you. Everyone at Avon has, and always does, an incredible job and it's such a pleasure to work with you all.

I'd especially like to thank Helena Newton, my copyeditor, and Amber Burlinson, my proofreader, for their amazing work. Thank you to Lindsey Spinks, my illustrator, for the absolutely breathtakingly gorgeous cover!

I'd also like to thank the amazing friends I've made along the way at Avon, especially Lisa Timoney and Amy Gaffney, and my friends in the Romantic Novelists' Association whose support and advice have enriched my life beyond words. Shout-out to Catherine Tinley, Lucy Morris, Ali Henderson and Saoirse Morrigan, the best people in the world!

And finally, thanks to my family for being so supportive and loving. I love you all so, so much!

If you haven't signed up to my mailing list yet, get on over there as I'm giving away a free novel! Here's the link bit.ly/3gbqMS0

Enjoyed *The Floating Amsterdam Flower Shop*?
Then you'll love the chateau series, also by Annabel French...

**A newly single woman. A handsome stranger.
A chateau that keeps bringing them together...**

ANNABEL FRENCH
Summer at the Chateau

A broken heart. An unexpected inheritance.
A life-changing summer...

The perfect feel-good romantic comedy
that will leave you falling head over heels!

Life has gone a little bit downhill for Naomi Winters...

ANNABEL FRENCH

Christmas at the Chateau

Will the magic of Christmas mend her broken heart?

Escape to the Swiss Alps with this festive, feel-good novel!

**Two friends. One wedding.
A love story that's long overdue . . .**

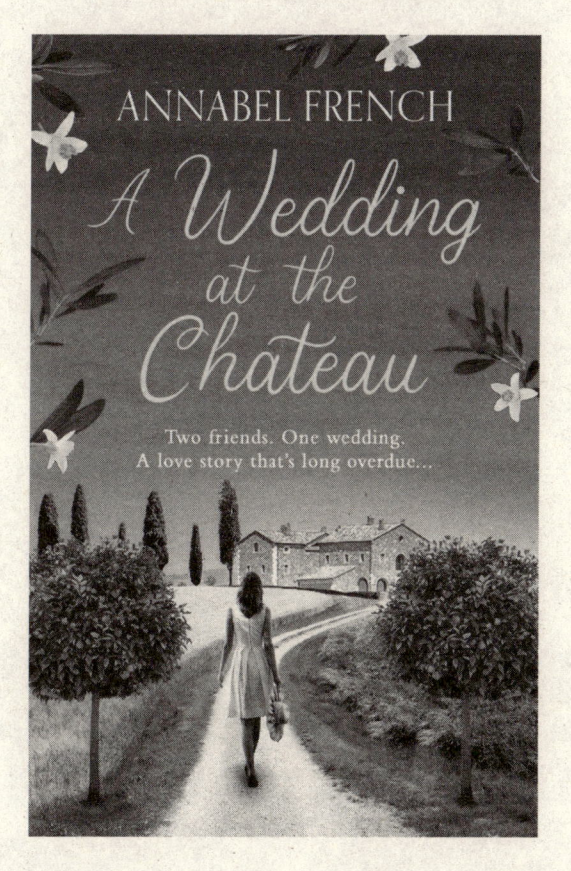

ANNABEL FRENCH
A Wedding at the Chateau

Two friends. One wedding.
A love story's that's long overdue...

A Wedding at the Chateau is a romantic and heartwarming story, the perfect summer read!